T0207908

With Pen in Hand

David Pitzele

authorHOUSE®

AuthorHouse™
1663 Liberty Drive
Bloomington, IN 47403
www.authorhouse.com
Phone: 1 (800) 839-8640

Published by AuthorHouse   12/17/2015

ISBN: 978-1-5049-6903-1 (sc)
ISBN: 978-1-5049-6901-7 (hc)
ISBN: 978-1-5049-6902-4 (e)

Library of Congress Control Number: 2015920989

Print information available on the last page.

I dedicated my first novel to my wife and six children.

I dedicated my second novel to my twelve
grandchildren. I now have thirteen.
I can't add Jack to that previously published novel
so he gets his own special mention here.

This novel is for my wife, my children, their spouses and my
grandchildren Thank you for inspiring me to be the best
person I can be. I think I still need a lot more work.

I want to acknowledge my son Brad. He has written the back
cover teasers for all three novels. Thank you, Brad.

CHAPTER 1

The Vigilante Killer had just claimed his thirteenth victim. The police were not fond of that name for this serial killer, but someone in the press had labeled him with it, and it stuck. Vigilante is one of those funny words, like the word *opportunistic*. Some people see it as evil, while others see it as something positive. This particular killer was targeting gang members in Chicago. He showed no special preference. It seemed that any gang member was fair game for him, regardless of affiliation. Initially, there hadn't been a lot of pressure to solve these cases. Gangs continue to be one of the biggest black eyes for the city, a city that most visitors rave about. The gangs represented everything that was wrong with the city and offered no redeeming features. The cops didn't have the numbers to adequately control their activities, much less take the streets back from them. There were approximately one hundred thousand gang members in the Windy City. It was too much for a city with financial challenges to contend with successfully. If gang members wanted to kill each other, so be it.

Gang members killing each other had been the way of the jungle in this part of the inner-city. Fortunately for the tourism trade, the killings mostly took place in gang territories. The places where tourists spent their time while visiting Chicago, remained mostly unaffected by these activities. Sadly, way too often, innocent people, good people, were killed simply because they were in the wrong place at the wrong time. Many people found themselves with limited options in where they lived because they couldn't afford the cost of renting or owning a home in a safer neighborhood. Housing was most affordable in many of these gang-infested areas.

Although they might not admit it publicly, many within the police department weren't all that upset with the Vigilante Killer. The killer was assassinating some of the worst people without taking the lives of innocents. Kids had one more thing to consider before joining a gang. It wasn't just the danger presented by other gangs, but also the threat of being killed by an unknown assailant.

The Vigilante Killer was a marksman. He found empty buildings that were often boarded up. He selected a good vantage point, waited for his target, and always took them out with one shot from afar. Despite having struck thirteen times, he had left no clues other than a few bullet casings and the bullets that had hit his victims, when they could be found. The police knew that the bullets being used were .50 BMG, fired from a sniper rifle. Beyond that, there was no physical evidence. The shooter killed in the dark of night. In all of his hits, only two people thought they had seen somebody who could have been the perpetrator. Neither could give a good description because they didn't get a good look at the man's face. They both described the man as black, with a full beard and wearing a stocking cap. They believed he was of average height and weight. That was almost like a non-description. This wasn't enough information to help in finding this ruthless killer.

It was after the third killing that they realized they were dealing with a serial killer, and the police started feeling some pressure to catch him. By the sixth victim, pressure had really mounted. There was definitely a serial killer on the loose; there was no denying it. He was only choosing gang members as his victims for now, but there was no guarantee that his focus wouldn't change. The city was getting bad press around the country. The mayor wouldn't tolerate it. He wanted the case solved, and he wanted it solved immediately. He exerted as much pressure as he could. The police commissioner was always under pressure, but rarely did he feel it like he was feeling it then.

Detective Fred DuKane and his partner, Bill Small, were assigned the case after the third killing. DuKane had distinguished himself throughout his career. His reputation was that of being one of the best detectives in the city. DuKane was on the smallish side. He stood five feet seven inches tall. Soaking wet, he weighed 165 pounds. He carried a little bit of a belly but still looked to be at a reasonable weight. A full head of hair graced his head, and he was not unattractive. He was an easygoing guy with a good sense of humor. Perseverance had helped him build a reputation as a successful detective. He had the ability to keep at it until he was able to build some momentum. Once that happened, there was no stopping him. Although he usually appeared to be laid-back, he had a fire burning inside, and it showed in his work.

Bill Small and Fred DuKane were an interesting team. Where Fred was white, Bill was black. As small as DuKane was, his partner was equally big. A better name for him would be Bill Large. The man was six feet, five inches tall. He was heavyset, and he had a huge presence but a small personality. He was quiet and introspective. The fellow officers in his precinct would describe him as a decent guy. He made DuKane's laid-back nature seem almost aggressive in comparison. Nothing seemed to affect him. Small had just partnered with DuKane in the last year. He proved to be a very average detective. Small was within a year of retiring. He didn't seem like he was losing steam because he never was a go-getter. DuKane took the role of lead detective in all of the cases they worked together, with no complaints from Small. The two men didn't seem to dislike each other, but for some reason, they also never grew as close as many partners tend to do. Some people thought that Small resented DuKane. Of the two men, Small was the more tenured, but everybody treated DuKane like he was the senior detective.

After two more killings and no real clues, DuKane was assigned to lead a task force with the mandate to bring the killer to justice. All that the task force had to go on was that the killer took out his victims within a block of their homes and did it in the dark of night. It was assumed that the killer was hitting his targets when they returned home at day's end.

On the task force, Small was no longer an equal partner in the investigation but just another member. He felt like it was a demotion, or at least a slap in the face. He didn't impede the investigation, but he didn't bring much to the party. DuKane didn't know if it was on purpose or just the way it was.

DuKane's task force interviewed every tenured gang member they could round up and talked to people in the neighborhoods where each killing took place. They came up with nothing. They closely inspected each location a shot had been fired from and came up empty, other than the casings. The two witnesses never saw the shootings. They only saw the apparent suspect walking away after they had heard a shot fired. The generic descriptions they gave offered little help. The killer wasn't just an ace shot, but knew how to stay under the radar.

DuKane's phone rang. It was the commander. He had DuKane's sergeant in his office, and he wanted DuKane to join them. DuKane asked, "Do you want me to bring Detective Small with me?" He knew the answer, but he couldn't resist asking.

"Just get your ass down here!" was the response.

DuKane knew this meant he was going to be verbally abused again. He walked over to the commander's office and knocked on the closed door. He heard the commander's voice instruct him to come in. As he entered the office, he saw the commander pacing back and forth, while his sergeant was sitting in a chair, staring into space, a grim look on his face. DuKane felt like a child who was about to be scolded for sneaking a piece of his brother's birthday cake that Mom had just baked for the party. He thought of cracking a joke but decided against it. He was told to take a seat.

The commander continued to pace. He looked like a bulldog as he went back and forth. Bulldog is only a good look for an actual bulldog. It's not such a good look for a man. He was small, even shorter than DuKane, standing five feet five inches tall. He had a squat physique. He could easily afford to lose forty or fifty pounds. His was not a good look. He was bald and had a constant scowl on his face, unless the brass was around. Then, he was all personality.

The silence was killing DuKane. He wondered why they couldn't start the beating and get it over with. Finally, the commander spoke. "I was at a meeting downtown earlier this morning. What do you think the topic was?" He glared at DuKane.

DuKane wanted to say the right thing, but the tension got the best of him. He'd worked too long and hard to become a good detective, and he *was* a good detective. He didn't deserve to be berated. He shot back at the commander, "I hope it was about updating the men's room and the locker room here at the station."

"Do you think this is some kind of a joke? The mayor is pissed. Heads are going to roll, and it's going to happen soon. I'm dependent on you doing your job. I haven't heard one positive thing from your task force in weeks. If I go down, I'm taking you with me."

The sergeant sat motionless. His arms were on the armrests of his chair, and his hands were folded on his lap. He appeared to be studying his hands. DuKane couldn't help but notice. *Thanks for backing me, Boss,* he thought. Meanwhile, the commander just glared at DuKane as if he was waiting for a response. DuKane obliged. "If you have some sage advice in all your wisdom besides 'solve the case,' I'm open to it. But if this is another session of let's beat on DuKane, I don't need it. That's what I have a wife for."

The commander's face softened a little. He almost looked like he wanted to smile but opted to resist. After all, he worked hard to build his reputation of being an ass. He wasn't going to let anybody ruin that reputation. The scowl returned to the man's face. "You're about one joke away from getting your ass kicked."

DuKane had never been threatened by someone above his level before. He realized the commander was in panic mode. He wondered if the man had been told at his meeting that his job was in jeopardy. DuKane chuckled to himself. How sweet that would be. It wasn't until the commander yelled, "What the hell are you smiling about? Aren't you getting that this is serious?" that DuKane realized he had let his amusement show.

"I get it, just like I got it yesterday, the day before, and the week before. These informal meet and greets are swell, but they aren't helping me. I get that we're all under a great deal of pressure, but these meetings are a waste of time. Nothing new comes out of them, and they only serve to piss me off. I'm not at my best when I'm pissed off. Let me do my job. Quit wasting my time. I want to solve this case more than anyone. It's the biggest case being worked under your leadership, but not the only one. It's my only case. It's taken over my life. So either let me do my job, or replace me as the head of the task force. But whatever you do, find somebody else to beat up on because I'm through with it." With that, DuKane stood up and walked out the door, slamming it behind him.

5

The sergeant sat, stunned, still silent, his eyes darting back and forth as if he were trying to figure out the safest place to look. The commander said, "Goddamn him! I should have assigned Marcus Jefferson to the case. He'd have probably broken it open by now. DuKane is running out of time. You keep the pressure on that bastard, because yours will be the first ass out the door if things don't get better soon."

The sergeant finally made eye contact and said, "I'm on it, Boss." They both knew it would never happen, but it at least allowed the sergeant to escape the commander's office before he had to take any real abuse.

CHAPTER 2

Fred DuKane arrived home early that evening. It was a Friday night, and he needed a break. He felt better than he had in weeks. He was done being the scapegoat. He wasn't worried about losing his job. He had a good reputation. About the worst thing the commander could do to him was to appoint a replacement to lead the task force. DuKane wouldn't like that because he got satisfaction from solving the tough cases, and he was determined to solve this one. But being relieved of the responsibility wouldn't be all bad. The stress he was constantly under couldn't be good for his health.

The family was already sitting at the table eating dinner when DuKane arrived home. The kitchen was a nice-sized room that hadn't been updated since the DuKanes moved in fifteen years ago. It didn't have a center island or granite countertops, but it was bright and had enough space for a round kitchen table and chairs. The room was very white, with white appliances, a white tile floor, and white cabinets. The walls were painted a steely gray, and it gave the room a modern feel, even without a recent update.

In the last few weeks, DuKane had been working long hours and had missed dinner with the family most nights. They hadn't expected him home in time and had started dinner without him. He realized that he should have called his wife and told her that he was on his way home. His wife, Ginny, got up and met him halfway across the floor and gave him a kiss. He got a "Hey, Dad" from his three teens, a daughter, Kelley, and

7

two sons, Patrick and Sean. He walked around the table and gave them each a kiss on their cheeks. Meanwhile, Ginny fixed a plate for him, and he sat down to eat.

Ginny asked, "How was your day?" Her stomach knotted up as she asked the question. DuKane was usually easygoing with his family, keeping things light and fun, but recently, he had become detached and sullen. She was hoping that she wasn't opening a can of worms by asking.

"There were no new developments with the case I'm working on." His family was aware of his current case. He didn't always bring them home with him, but the real tough cases seemed to work their way into the family discussions. "I had it out with the commander today. I said some things that needed to be said."

"Like what?" Ginny asked.

"You know that he has been making me meet with him on a daily basis. The meetings consist of nothing more than him screaming and carrying on. It's just so counterproductive. I let him know I was done with it. Unless he had something positive to add, I was through with his nonsense."

"How did he react?"

"I'm not sure. As I stormed out of his office, he looked pretty surprised, but I didn't wait for a reply."

"Was Bill with you in the meeting?"

"No, I get all of the grief because I'm heading the task force. It sure makes me feel special."

"What about your sergeant, was he there?"

"He was, and as usual, he didn't try to defend me or take any of the heat off of me. He was a decent cop, but as a boss, he's awful. He knows how hard we're pushing on this case, but he acts like he's clueless."

"Dad, why doesn't he stick up for you?" DuKane's oldest son Patrick asked.

"The commander's a bully. It's less painful for the sergeant to watch me take the brunt of it. I have no respect for either of them. The commander knows how to suck up to higher-ranking people and to put on a game face in front of them. Unfortunately, he doesn't show any respect for the people working under him. I see it all the time. It's not the best people who get ahead; it's the ones who play the game. The commander doesn't care about the case or people being murdered. He cares about looking good to his superiors. Karma being what it is, he'll get his in the end. Let's change the subject. How did your first week back at school go after a nice long summer?"

DuKane and Ginny were raising good kids. Even though all three were teenagers, they maintained a loving relationship with their parents. They had their share of flare-ups, as you might expect from teenagers, but for the most part, they all got along. Theirs was a warm household built on love and respect.

The kids all shared stories of the new school year. DuKane was all detective, asking lots of questions. There was plenty of laughter. The kids made fun of each other and of their parents. It was all good fun. They sat at the table for a good hour before everyone pitched in to quickly clean up the kitchen. Two of the kids had plans with friends and were soon out of the house.

Fred and Ginny watched a movie with their youngest son, Sean. Halfway through the movie, Ginny put it on hold and made some popcorn. It was a nice, laid-back evening. It was just what Ginny and Fred needed.

Later, as they lay in bed, Ginny said, "This was such a nice evening. We haven't had one of these in what seems like forever. I could tell the kids really enjoyed themselves during dinner. They seemed so happy to have their father back again."

"Look, Ginny, I'm sorry. I know these past few weeks have been difficult, and I haven't handled it well. I honestly don't know which has been worse, having the case hanging over my head or the resentment and frustration building up over the commander's actions. None of my past experiences have prepared me for what I'm going through right now. I've worked under difficult commanders before, but never felt abused like under this jerk."

"I get it, Fred. Maybe you should beg off of the case."

"No. That's not the answer. The reason I seemed better tonight is because I am better. The case is still there, and it's really big, but I faced the commander head-on. I'm really done with his shit. The abuse is over with because I won't allow it anymore. He's stuck with me, and frankly, as far as I can see, he's lucky to have me. Standing up to him relieved a ton of pressure. I feel better than I have in weeks. I actually think that I'm going to get a full night's sleep tonight."

DuKane did get a full night's sleep. Saturday was another fun day for the family. They were active, going for a bike ride and playing three on two basketball. Fred and Ginny went on a date Saturday night, enjoying a long dinner at one of their favorite restaurants. Fred slept like a child Saturday night, without a care in the world.

Sunday night was a different story. DuKane fell into a deep sleep easily enough. A few minutes after three, though, he found himself wide awake. It had occurred to him while sleeping that there might be a pattern to the killings. He needed to get to his desk at work to see how the pieces fit together. He wondered why he hadn't noticed this sooner. He felt wide awake and refreshed. He got up and headed to the shower. Within an hour, he was sitting at his desk.

CHAPTER 3

Once at his desk, DuKane laid down a blank piece of paper in front of him. With a ruler, he made five columns. He listed the victims' first names in order of their deaths in the first column and their last name in the second column. In the third column, he listed the gangs they were affiliated with. In the fourth column were the days of the week and the date of their deaths. The fifth column had the estimated tenure with the gang. It didn't take him long to put the chart together. He had all of the information at his fingertips.

The Chicago Police Department has a written Gang Violence Reduction Strategy. The cornerstone of the strategy is the Gang Audit. The commander of each district is required to conduct at least one audit per year for his district. The Gang Audit is designed to gather the following intelligence from each district: gang name, gang faction name, territorial borders, faction size, alliances, conflicts, organizational level, and propensity for violence. The Gang Audit is the foundation of gang intelligence in each district and is regularly reviewed and updated.

The audit serves to identify the hard core members of each gang. Only ten percent of gangs are made up of hard core members, long-time members who are most likely to remain with the gang for the rest of their lives. They're not the younger kids who are hustling for the gangs on the streets, doing the grunt work. They're the leaders, the ones making decisions. When attempting to dismantle a gang, these are the people who are targeted.

DuKane had the epiphany that all thirteen of the Vigilante Killer's victims had been hard core gang members. How did the killer know who the police had identified as hard core? As the detective studied his chart, something else jumped out at him. All thirteen victims were from only five different gangs. For some reason, that hadn't occurred to him before. That in itself wasn't surprising. He also noticed that the five gangs were the same five that rated the highest for their propensity for violence according to the gang audit for the district. That couldn't be a coincidence. DuKane wondered if the killer was somehow gaining access to the audits. He felt sick to his stomach as he realized that the most likely scenario was that the killer was a police officer. The only other possibility was that the man was really astute.

DuKane continued to study his chart. He noticed something else. Although he had struck on different days of the week, the killer was shooting only one person per week. He was consistent. He never skipped a week, and he never killed more than one person in a week. DuKane also saw that the killings took place on weeknights and not on weekends. He wondered why the killer never struck on a Friday, Saturday, or Sunday night. Perhaps he was divorced and had his kids on weekends. He gave it more thought, and another idea came to him. Another possibility was the killer lived outside the city and came to the city each week to do his daytime job and returned home only on weekends. He wondered if either scenario could give him direction in finding their man. He decided it would only help if they had suspects, but without any, it didn't do much good. Although it might not be useful now, he wanted to share it with the team. Somewhere down the line, having this knowledge might lead to a break in the case.

DuKane couldn't believe no one had noticed it before, but as he studied the sheet, something else jumped out at him. How could they all have missed it? As he looked down the first column, it hit him over the head like a ton of bricks. It was so obvious. The first names, in order of their deaths, were Andres, Bayden, Cle'von, Darrel, Earnell, Foster, Germain, Hakim, Isiah, Je'von, Kendrich, Leeshawn, and Marvin. The victims were being killed in alphabetical order, by the first letter in their first names.

DuKane realized that this information was going to be a big help in solving the case. Then he started wondering why the killer was following a pattern that the police were bound to see eventually. He couldn't make sense of it, but he was elated with what he had uncovered.

The task force had a standing appointment at eight every morning. During those meetings, they would discuss what had transpired during the previous day relating to the case. Also discussed were each man's responsibilities for the current day. Other than DuKane, the other members of the team all had other cases that they were responsible for investigating, even DuKane's partner, Bill Small. It was important for DuKane to assign tasks on a daily basis so that the other members didn't get so wrapped up in their other cases that this investigation didn't get the attention it demanded. The meetings had become rather short because the detectives were running out of productive activities. They needed more to go on, to widen the scope of the investigation.

Partners Marcus Jefferson and Jerome Hector were the third and fourth members of the task force. They had been transferred from the Belmont Station to the Gresham Station on South Halsted Street because the case load there demanded more police support. Jefferson had been offered the sergeant's position with the Belmont District but opted to remain a detective. He was considered by many to be the best detective in Chicago. Hector was young but was quickly proving to be a very capable detective in his own right. They were welcome additions.

Just prior to their transfer, they had cracked another serial killer case taking place in the city. The victims in the case were all homeless men. It also had high visibility. It was the first time the two of them had been partnered. While working that case, Hector saved Jefferson's life. That had helped them to form a strong bond. Prior to that, the two detectives had actually been at odds with each other, almost coming to blows at one point.

There were four other members of the task force: James Caulder, Bruce Winston, Clancy Bright, and Vicky Soderheim. All four were capable detectives. All but Soderheim were very experienced. Soderheim had been promoted to the position just months before being assigned to the task force. The commander thought that having someone with a fresher perspective might be a good thing. All eight detectives got along with each other, although Bill Small didn't interact much with the rest of the team. He seemed to take it all in but never offered any more than what was asked of him.

DuKane was a good leader. He had a vision of how they were going to solve this case. He made sure that everybody on the team understood it and bought into it. He was firm on his expectations, and he held people accountable. He managed people with tact and honesty. He was of good character, and it came through to the group. He also had a good sense of humor and used it to relieve tension from time to time. It was fair to say that the members of the team, both collectively and individually, felt bad that they weren't having more success under DuKane's leadership. They were aware of how unreasonable the commander had been and the abuse DuKane was suffering at his hand. But through it all, DuKane never passed the pressure onto the team, although his frustration was clearly visible from time to time.

At five minutes after eight, the meeting officially started. Every member was in attendance. They reviewed the past week's activities. Afterward, DuKane passed out copies of the chart he had created earlier that morning. He reviewed his findings. The other detectives were equally surprised that none of them had noticed the killings had an alphabetical element to them before now. DuKane asked, "As you look at the chart, am I missing anything in my findings?"

The room went silent for a few seconds. DuKane scanned the room. Everybody was studying the chart. After a little bit longer, Jerome Hector spoke up. "I'm not sure if this is something or not. I noticed that four of the killings have taken place on Monday nights, and there were three killings each on Tuesday, Wednesday, and Thursday nights. I don't know if there is a pattern here or if this is random, but it would seem that the next attempt will be this Tuesday, Wednesday, or Thursday night."

"Jerome, I think you have something. I can't think of a reason the killer would try to maintain an equal number of killings per night, but it appears that might be important to him."

Studying the chart DuKane had given him again, Hector responded, "Knowing when the guy might strike again is good, but it doesn't put us any closer to the big question: who is the killer?"

"No, it doesn't. But it gives us direction for a next step. Let's assume that the guy will strike Tuesday, Wednesday, or Thursday night this week.

We can also assume that the victim will be another hard core member of one of the five most dangerous gangs. All indications are that his first name will begin with the letter N. I went through the roster of hard core members of the five gangs being targeted and came up with seven guys whose first name begins with an N." DuKane passed out another sheet of paper. On it were the names of the seven gang members: Nate, Nelson, Ned, Nemiah, Nolan, Nieko, and Neville.

"You've been a busy guy this morning," Jefferson said. "I'm impressed with what you accomplished."

"Thanks, but we still have a long way to go. At least now I do have a plan that makes me more optimistic. It requires lots of moving parts, but if we execute, it should work. I will clear it with The Bulldog, but I'm pretty sure he'll go along with it. He's desperate for closure on this case." Nobody had used that nickname for the commander before, but everybody knew exactly who DuKane was talking about. They laughed.

"I know you aren't looking to work evenings," DuKane said, "but for the next three days, I need you guys to bite the bullet. I'm going to assign each of you to one of the seven targets we've identified." DuKane looked at Vicky Soderheim. "Because there are eight of us, and you are the least experienced member, Vicky, I'll work with you. The other six of you will be assigned to work with a uniformed officer. Our seven teams will all be in unmarked cars. We know that each of these killings have taken place at night, and they have all occurred within a block of each victim's home. We know where each of our possible targets live. Starting tomorrow evening, after dark, for the next three days, each of you and your assigned partner will be camped down the block from your specific target's home."

Bruce Winston said, "Aren't you worried that we might be spotted by either the target or the killer? We tend to stick out in these neighborhoods. We might only have one chance to get this right."

"I agree with your sentiment, but I don't know of a better option. Does anybody have another idea?" Nobody responded. There was silence in the room for several seconds, and then they moved on.

"Are we going to wait for the killer to shoot before we take any action?" Hector asked.

"Jerome, I don't see any other viable option. It might mean one more death, but if we do what we have to do, it will be the last of it. We can hope that the shooter has an off day and doesn't take his target out. Once a shot is fired, we have to hope that the shooter casually tries to walk away as the two witnesses had described. As soon as a shot is fired, call for backup and make the shooter your focus. We'll have to ignore the victim because we don't want to miss the shooter while trying to attend to the victim. Our job is to apprehend the killer. It's the medical professional's job to treat the injured. Be alert, and be careful, real careful. We don't want to lose one of us. We're dealing with a very dangerous man."

The team sat in silence as they all thought about the task ahead of them. After a little while, DuKane thanked the team and told them he would get back to them with specifics after talking to the commander. The meeting broke up.

Jefferson and Hector walked away from the meeting together. Jefferson said, "I think DuKane did an amazing job in putting the pieces together and recognizing the killer's tendencies. The chart was a creative idea. I'm sure we'll steal the idea at some point. While reviewing his chart and his findings, he indicated that a cop might be involved. It would seem that we should be investigating that possibility in some way, internally. It leaves me wondering why we're not. I almost challenged that, but we're the new guys here. I don't want to give the impression that we think we know everything. I've known DuKane for a long time now. He's a good detective. I guess I'll just trust that he knows what he's doing."

"Perhaps he's working that out with the commander," Hector responded.

"I hope so."

CHAPTER 4

The city of Chicago had initiated a project to help eliminate gathering places for gang members and to continue an on-going process of improving neighborhoods. The project called for abandoned houses that were falling into complete disrepair to be torn down. A vacant lot was certainly easier on the eyes than a house that was boarded up, with peeling paint and a sagging roof. Not only were these homes unattractive, but they presented risks to the safety and health of the neighbors.

A company was contracted to tear down a house in the Auburn Gresham Neighborhood. The house had been vacant for at least three years. There was graffiti on the outside walls, and it appeared that someone had torn some of the siding off. From the outside, it looked like it would need a lot of work if it were to ever become habitable again. The two workers who were there to do the demolition agreed that the house could've been a gem if it had been cared for. It was a shame that it was coming to such an inglorious end.

The men ripped the board down that was covering the front doorway. The gas, electric, and water had been shut off years ago. Even so, the utility companies were contacted to coordinate efforts to be sure it was safe to proceed with the demolition. The two men were tasked with double checking to be sure everything was ready to go. They each had on hard hats with built-in flashlights. With very little natural light inside the house, it was mostly dark and somewhat eerie and had an unpleasant odor. They wanted to be sure they knew what would be involved with this particular demolition. Very occasionally, when getting ready to tear down a home, they'd find something of value within the house. They had their eyes open, trying not to miss a thing.

The house was two stories, with a cellar underneath. After walking through the first and second floors, seeing nothing unusual, they headed down the cellar steps. One of them said to the other, "There sure is a lot of crap down here." The two upper floors had been gutted. Even the walls weren't intact. The plaster had been ripped off, and the wiring and pipes behind them had been exposed. That's why they were surprised that the basement still had things lying all around, even if the things looked like junk. As they sifted through the mess, it made sense why these things hadn't been taken. They saw nothing of value. Everything was grungy. They found old rags, bedding, paint cans, and rusty hardware. They came across what they guessed to be old kitchen cabinets that had been reduced to a nasty pile of rotting wood. The doors were missing. One guy said, "I wonder where the doors are?"

"I'm sure they're here somewhere," his partner replied. The two men headed toward opposite corners of the cellar, and the second man said, "This is disgusting. There's a cot over here that I don't think a rat would lie in. I wonder if it was this gross when the people who lived here were still in the house. It's sickening." He kept walking, and then yelled, "Oh SHIT! Get over here, right now."

The other guy maneuvered around the mess and joined his co-worker as quickly as he could. They found themselves looking down at a human skeleton. "We need to call 9-1-1. This house will live another day, unlike this poor bastard."

• • • •

Detectives Jefferson and Hector were assigned the case. Theirs was an interesting partnership. Jefferson was in his forties, married with two teenage children. He was African American, standing six feet, two inches tall and weighing a lean 185 pounds. He'd had to work really hard to be promoted to detective. Hector was only twenty-eight when he was promoted, and Jefferson resented that it had been given to him much too easily.

Hector couldn't have been more different than Jefferson. His mother's family was from Mexico, and his father was a Russian Jew. He was five feet, ten inches and weighed a beefy 225 pounds. He was thick and as strong as an ox. He was single, but vigorously playing the field.

There was no way to know at this point how the body came to its demise. It could have been a murder, a suicide, or from natural causes. It was up to the detectives, along with the crime scene technicians and medical examiner, to determine the cause of death. They arrived on the scene within short order. The two men who had uncovered the skeleton were waiting in front of the house. They talked for a little while, but of course, the men had no information that would be helpful. Hector got their names and contact information in case the detectives wanted to confer with them again.

As they were wrapping up the discussion, two people from the crime lab arrived. The two of them and the detectives proceeded into the house and headed to the cellar with flashlights in hand. It had a very musty odor, but the corpse, or what was left of it, was way past the stage where its odor would be overwhelming. There were two very small windows, high on the wall on one side of the basement. Both had been boarded up. The skeleton was halfway between the windows, approximately five feet from the wall. Jefferson moved carefully toward the skeleton, making sure not to hit his head on anything above. The rafters supporting the first floor were only two or three inches over Jefferson's head. Hector, being shorter, had no concerns, nor did either of the technicians.

The skeleton was lying on its back. There were rotten shoes sitting on the feet and rags covering small areas on the corpse. Jefferson guessed that rats had probably ripped through the clothing to get to the flesh. Part of a T-shirt still circled the neck. It looked like it may have been white at one time, but the scrap remaining appeared to be a deep reddish-brown color, with some areas almost black. After taking pictures from every possible angle and shooting a video of the remains, one technician carefully put a slit in the collar, removed it gently, and bagged it. He proceeded to do more of the same with the remaining material that was still intact. The bags were labeled so the techs would know exactly which part of the body each piece had come from. He also removed and bagged what was left of the shoes.

The other technician took scrapings from the floor surrounding the skeleton. The two of them worked from one end of the cellar to the other, looking for anything that might be evidence. It was a time-intensive endeavor due to the amount of debris scattered around. The only thing that seemed useful was a shard of glass that was lying next to the skeleton. It was shaped like a shiv, and it was very dirty. It appeared to have some of the same dark reddish-brown coloring on it that was found on the remains of the collar of the T-shirt. The techs felt like they had a real solid clue as to the cause of death, but they had to get back to the lab and run some tests.

Meanwhile, Jefferson and Hector went searching to try to determine where the glass came from. It didn't take long to find what they were looking for. Although both basement windows were boarded up, the glass in one of them was intact, while the other window had only small pieces of glass still remaining around the edges. There was no glass on the floor under the window, though, so they went outside. They found pieces of glass lying next to the house under the little window. Jefferson said, "Let's be sure that the techs collect this glass to try to match it to the piece found inside."

"With the glass lying on the outside of the house, we can assume that the window was broken from the inside. We also know that the window was broken prior to the opening being boarded up. Somebody had to reach through the window frame to retrieve the piece of glass. Doesn't that seem like a strange murder weapon or a weird way for someone to commit suicide?" Hector said.

"At this point, we don't even know for sure if the guy died of natural causes," Jefferson responded. "But assuming that he committed suicide or was killed, it's strange. I'm trying to imagine the scenario, and frankly, nothing seems to make sense. If it was a murder, I can't imagine it was premeditated. As you said, the choice of weapon doesn't make sense. On the other hand, it's hard to believe it was a crime of passion. Who would've thought to break a window and recover a piece of glass to use as a weapon?"

"I'm trying to picture a heated argument where one person broke a window and turned toward the other person with a sharp piece of glass,"

Hector mused aloud. "I would think the victim would try to get away. Yet the body was fairly close to the broken window."

"It appears as if we really have a mystery here," Jefferson agreed.

The detectives returned to the cellar. The techs were still searching through the rubble. They had collected a few odds and ends, but they didn't think they had found anything else that would help in the investigation. One of the techs indicated that he and his partner would have to return to the house with their battery-powered search lights. They needed more light than their flashlights were supplying. They would be able to set the lights on tripods. That would allow them to do a much more thorough search.

Jefferson told them about the glass on the outside of the house. The four men made one more quick walk-through of the inside of the house and then headed outside. The detectives searched for more evidence, while the techs collected the glass. No other evidence was uncovered. The techs returned to the lab to pick up additional lighting. The detectives went back to the station to report what they found to their sergeant.

CHAPTER 5

After walking out of his meeting with the task force, Fred DuKane's next stop was his sergeant's office. Sergeant Dirk Trout was sitting at his desk, pecking away at his keyboard. The office was small and cramped. The entrance wall was made mostly of glass, so the sergeant could keep an eye on activity within the squad room. In Trout's case, the glass had little use. He usually kept the blinds down. DuKane always wondered if it was to keep his own activities private or if he didn't want to know what was going on. DuKane didn't think that Trout didn't want to do his job, but he was smothered by an overbearing commander who seemed to go out of his way to make Trout look small. He gave Trout little opportunity to do the job he had been tasked with. The Bulldog was a control freak with a nasty personality.

DuKane, like most of his colleagues, had mixed feelings on the issue. They felt sorry for Trout but believed it was partly his own fault for not standing up for himself, or even more importantly, for his men. As DuKane entered the office, Trout asked, "What do you need, Detective?"

DuKane gave the sergeant a recap of the conclusions he had made in the Vigilante Killer case and how he came to them. He outlined the plan that he and his team had put together for capturing their target. As he finished his oration, he sat patiently and waited for Trout to respond. Throughout his review, Trout sat silently, never indicating that he agreed with what he was hearing, nor that did he have a problem with any of it.

He was emotionless and never even nodded to indicate he was taking it all in. DuKane continued to stare at Trout, waiting for some response. He assumed Trout was mulling it over, trying to figure out what the commander was going to say. Apparently, he never figured it out. When he finally did speak, he said, "Let's go talk to the commander and see what he wants us to do."

DuKane took that as a positive. It seemed as though Trout's main mission was to avoid the commander as much as possible. He must have been feeling good about what he heard or there was no way the two men would be going to ask for an audience with The Bulldog.

As the two men neared the commander's office, he was approaching from the other direction. He looked at the two of them and scowled. "I was just getting ready to summon you two for our daily powwow. The news better be good."

"We're doing fine, Commander. Thanks for asking," DuKane responded.

The commander was not amused. "As usual, you're just a riot. If you don't get this case solved soon, perhaps you can start a new career as a comedian."

The three men entered the office. The commander took a seat behind his desk and motioned for the other two to sit across from him. As usual, Trout went silent. DuKane got right to it, not waiting for the commander to speak first. He went through the same story he'd shared with Trout. The commander listened intently, nodding his head to indicate he was getting it. When DuKane finished, the commander responded immediately. His initial response was to give DuKane hell for not putting his chart together sooner and for taking so long to get to this point. DuKane was getting pissed off and was getting ready to bolt, but then something shocking happened.

The commander said, "In spite of being late to the party, you did some nice police work. This is what I've expected from you all along. You have the ability to be a star, and finally, you're showing signs that you get it."

DuKane sat dazed. He hadn't expected a compliment from the commander, even if it was a backhanded one. The commander proceeded to talk about the plan for catching the killer. He had some suggestions, but nothing that significantly changed the plan. That also surprised DuKane.

He had been afraid that the commander would come up with something completely different from what he was proposing. The meeting ended with DuKane feeling better than he had in a long time.

After leaving the meeting, DuKane contacted each of his team members. He communicated that the plan was a go, and he gave directives for each member pertaining to his or her assignment. The pieces were all in place, and everybody understood their responsibilities. DuKane called his wife and told her that he was headed home. He was going to be putting in some longer days and wanted to get some extra family time before jumping in.

• • • •

As the DuKane's were finishing dinner that night, the youngest son, Sean said something about becoming a cop after he graduated from college. The boy was an eighth grader. DuKane said, "I'm impressed that you already know what you want to do when you grow up. I didn't know what I wanted to do until I was an adult, and I still wonder if it was the right thing. I'm not crazy about your choice of professions, though, Son. After we clean up the kitchen, let's sit down and talk about it."

The oldest son, Patrick, chipped in with, "I'm going to sleep better at night knowing that you're a cop. For sure, the world will be a safer place."

"Don't count on sleeping well because you'll be in prison," his little brother replied. "I know the things you've done. You're the first person I'll arrest." The boys smirked at each other, and DuKane just shook his head.

DuKane, his wife, and Sean stayed in the kitchen after clean up. They sat at the table and talked. DuKane asked his son why he wanted to be a cop.

"I like to solve puzzles, and I'm good at it. Your work seems really interesting. You get to meet a lot of people, and you help people."

"What do you see as the downside to being a cop?" DuKane asked.

"I know at times you have a lot of pressure on you, and you work long hours. My guess is that no matter what I choose to do, there'll be pressure, so I might as well do something that I'm interested in doing."

"It sounds like you get it, but you're leaving out one big piece."

"What's that?"

"It's dangerous being a cop. We put our lives on the line every day. Also, as your mother will tell you, being married to a cop is tough. I know that she worries about me all of the time." He looked at Ginny and asked, "You do still worry about me, right?" She just smiled and nodded.

"Dad, it sounds like you're trying to talk me out of being a cop."

"If you told me you wanted to be an accountant, I couldn't tell you much about the work. But you said that you want to be a cop, and I know all about that. I'm just trying to make sure you understand what you'll be getting yourself into. In the end, you'll do what's best for yourself, and I'm sure that you'll make us proud. I'll tell you what. Next summer, I'll arrange for you to spend a day in the field with a patrol officer so that you can see what the job is really about. How does that sound?"

"Very cool, Dad. Thanks."

DuKane moved over to his son and gave him a kiss on his forehead. Ginny rose also, and she and Fred walked toward the family room as their son headed to his room.

"What are you thinking?" Ginny asked.

"I'd rather he find something else to do. He's a bright kid with a good personality. He could be whatever he wants to be. I'll support whatever decision he makes, but I hope when he sees the grunt work and the reporting that a cop does, he changes his mind."

"You're a good man, Detective DuKane. I'm glad I picked you to be my children's father."

"Me too."

CHAPTER 6

After hearing from DuKane with final instructions for the following day, Detective Marcus Jefferson got a call from one of the men in the crime lab. The two techs had returned to the house where the skeleton was found. Armed with spotlights, they had done a thorough search. The crime lab technician explained what they had been able to find with the better lighting. "We assumed that rodents had gotten to the body because the pieces of clothing on the scene were so tattered. We were also able to verify that maggots shared in the feast. There were sufficient amounts of pupae casings in and around the body to indicate that they were there. We also found what looked to be fine sawdust, which we identified as beetle droppings. It's no wonder that all that was left of the man was his skeleton."

"Believe it or not, this is the first case I've worked where only a skeleton was left of the body. Remind me what pupae are."

"In layman's terms, when fly eggs hatch, they are at the larvae stage and are commonly known as maggots. The purpose of the maggot stage is for the insect to gain nutrition prior to their final stage of development. In that final step, they go into the pupae stage, where they have a shell that encases them, very much like butterflies in cocoons. In three to six days, they develop legs and wings and become full-grown flies. After they move on, the pupae is left behind."

Suppressing a shudder, Jefferson said, "How delightful."

The tech continued to summarize their activities during their second trip to the house. After taking additional pictures and video, they had transported the skeleton back to the lab. They were able to transport it without doing any damage to it. "We have more work to do, but we believe that we know how the man died," the tech said. "We also collected something from the scene that you need to see. Why don't you come over to the lab?"

Jefferson collected Hector, and the two of them headed over. They met with the chief tech. After a few pleasantries, Hector asked, "What do you think the cause of death was?"

"Understand what I'm about to tell you isn't conclusive yet, but we believe that it'll prove to be right. By the way, we know for sure that the skeleton is a man's. It appears that he was stabbed multiple times by the shiv-like piece of glass found next to the body. From the nicks on the vertebrae and sternum, it appears that the neck and chest were the main targets. It's possible that the guy was cut in both the external and internal jugular veins. His heart may have been hit too. If we're right, the victim would've bled out fairly quickly, within a few minutes."

"How do you know that the guy didn't cut himself?" Hector asked.

"We don't know for sure, at least not yet. However, if the guy did this to himself, it would be the most unique suicide I've ever seen. Usually, people who cut themselves in attempting suicide, go for their wrists. I've never seen a case where someone used a piece of glass to commit suicide. We know that there is blood on both ends of the glass. My assistant is checking to see if the samples match each other. Our guess is that we'll find a second person's blood."

"It looks like we have a murder case on our hands. You said that you had something that we needed to see. What is it?" Jefferson asked.

"In the corner of the cellar was a rickety old workbench. Under the bench, we found a journal of sorts. I've leafed through it. It appears that it was written as a diary. I haven't examined it in detail, but it seems as though it was written by a woman who was being held captive."

Surprise flashed on both detectives' faces. Hector asked, "Can we have the journal?"

"Not yet. There was a sleeve for a pen on the inside cover, with a pen still in it. We need to do some work with it first, checking for fingerprints,

DNA, and other possible markings or stains that might be useful from either the journal or the pen. We can probably have it for you late tomorrow morning."

Nodding, Jefferson said, "Please give me a call when you're ready to release it to us. Do you have anything else?"

"Not yet. We hope to use dental records to identify the victim. Frankly, we don't have a lot more to go on."

The detectives thanked the tech and headed out the door. As they walked, Jefferson asked Hector what he thought they should do next. Jefferson already knew the answer, but he had learned through partnering with Hector that he was touchy about being told what to do. Hector knew what Jefferson was up to. He chuckled to himself. This worked for him. He said, "Why don't I check records and see who owned the house prior to it going vacant? Once we have that, we can start checking the background of the owner or owners."

"It sounds like a plan. Let's go see the sergeant and fill him in."

They approached the sergeant's office. He was on the phone but motioned them to come in. Jefferson couldn't help but grin. The sergeant was not talking, only listening. Occasionally, he nodded his head. Obviously, the person on the other end of the line couldn't see the sergeant moving his head. Even a grunt would've been more useful. At least that person on the other end of the line would've known that the sergeant was still on the line. Hector noticed Jefferson grinning but had no idea why. At the end of the conversation, Trout uttered his first words. He said okay just before he hung up.

Trout looked at the detectives and raised his eyebrows. Hector reviewed their conversation with the lab technician. Trout never asked a question or made a comment while Hector was speaking. He did make eye contact with Hector, and that was good. You couldn't always count on that from Trout. When Hector finished, Trout finally spoke. "The Vigilante Killer is your priority for the next few days. We can talk about this investigation after we capture the Vigilante."

The detectives waited for more, but that was it. Jefferson said, "Okay then, we'll be on our way." His voice was uncharacteristically high as he said it. Hector couldn't help himself. He broke out laughing. He just found dealing with Trout to be so bizarre, and Jefferson's remark seemed so amusing. The more he tried to stop laughing, the harder he laughed. Soon, Jefferson found himself laughing as well. He wasn't even sure why Hector was laughing, but the man seldom laughed, and it was just so contagious.

But it wasn't contagious enough to get Trout laughing. He just watched in silence as the detectives walked out of his office, still laughing. He had no idea what was so funny. It was apparently over his head, and he was okay with that.

CHAPTER 7

At six thirty on Tuesday evening, DuKane and Detective Vicky Soderheim left the station and headed for a local restaurant. Over dinner, they reviewed their plan for the evening. DuKane made sure that Soderheim understood that the priority wouldn't be the victim. It would be capturing the killer. He was very emphatic. That seemed counterintuitive to Soderheim, but it had to be at least the fourth time she was told the same thing. She was new enough that she didn't want to rock the boat by protesting. She would do as she was told. Conflicting emotions haunted her. She was nervous because she'd never been involved in anything like this before. But there was a certain excitement about it too. She wouldn't admit it, but she was glad that she was partnering with DuKane and not a uniformed cop as the other detectives were. This would be a good learning experience for her.

Over dinner, after reviewing the plan, the detectives mostly made small talk. They got to know each other a little better and gained some comfort with each other. DuKane was favorably impressed with Soderheim. She was bright and committed. He had no doubt she could become a good detective at some point, but she was awfully green. When he had been coming up through the ranks, by the time somebody made detective, they were much more experienced and worldly then Soderheim. Times were changing, and he realized that he had no choice but to accept things as they now were. He knew that he only had a few days with her, and he decided to try to mentor her as much as he could while they were together.

They would be spending a lot of time in the car. He wouldn't have anything better to do. He believed that she would welcome any advice he could give.

It started getting dark around eight fifteen that night. At eight forty-five DuKane and Soderheim were parked half a block down from the home of Nemiah Parker. He was suspected of killing several people, but the police had never been able to make a case against him. At one time, they'd had a witness to one of the murders. She agreed to testify. She indicated that she was sick of gang violence, and that seeing Parker shoot a teenager would give her nightmares for the rest of her life. As the trial date approached, though, the woman changed her story. It was obvious that Parker or one of his cronies had gotten to her. The prosecuting attorney couldn't get the woman to cooperate after that.

Soderheim could feel a tense excitement when she realized that there was a vacant apartment building within shooting distance of Parker's house. Suddenly, the situation felt very real to her. She said to DuKane, "Did you notice the boarded-up building?"

"You don't think we landed on Nemiah Parker by mistake, do you? I scouted out all of the targets' neighborhoods before I assigned one to each member of the task force. Some of the other targets live in areas that provide similar circumstances, but Parker has the worst reputation. He would be the guy I would go after first if I were the Vigilante Killer."

"You really want to be the guy to capture this killer, don't you?"

"Yes, but I also thought that as the head of the team, I should take the riskiest assignment."

"Do you mind if I ask you something?" she asked.

"Go ahead."

"Okay. Yesterday, at the task force meeting, you indicated that a cop could possibly be the killer. You didn't say any more about it after that. Shouldn't we be pursuing that angle?"

"That's a good question. Here's what I'm thinking: even if it's a cop, if our plan works, we'll catch him."

"That makes sense, but if it's a cop and he hears about the plan, he might not strike this week, and we won't catch him."

"True, but think about this: For thirteen weeks in a row, the killer has stuck. He has established a pattern. If the killer doesn't strike this week, we can assume that he is a cop and he knows our plan. Why else

31

would his pattern suddenly change? If that's the case, we'll initiate an internal investigation. With what we know, we'll have a good chance of catching the guy. We know that he's African American, of average size and build, and probably has a full beard. We also know that he is a crack shot. Through background checks, we'll be able to narrow the list down considerably. My guess is that we identify the guy within a few days."

"Wow, you really thought this through. I'm impressed. Why do you say he *probably* has a full beard? Isn't that what both witnesses said?"

"They did, but we don't know if it's real. He may have been wearing a fake beard to disguise himself."

"I was kind of thinking that myself."

For the next hour, DuKane laid out different case scenarios and challenged Soderheim to tell him how she would proceed. She did relatively well, but in a few situations, DuKane presented alternatives that he believed would be more effective. She couldn't help but agree with him. He had a nice way of presenting his side without making her feel small or inferior. He made it obvious that he was trying to teach her and not impress her. He was quick to compliment her when she nailed it, and that meant a lot to her. She liked Detective DuKane and felt good that he cared enough to want to share some of the things he had learned through his years of experience on the job.

Suddenly, Soderheim heard a loud noise that made her jump in her seat. The windshield shattered. In shock, adrenaline pumping through her, she looked over at DuKane in the passenger seat, eager to follow his lead. The only thing keeping him from falling forward was that his shoulder harness was still fastened. She saw blood pumping out of his upper chest. She was ravaged with fear and froze for a second. Her heart was beating so hard that she felt like she could hear it; *pump, pump, pump*. She wanted to try to help DuKane, and then she remembered what she had agreed to do if the shooter showed up. She radioed in for help. She screeched, "Officer down, officer down!" She gave her location. She looked over at DuKane. He was either unconscious or dead. She started crying and got out of the car. She didn't like it, but she had committed to making the perp the focus, and that's what she was going to do.

Soderheim ran for the vacant building with gun drawn. She was more scared than she had ever been in her life. No amount of training prepares you to face a killer head-on. You can go through simulations, but reality is a whole different ballgame. She continued to cry as she ran. Even with fear gripping her, she couldn't quit thinking of DuKane slumped over, looking lifeless. She told herself to focus. She found the front door to the building boarded up. She heard sirens. She thought, *Thank God, please let DuKane be okay.* She raced between the vacant building and the one next to it, toward the back. There was a back stairway leading up to the second and third floors. She looked in all directions and didn't see anybody. The stairway was not in good shape, but she saw no other option. With deliberate care, she climbed the stairs. They seemed to be floating in the wind as they swayed with each step.

There were two apartments on each floor. She could see that one of the entrances on the third floor was not boarded up. She knew where she was going now, but the fear was overwhelming. She thought to herself that it would be better to take a position to cover the doorway and wait for the shooter to come to her. She wondered if that was the right thing to do or if it was the fear talking. She wasn't going to succumb to it. She continued up the stairs with both hands on her gun, eyes wide open.

As Soderheim got next to the doorway, every instinct she had was screaming at her to turn around. She peeked around the corner and drew her head back quickly. She waited. There were no sounds from inside. She got down on her knees, took a deep breath, and crawled into the doorway ever so slightly. Her eyes felt like they were coming out of her head as she stared intently. It appeared that she was at the kitchen of the apartment, and as best she could see, nobody was there. She got to her feet and proceeded slowly from room to room. If the perpetrator had been there, she had missed him. She went racing down the weakened stairs. Now it was time to get back to DuKane. She cried the whole way back to the car.

CHAPTER 8

As soon as he received the call of an officer being down, Marcus Jefferson and his uniformed partner went racing to the scene. The call to action had come from Vicky Soderheim, so everybody knew that DuKane had to be the victim. Jefferson also assumed that the Vigilante Killer must have been the shooter. It was upsetting to Jefferson that a cop had been shot, but it was especially disturbing that it was DuKane. In Jefferson's mind, DuKane represented everything that was good, both as a detective and as a man.

Jefferson's uniformed partner was driving. Jefferson's phone rang. He saw that it was the commander. The only other time Jefferson had received a call from the commander was just after he was told of his transfer. The commander had called to welcome him aboard.

"Hello, Commander," Jefferson said. "Is it DuKane?"

"Yes."

"Is he going to be okay?"

"It's too early to tell. He's alive, but he's hurt bad. They have to take him all the way to Northwestern Memorial Hospital. It just pisses me off that we don't have a decent adult trauma center on the south side of the city. I'm going to the hospital. I've sent Trout to break the news to DuKane's family and to drive them to the hospital. Are you anywhere near the site of the shooting?"

"We're less than two minutes away. Did we get the shooter?"

"No."

"How is Soderheim?"

"She's not hurt, but she's a mess. I need you to manage the scene. I don't want anybody talking to the press. We'll handle that. Go through the area with a fine-tooth comb. This killer has gone too far. Get something that will help us. Also, take care of Soderheim. At this point in her career, something like this could derail her. She's an asset. I don't want to lose her."

"I'll take care of everything as best I can, but please call me or have somebody call me as soon as you know anything more about how DuKane is doing."

When Jefferson got to the scene, there were flashing lights everywhere. People in the neighborhood had come out of their houses, and the street was filled with a small crowd. Crime scene tape had already been used to wall off the area around DuKane's car and the area surrounding the building where it was suspected the shooter took his shot. Jefferson had just missed the ambulance pulling away with DuKane in it. Jefferson's partner, Hector, had been one of the first people on the scene. When DuKane's regular partner, Bill Small, appeared shortly after his own arrival, Hector had looked for him to take control, but he didn't, so Hector had. He was doing all of the right things. There was no need for Jefferson to take over. He shared what the commander had said to him about talking to the press. He said to Hector, "Please instruct all of our guys on the scene not to talk." He then asked, "Where's Soderheim?"

Hector pointed to a patrol car. Jefferson walked over to the car. Soderheim was in the passenger seat, with a uniformed cop in the driver's seat. The windows were open. Jefferson walked up to Soderheim. She looked up at him. He could see that she was totally distraught. He placed a hand on her shoulder. No words were spoken. They just stared at each other, neither knowing what to say. After a few seconds, Jefferson said to the uniformed cop, "If you don't mind, let me take your place. I'd like to talk to Detective Soderheim." The officer agreed and got out of the car. Jefferson took his place behind the wheel.

Jefferson wanted to ask Soderheim how she was doing, but he already knew the answer. Instead, he asked, "Did the paramedics indicate how DuKane was doing?"

"It was awful. He never gained consciousness. The paramedics didn't communicate with us at all, and Hector ordered us to stay away so they could focus on DuKane. He didn't look good."

"Why don't you tell me what happened."

Soderheim described what happened. He assured her that she had done exactly what was expected of her. "Vicky, you know you're not responsible for the shooting. There was no way any of us could've prevented it. You did the right thing in pursuing the gunman. It sounds like you handled the situation exactly like you should've. You can be proud of your actions."

"I'm not proud at all, Marcus. I didn't move quick enough to apprehend the guy. I accomplished nothing."

"It sure sounds to me like you jumped into action. I don't know what else you could've done."

"I have to tell you something. Before tonight, I thought I was brave, but I discovered that I'm not. In fact, I feel like a coward. I was so scared that I was shaking. Maybe I'm not cut out for this work after all."

"Vicky, you have it all wrong. Brave doesn't mean not being scared. In fact, in the situation you were in, not being scared would be idiotic. The definition of brave is doing what needs to be done in spite of being deathly afraid to do it. That's exactly what you did. I assure you that many cops would've waited for backup. What you did was amazingly brave."

Soderheim looked into Jefferson's eyes, trying to read him. Was he being sincere or was he just trying to make her feel better? She realized that either way, she was feeling a little better about herself. What Jefferson had said made sense to her.

"Can I go to the hospital?" she asked. "I need to be there."

"Yes, I'll ask the officer to take you."

After sending the patrol officer back to his car to transport Soderheim, Jefferson spotted Hector and walked over to him. "The commander asked me to manage the crime scene, but it appears that you have it under control. Do you need anything from me?"

"Thanks. I think everything's under control. Uniform cops are interviewing the bystanders and neighbors. The crime scene techs recovered the casing from the third-floor apartment." Hector pointed to the window the bullet had come from. It was still boarded up, but apparently, the shooter had created enough of an opening in the plywood covering the window to get a clear shot.

Jefferson said, "This has really turned ugly. The shooter must be a cop, or he has access to information he shouldn't have. The only thing worse than a cop being shot, is when the shooter is another cop."

"Is it possible that the killer was in position to shoot his next victim when he spotted DuKane and Soderheim and assumed they were cops?" Hector said. "They kind of stick out in this neighborhood; even unmarked, a cop car looks like a cop car."

"That's a possibility, but we had seven cars out there tonight. It seems strange that it's the head of the task force who gets shot. I believe it was a warning from the killer to back off." Hector nodded his head as if to say that could be right. Jefferson said, "Let's finish what needs to be done and get to the hospital."

CHAPTER 9

It was two thirty in the morning when Jefferson and Hector arrived at the hospital. DuKane's family, the other members of the task force, the commissioner, Sergeant Trout, and various other cops were there, silently waiting for word on DuKane's condition. He had been in surgery since sometime after ten. The people who knew Jefferson and Hector nodded at them, but nobody spoke. Jefferson spotted a woman with three teens sitting beside her. He and Hector walked over to the DuKane family and introduced themselves.

With a hollow feeling in his stomach, Jefferson said, "I can't begin to tell you how sorry we are. Your husband's special. He's a hero." Jefferson looked at each of the kids one by one and said, "He loves you guys, and I'm sure he'll fight like hell to survive this."

Mrs. DuKane thanked Jefferson.

Vicky Soderheim was sitting by herself. She had the look of a sad puppy. Jefferson headed over to her with Hector a half step behind. Jefferson sat down beside Soderheim and put an arm around her shoulder. She had been looking down. She glanced over and gave him a half wry smile and looked back down. He knew that there was nothing to say that was going to help her. They sat there in silence.

Occasionally, the sound of people whispering could be heard, but for the most part, the room remained silent. It stayed that way until close to three fifteen, when a man in surgical scrubs walked in. He moved to Mrs.

DuKane and introduced himself. He was Fred's surgeon. She stood up. He asked her if she wanted to talk to him alone. She said, "These people are Fred's extended family. Please, just tell us what's going on." She was really scared that the doctor had bad news. Why else would he ask her if she would rather hear the news alone?

The surgeon looked her in the eyes and said, "Your husband made it through the surgery. The bullet nicked his heart. He lost a lot of blood and was in bad shape. To be honest, I wasn't confident that he'd make it, but somehow, he did. It's still touch and go. He's in critical condition. He is still in grave danger. We'll have a nurse monitoring him around the clock for the next few days. From this point on, every day that he survives, his chances improve. So for now, we just want to get him to tomorrow."

"Can we see him and let him know that we're here?"

"The immediate family will be able to see him in a little while, but he won't be conscious. He'll be heavily sedated. We don't want him moving. You'll be able to talk to him, but he won't hear you."

"Thank you, Doctor." With that, Mrs. DuKane broke out crying. Her daughter Kelley hugged her mother. Patrick and Sean each put their hands on her shoulders. Kelley began crying and so did Patrick.

Hector looked around the room. Although he could still see concern, the atmosphere was more positive. He was surprised when he looked at Bill Small, DuKane's partner. There were tears running down the big man's face. Although you would never know it watching the two men interact, apparently Small cared about DuKane after all. Hector was pleased to see it.

The doctor told Mrs. DuKane that someone would come get the family as soon as they got her husband situated and comfortable. She thanked the doctor again. He smiled at her and walked away. The commander walked over, gave the woman a hug, and said, "We'll give you your privacy now. Here's my card. Please keep me in the loop concerning Fred's condition. We'll pray for him." She thanked him.

The commander spoke to the other people in the room. "Thanks for coming out to support the DuKane family. Let's allow the family to have time to themselves. Mrs. DuKane will let me know of any changes in Fred's condition, and I'll be sure everybody here gets the word."

With that, people started moving toward the elevators. Jefferson was surprised that the commander showed compassion, and even more surprised that it seemed genuine.

• • • •

When Hector arrived at the station the next morning, he had a message from the chief lab tech. The journal that they had found at their crime scene was ready for pick up. Hector went to retrieve the book. He asked the tech if they were able to get prints or DNA off of the book and the shiv. The tech said, "We got prints and DNA off of both, but we don't have time to do anything with them right now. Working on the DuKane shooting is our priority. We'll call you when we have something for you. For what it's worth, we found two different blood types on the shiv. It supports our theory that the death was a homicide and not a suicide. Hopefully, I'll have something for you in a few days."

"Thanks. Were you able to obtain any worthwhile evidence from the DuKane crime scene?"

"It's hard to say. We found a variety of things in the abandoned apartment that do provide partial prints and some DNA, but we have no idea if they're the killer's or not. We're going chase down what we have and see where that takes us."

"Do you know for sure whether the shooter last night was the Vigilante Killer?"

"One of my guys is on the way back to the lab from the hospital. He picked up the bullet. We should have that answer very soon."

"We're counting on you to give us some solid evidence," Hector said, then walked back to his desk. When he had left for the lab, Jefferson hadn't arrived yet, which was odd because Jefferson almost always got to the station before Hector. As Hector approached his desk, he saw Jefferson sitting very still at his own. Hector shared what the lab tech had told him. Jefferson looked distracted. "What are you thinking about?" Hector asked when Jefferson didn't respond.

"I can't get DuKane's shooting out of my head. I can't remember someone targeting a cop before. It doesn't make sense to me. I'm trying to wrap my head around this thing," Jefferson answered.

"It's crazy. Whoever shot DuKane has made the biggest mistake of his life. We'll get him."

Jefferson nodded. "It's weird not having our morning meeting with DuKane. I wonder if we should go see the sergeant and find out what he wants us to do."

Jefferson's phone rang. He could see that the call was from the commander. "Hello, Commander. Have you heard anything more about Fred's condition?" he asked.

"He's stable. That's a positive for now. I need to talk to you. Come to my office."

"I'll be right there."

CHAPTER 10

The door was open to the commander's office when Jefferson arrived. He motioned for Jefferson to come in. Sergeant Trout was already sitting across from the commander, and Jefferson sat in the chair next to him. Trout nodded at Jefferson and then looked at the commander, waiting for him to initiate the discussion. The commander looked pensive and remained silent for a few seconds. He got out of his chair and began pacing. Jefferson got impatient and asked, "What's up?"

"What's up is that we have a real mess on our hands. Although they're sensitive that a cop was shot, the press is all over us for letting the Vigilante Killer get one of ours before we could get him. They're accusing us of being incompetent, maybe even stupid. You can't imagine what the mayor has said behind closed doors. We need to get this guy, and we need to get him now." The commander went silent again as he continued to pace. His look had gone from pensive to bulldog.

"Jefferson, I'm appointing you to take over the task force, but I'll have no patience. You'll need to take decisive action and make things happen quickly."

The room went quiet again. The commander stopped pacing, turned toward Jefferson, and stared at him. "I want to catch this guy as badly as anybody else, Commander," Jefferson said. "He shot, and for all we know at this point, killed a good man. It makes me sick. But I'm not willing to lead the task force."

"What the hell are you talking about?" the commander shouted. "I didn't ask you if you wanted the assignment. I'm telling you that it's your assignment as of right now."

"And I'm telling you that I refuse to take it!"

"That's grounds for dismissal."

"If you think dismissing me is the answer to your problems, then do it. If you think that you have problems with the press now, dismiss me. I'd love to go to the press and tell them all about you."

"What the hell does that mean?"

"You were treating DuKane like he was some piece of shit. He's been a great detective for a long time. But you berated him and put tremendous pressure on him without offering any real help. He suspected that a cop might be the killer, yet because of the pressure, he went ahead with the operation that got him shot. I'm sure if DuKane didn't feel that he was a failure due to your treatment of him, he would've concentrated on finding the dirty cop instead of pulling an operation this risky."

"That's a load of crap. He came to me with his decision. I backed him by giving him the okay for the operation. If there was a better course of action, it was up to him to come to me with it. It's on him. You're a coward. That's why you don't want to head the task force. You're afraid that you'll get shot next."

"The thought of being shot does scare me. I'm not embarrassed to say it. But that's not the problem. The problem is that if I take the job, I won't get the support and backing I need from you. When you told me that you wanted to me to lead the task force, the first thing out of your mouth was that you would have no patience. It sounds to me like you plan to start off with me just where you left off with DuKane, being a horse's ass. I don't need that in my life. Intimidation isn't leadership. You put so much pressure on DuKane, he wasn't himself, and he wasn't thinking clearly."

"How do you think the mayor treats me?"

Disgusted, Jefferson said, "And how do you like it? Is it working for you? Are you doing your best work? I sure hope that you're capable of more. I have worked for a variety of commanders. You don't want to know where I rank you."

Jefferson couldn't believe what came out of his own mouth. Trout looked like he had been run over by a truck. He was dumbstruck but silent, as always. Jefferson's heart was racing. He was perspiring. The commander began pacing again. The room became uncomfortably quiet. Jefferson had more he wanted to say but realized that he had probably said way too much already.

The commander stopped pacing again and looked at Jefferson. The two men were locked in eye-to-eye contact. Jefferson braced himself and waited to be verbally attacked. The commander finally spoke. "The mayor specifically told me that he wants you to take over the task force. It wouldn't be good for either of us if you don't do as he wants. I'm not at all happy with the things that you said. But we have to find a way to make this work. What's it going to take for you to accept this assignment?"

The room went silent again. Jefferson contemplated what had just happened. He didn't know what to do or say next. As he thought about it, to a certain extent, he realized that he'd like to take over the task force. He wanted nothing more than to catch the killer. On the other hand, he had a wife and two teenage kids, and like DuKane, a happy family life. He realized what he had to do.

"If I take the job, I have expectations. I expect that you'll trust in me and leave me to do the job. I won't do daily meetings, and I won't let you bully me. If I have something to report, I'll report it to both you and Trout. If I need anything, I'll get in touch. Unless you have something that we can use, leave me and the other members of the team alone. That's it."

Again, there was a silence. It looked like the commander was trying to come to terms with how this meeting had turned out. It was in no way what he had anticipated. It was his first official meeting with Jefferson. He'd heard that Jefferson was a professional who was easy to manage. In light of what had just happened, he wondered if Jefferson's last commander had given a glowing report on him because she wanted to get rid of him. In either case, Jefferson was a very successful detective, and this case required the best. The commander realized he had few options.

"I have to report to the commissioner on a daily basis, and he talks to the mayor at least once per day. They expect daily progress reports. The mayor isn't going to get blindsided by the press. I need daily reports."

"I'll send you an e-mail at least once per day letting you know what we're doing and the progress that we're making." The commander nodded his head as if to say yes. Again, the room went silent. If looks could kill, Jefferson would've been a goner.

Jefferson started thinking about the task ahead of him. There was a knock on the door. The commander called out, "Come back later. We're in a meeting."

A voice said, "I have some information that I think you'll want right away."

"All right then, come in."

It was the chief tech from the crime lab. "Commander, the bullet that shot DuKane came from the same gun the Vigilante Killer has been using. He's definitely the shooter."

"There's no surprise there. Do you have anything else?"

"Not yet, but we're getting close to sorting through the things found at the crime scene."

"Detective Jefferson is taking over the task force," the commander announced. "Get him whatever you find as soon as you can." With that, the tech exited the office, closing the door behind him.

Jefferson frowned. "It's not just a coincidence that the killer happened to be in that neighborhood. He was targeting DuKane. He shot him as a warning to us to back off."

The commander responded, "Trying to kill a cop is more than a warning, it's a challenge. He thinks that he's better than the police."

"That may be true, but he didn't try to kill DuKane. In all of his kills, he's hit the victims in the middle of their foreheads. He shot DuKane in the upper chest. My guess is that he meant to hit DuKane somewhere less serious, but DuKane must have moved at the worst possible moment. This guy is a crack shot. If he wanted to hit DuKane's heart, the bullet would have hit almost dead center."

"Perhaps you're right," the commander agreed. "How did the perp know where DuKane would be? For the most part, only the task force knew where each member would be. Nobody on the task force fits the description of the killer."

"I can only think of three ways. The killer could be another cop at this station, and he works at keeping up with everything going on here. The conference room is bugged. Or someone on the task force is feeding information to the killer."

"That makes sense. What do you plan to do?"

"Give me time to think through everything, and I will devise a plan. I'll try to have something to you no later than tomorrow."

The commander wanted to demand that Jefferson provide a plan sometime before the end of the day, but he bit his tongue. He didn't want to start out on a bad foot. He had to make this relationship work. He said, "Get me something as soon as you can."

Jefferson nodded and quickly left the office.

CHAPTER 11

Hector's desk butted up to Jefferson's, with the front of each facing the other. As Jefferson returned from his meeting, their eyes met. Hector waited for Jefferson to tell him what was going on, although he was pretty sure that he knew. Jefferson said, "I've been assigned to head the task force." He showed no emotion.

"I assumed that's what the meeting was about. How do you feel about it?"

"I couldn't sleep much last night because I realized that this might happen. I have mixed emotions. Going into the meeting, I knew that I couldn't put up with the commander's constant crap. I was prepared for him. I let him have it, sharing my real feelings with him. I know that he needs me right now. If ever there was the chance to tell him how I felt, this was it. So, I did."

"I was on the other end of one of those come-to-Jesus meetings with you when we first started working together. I know how that feels." Hector chuckled when he said, "I'm still getting over it. I would've loved to witness your meeting. How did the commander react?"

"Much better than I expected. He agreed to let me do the job without his constant interruptions and interference. I told him that I refuse to let him beat on me. It probably ruined his day, but he agreed. It'll be interesting to see what our relationship is after this case has been cleared."

"Did the commander have any new information regarding DuKane or the shooting?"

"Yes. We heard from the lab, and the bullet that hit DuKane came from the Vigilante Killer's rifle."

"I think we all knew that already. Have you formulated a plan yet?"

"I have some thoughts as to how I want us to proceed. Let's take a walk, and I'll fill you in."

They headed to the front entrance of the station and started walking around the block.

"I didn't want to talk inside," Jefferson said once they had left the building. "We can be pretty sure the shooter is either a cop or a cop is feeding him information. We know for sure the shooter is a sniper. I'm going to review the backgrounds of all cops, regardless of rank or position, who work within the station. I want to see if anybody was a military sniper before joining the force."

"Why are you looking at everybody? We know that the shooter is black, and of average size and weight."

"That's probably true, but I'm not willing to assume it is guaranteed. Most people don't realize this, but military snipers are almost always paired with another soldier who serves as his spotter. The spotter is every bit as important as the shooter, and the shooter is totally dependent on him. The two witnesses could have seen the spotter if there is one. Snipers are not only trained in shooting, but they are also experts in areas such as stealth, using camouflage, infiltration, and keen observation techniques. If the shooter didn't want to be seen, he wouldn't have been. I'm thinking he let a few witnesses see him to make us think he is working alone. It's possible that the shooter isn't the cop, but the spotter is."

"I have to admit, I didn't realize snipers work with spotters. I guess I never gave it much thought. Why didn't you ever say anything at any of our task force meetings?"

"It just occurred to me recently. I planned to talk to DuKane about it, but never had the chance. I didn't mention it at our task force meeting because I was concerned that a member of our team might actually be the spotter." Hector reflected on what was being said. Jefferson started talking again. "I thought about saying something, but I held back. After all, I had no evidence to indicate that there is a spotter. But if the shooter isn't a cop, and he has a spotter, that person must be a cop. How else would they have inside information?"

"This gives me a better understanding of the situation. I wondered how the shooter got away without Soderheim getting eyes on him. But as you said, the guy would be an expert at being stealthy and at using camouflage."

"That's right. I didn't mention this, but snipers are also trained to establish escape routes prior to taking any shots. The guy or guys are going to be awfully hard to find."

"Do you think the killer is still going to take another victim this week?"

"Yes, I do," Jefferson replied.

"Well, that means he is probably still on the letter N. Of the seven guys we targeted whose first name begins with N, I think I heard DuKane say that only three of them have vacant buildings on their blocks. Why can't a few of us do a stakeout around those buildings?"

"There are two reasons. I don't want to put any more cops in harm's way until we have a better handle on things. Snipers are capable of hitting their targets from a mile away. The vacant building could be several blocks away, as long as the killer can get a clear shot. Our chances of catching the killer at the scene are very low. His training to disappear and stay off of our radar is much better than our training to spot or find him at the scene. We need to find a different way. Unfortunately, I haven't figured out what that way will be yet."

"While you're checking out the backgrounds of the personnel in our station, I'll start doing work on the other case. I'll find out who lived in the house where the skeleton was discovered before it went vacant. Hopefully the lab guys will get a chance to identify the remains soon."

CHAPTER 12

It was seven thirty on Wednesday evening. The Vigilante Killer sat at a bar nursing a beer. He had arrived around seven and patiently waited for his companion to show. He wanted to order something to eat, but he would do the polite thing and wait. Shortly thereafter, the companion appeared. The two men gave each other half-hugs like men do. They sat down. The bartender came over. The companion ordered a beer, and both men ordered a hamburger. As the bartender walked away, the men talked in hushed tones. The killer asked, "Have you heard how DuKane is doing?"

"It's almost twenty-four hours and he's still hanging on," the companion said. "That's as good as it's going to get for now. Why did you shoot him in the heart? I told you it was a big mistake going after him. And why didn't you stick to your plan for a nonthreatening shoulder shot you?"

"That was the plan. I was aiming for above his heart. I had the spot I wanted to hit locked in my sights. As I started pulling the trigger, his chest began rising, as if he were repositioning or taking a deep breath. I tried not to shoot, but I was too far into it. I didn't anticipate the movement. I'm not happy about it. I take pride in doing exactly what I want to do when I shoot. But stuff happens."

"This isn't good. We better hope that he makes it. Shooting a cop is really bad; you invite every other cop in the city to take part in your capture. Killing a cop is even worse. I knew I should've stopped you."

"I had no choice. He was starting to figure me out. He saw the patterns to what I was doing. It was just a matter of time before he put the whole thing together. I couldn't chance it. Now he's out of the picture. It's better for me, and it's better for you."

"I told you not to follow a pattern. I knew somebody would figure it out eventually."

"And I told you that I wanted to use a pattern so when the information became public, the cops would be humiliated for not coming up with it sooner. It took them thirteen hits before someone put it together. The cops are incompetent, and this will demonstrate it to the public."

"The public will never know any of this."

"You're wrong. I plan to call a reporter from a burner phone and give him the story. I'll lay out the whole thing. This not only will be in local papers, but it will go viral. The Chicago Police Department will be exposed for what they are. Besides, I realize that you don't see the cops as the enemy, but they're partially to blame for my actions. They know who killed Anthony and Roland, and yet they never made a case against those punks."

The companion heaved a heavy sight. "You've already killed both of those guys. You've avenged your brothers. It's time to back off before you get yourself caught."

"Maybe I've avenged my brothers, but what about all of the other families that are losing loved ones to gang violence? Who's avenging those needless deaths? It certainly isn't the cops. Even when they know who the killers are, they seldom get enough to prosecute them. They're not putting in the effort it takes to put these criminals behind bars. Every gang member I've taken out has had his share of kills. I'm going to keep killing until I'm caught or the disruption to the gangs becomes too much for them to survive."

"You're no better than the people you're hunting when you shoot—and in this case, possibly kill—a cop. The guy you shot is a good family man. You can't justify what you did to him. He does his job. He's not a slacker. You wanted to scare the police off, and instead, you've initiated a call to action. I'm mad at myself for not stopping you. If DuKane dies, I'm done feeding you information. This whole thing makes me feel conflicted, at best. When you eliminated your brothers' killers, I was okay with that.

51

Maybe I even felt good about it. But I'm not feeling good about the other killings."

"Why not? Other than the cop, I haven't shot anybody who didn't deserve it. The world is a better place without those guys."

"You're not the judge and jury. There are back stories to each one of those guys. Without the back stories, you don't know why these guys ended up being who they are. Most of them have had sad lives."

"Does that give them the right to ruin other people's lives? Not in my book. I can understand Anthony being killed. He joined a gang. When you live by the sword, you die by the sword. Anthony put himself in harm's way. Nonetheless, I think about him every day. But there was no justification for killing Roland. He was a good kid doing all of the right things. He was a good student. Although he was only a sophomore, he was all-city on his high school basketball team. There was little doubt that he would've scored a scholarship to college. For him to get shot and killed while playing a pickup basketball game in the park is wrong—real wrong."

"And you've avenged that killing. It's time to end this."

"When I was fighting in the Middle East and I got word of Roland's death, it destroyed me. All I wanted to do was finish my tour and get back home. I wanted to change the world. I don't know how else to do it. I know what I'm doing is right. There's a dark cloud following me around. I can't get rid of it. I can't laugh, I can't love. It's hard for me to even be alive a lot of the time. How many other people have lost loved ones to gang violence and feel just like I do? I pray that what I'm doing is giving them some relief. Perhaps they can get their lives back."

The companion sat in silence. He understood the pain and sorrow that the other man was feeling. He realized that the man wasn't all wrong. But, it just felt so wrong. He wasn't going to change the other man's mind. He had tried over and over. It always ended in the same place. There seemed to be no argument that was the least bit effective. His eyes got watery as sadness overcame him. He didn't know what to say. They sat in silence for a while. Then the companion said, "You really didn't do yourself any favors in shooting DuKane. I hear that Marcus Jefferson is now heading the task force. If there's a better detective than DuKane in the Chicago Police Department, it's Jefferson. If he gets close, are you going to shoot him too?" There was no response.

The bartender walked over with their food. The killer said, "We'll each take another beer." The bartender poured them each a draft and set their beers down. The two men sat quietly as they ate their dinners. The companion knew there must be something to say, but no words came to him.

The killer was tired of justifying his actions. He had no doubt that he was making a greater contribution to his country by killing punks than he had with terrorists in the Middle East. He was at peace with his actions.

CHAPTER 13

As the first order of business on Thursday morning, Marcus Jefferson was introduced to the team as the new head of the task force by Sergeant Dirk Trout. There was no applause or fanfare. It wasn't a happy moment. It mostly served as a reminder that DuKane was fighting for his life.

Vicky Soderheim had taken Wednesday off but was back to work. Her normal partner, Clancy Bright, sat next to her. He kept looking over at her to see how she was doing. He didn't like what he saw. She appeared to be tired, and was lacking her usual enthusiasm. Yet, she insisted that she was ready to do whatever it took to find the guy who had shot DuKane. She didn't tell anyone that she had revisited the minutes around the shooting hundreds of times in her mind. She didn't want the images taking over her thoughts but couldn't seem to stop them. In reality, she shouldn't have been back at work. Sergeant Trout insisted that she get counseling immediately. She agreed to see a department counselor that day after the meeting and hoped to get some relief.

Trout sensed a certain tension in the room. He doubted that it had to do with the appointment of Jefferson. Jefferson was well-respected. He realized that people's thoughts were probably with DuKane. "I talked to DuKane's wife this morning. The doctors are pleased with his progress. They still consider him in critical condition, but he's showing steady improvement. He's conscious, and they're keeping him comfortable. There are still no guarantees, but the doctors are optimistic."

Trout told the team that from this moment going forward, whatever was discussed amongst the team had to stay with the team. He didn't want anybody sharing anything with non-team members. He said, "The Vigilante Killer is almost for sure a cop, or is getting insider information. At this point, I still trust everybody in this room, but my concern is that some of you might be sharing information with someone else. You know how that is. One cop tells another, and he tells three more, and before you know it, a hundred cops know everything. We have to eliminate those issues. Does everybody understand that?" Everybody nodded their heads. Trout said, "Jefferson, why don't you take over and fill us in on where you're at now?"

The remaining seven members of the task force, including Jefferson, were sitting at a rectangular table in a conference room. The sergeant had been standing. He took a seat. Jefferson didn't get up. He looked around the room, trying to make eye contact with each member. Everyone returned the eye contact other than Bill Small, who appeared to be trying to stare a hole into the table in front of him. Jefferson wondered if it was because he thought he should have been the one to take over the task force or because his partner was in critical condition. Either way, Jefferson had to move on. "As Sergeant Trout indicated, we think that the killer is a cop or is getting inside information. Based on the gangs he has targeted and the members he has killed, we're fairly certain that he's had access to our gang audit. In addition, DuKane was shot with purpose. It wasn't just a coincidence. The killer knew where DuKane was going to be. That information had to come from the inside."

Bruce Winston, one of the more experienced detectives on the task force, asked, "Do we have any idea why someone would work with the killer, assuming it isn't a cop doing the killing?"

Jefferson responded, "We can only guess at this point. Perhaps the insider believes in what the killer is doing. The insider might be frustrated because he's seen too many gang members get away with murder. On the other hand, it could be that the killer has remained anonymous to the insider but has threatened the cop's family. The cop feels like he has no option. I'm sure there are other scenarios, but we would need more information to be able to understand a motive for aiding a killer."

David Pitzele

Trout broke in. "Marcus, why don't you bring everybody up to date with what you accomplished yesterday?"

"Okay. Initially, I researched all personnel working out of our station to see if any had served as snipers while in the military. I found that there were none. Next, I researched the entire police department, with a lot of help from Detective Hector and our Human Resources Department. We found that there are five African American men in the Chicago Police Department who have served as snipers in the United States military. Jerome did a lot of work checking assignments and reports submitted by these men to try to understand if any could be eliminated as suspects. As an example, one of the ex-snipers was working a bad traffic accident when one of the killings took place. Hector was able to talk to other officers who were working the accident with the man. They verified that he was at the scene for the entire operation."

"How many of these guys are still viable suspects?" Winston asked.

"We found two who could be possibilities. They both work days, meaning they usually have their nights free. They're both about average size, which includes a fairly broad range of men. One has a beard, and the other doesn't, but we don't know for sure whether the killer has a real beard or fake one. The one without the beard is single with no children. However, the guy with the beard is divorced and has one child. If we get more on him and he appears to be a viable suspect, we'll check into if and when he has his child. We don't want to involve the guy's family in any way unless we have to do so."

Trout drew the attention again when he said, "Jefferson will lay out our plan, but as I said before, nothing leaves this room. Don't even tell your spouse." Trout looked each person in the eye, one by one, to emphasize the point. Jefferson was impressed. He'd never really seen Trout take much of a stance on anything before. Perhaps the man had more to him than he'd been given credit for.

"Late yesterday, I met with some folks from the FBI," Jefferson informed the team. "They agreed to put surveillance teams on both cops from the time they leave work until the wee hours of the morning."

Another member of the task force, James Caulder, asked, "Why the FBI? Why not use our own guys?"

"That's a good question, James," Jefferson answered. "It all has to do with making sure an insider doesn't get wind of our plan. We're concerned that if we use cops for surveillance, word might get out. We want to be sure that the killer doesn't become aware of our plan. He might just shut down, figuring the risk isn't worth it, and then we'll be nowhere." Although Caulder nodded his understanding, he didn't look all that happy about it. Jefferson considered pursuing the discussion but elected not to. He would just let it go.

Soderheim asked, "How long has the FBI committed to work with us on this?"

"There's no clock on it. They'll participate for as long as it takes. We hope that the killer either plans to make a move tonight or next week, at the latest. I guess if he's spooked for whatever reason, it might take him a few weeks to get back into it. But I can't imagine that he plans to quit at this point."

"What will we be doing while this operation plays out?" Winston asked.

"I'll continue to explore other options and look for other possibilities while digging deeper into these killings. I may ask for support from some of you guys at some point. But for now, the rest of you can concentrate on your other cases."

Soderheim asked if Jefferson planned to continue their morning meetings. "No, there's no real justification, for now. That can change at any time. I'll call meetings as needed. If anything worthwhile transpires, I'll be sure to let everybody know." Jefferson thanked everybody for their time and adjourned the meeting.

CHAPTER 14

Jefferson and Hector remained in the conference room as everyone else shuffled out. Jefferson got up and closed the door. "How do you think the session went?" he asked.

"It went fine. I think people were surprised that they didn't have assignments, but nobody seemed disappointed by that. I'll tell you what concerns me. How do we know that one of the other members of the task force isn't possibly feeding the killer information? I was thinking maybe you shouldn't have revealed your surveillance plan to the group."

Jefferson nodded in agreement. "I talked to Trout about that before the meeting. He said he trusted everybody on this team, and he wanted to keep them in the loop. He talked about being transparent. I was wavering between sharing and not sharing, so I didn't disagree with him. Here's what we know: Neither of us is leaking information. We can be certain that it isn't DuKane. I'm fairly certain it isn't Vicky Soderheim. I don't believe the killer would shoot DuKane with her in the car if she were the mole. There would be the risk of the bullet ricocheting and hitting her. Besides that, her reaction to DuKane's shooting was real. She was very upset and even talked to me about quitting the job. That leaves James Caulder, Bruce Winston, Bill Small, and Clancy Bright. I plan to keep a close eye on those four."

Hector frowned. "To be honest, that doesn't leave me feeling very comfortable."

"What's the issue?"

"Unless you plan to tail all four of them, I'm not sure what keeping an eye on them does for us."

Jefferson nodded; he saw his partner's point. "Mr. Transparency, Sergeant Trout, has agreed to have the IT department review all four men's computers. They'll be looking for any suspicious communications. They'll check to see the kinds of things each man has researched. They actually have a laundry list of things they can check for to give us a clue. It isn't perfect, but it's what we can do. If we get any indication that one of these guys is dirty, there are other steps we can take, and we will."

Hector shrugged. He wasn't pleased, but he didn't have any other ideas. "How do we know Dirk Trout isn't the guy we should be looking at? He knows everything that the rest of us know. DuKane had indicated that Trout was always very low-key at the daily meetings with the commander. It's too perfect. Nobody would suspect him."

"Apparently you do."

"What do you think?"

"That never entered my mind, but it's a valid point. Trout never brings anything to the table that can help us. Although the commander is all over this, Trout hasn't put any additional pressure on DuKane or any of us to solve this thing. It's almost like he doesn't care. We've taken that to be his style of staying out of harm's way. It's possible that there's more to the guy than we think. With that said, it's still too big of a leap for me to buy in."

"I tend to agree with you, but let's keep the possibility alive as we move forward," Hector suggested.

"I'm going to do some background work today. I want to see if the four members of the task force we have penciled in as possible moles have a history with gangs while on the job. I'll go through their files and check with past supervisors and see what I can uncover."

Hector agreed, and they both got busy with the tasks at hand.

• • • •

The day went fast for Jefferson. He called his wife, Aubrey, around six and said that he would be home by six thirty. He walked in through the back door from the garage. As always, his faithful collie, Bossy, was standing at the door with her tail going a mile a minute, waiting for him to come in. The celebration lasted for a good thirty seconds. As Bossy settled down, Jefferson walked into the kitchen, where Aubrey was patiently waiting her turn. Their greeting for each other was not as enthusiastic, but they enjoyed a long hug and kiss. "Are the kids here?" Jefferson asked.

Aubrey nodded Jefferson's kids were both involved in fall sports at the high school and usually got home just before six. His son, Donnell, was a senior and played on the soccer team. His daughter, Alicia, was a freshman and a member of the cross country team. Both were average athletes but excellent students. They were good kids. Jefferson felt like the only times he saw them were at dinner and when he attended their sporting events.

Aubrey put dinner on the table, and the family enjoyed a good meal together. Donnell was a quiet kid. He had a dry sense of humor, and he often had the family laughing heartily when he did talk, but it wasn't often. Alicia was a motor mouth. Perhaps that's why Donnell didn't talk much. He didn't get the chance with Alicia around.

After dinner, on many nights, Jefferson and Aubrey took Bossy for a walk when the weather was tolerable. It was early September. The weather couldn't have been any better, just above seventy degrees. As Jefferson put on Bossy's leash, she started pulling so hard that she almost dragged him off his feet. Bossy was an excitable dog who loved any attention that she could garner.

As they walked, Aubrey asked Jefferson how his first full day as the head of the task force went. "It went as expected. We've a plan in place, and now it's just a matter of time to see if we have the right idea or not."

"What do you think, Marcus? Is it the right plan?"

"I'm not so sure, but it's a starting point."

"Of course, I have to ask what Hector thinks of it."

"He's Hector. He questions everything. It makes him a pain in the rear, but it also makes him a good detective. Today, he suggested that we need to think about Trout as a possible mole. I hadn't thought of that, but it's a possibility. It's a long shot, but stranger things have happened."

"I sure hope it's not Trout. I'm nervous enough about you taking this assignment. I would hate to think that your boss is the enemy."

"He sure has a good cover if he is. He seems totally harmless, and he doesn't come across as being that bright."

"Didn't you tell me that he was a decent detective?"

"In his day, he had a good reputation. But he also had a partner for close to eight years who was the alpha and was really good. I'm not sure if the partner carried him, or if he actually was good at what he did. He sure is a dud as a sergeant. Enough about the case, though. Tell me about your day."

"It's a new day in the library. Teachers used to frequently bring their classes into the library to do work on papers and projects. Now they seldom do. Classroom teachers have technology at their fingertips. This is the first year that the library is being used for study halls, and I've become a high-paid study hall monitor. I'm doing all kinds of things that I've never done before."

"Did you say high-paid?" Jefferson asked sarcastically.

"Be careful, Buster, or you might find out how you like paying the bills without my check."

"Steady, girl, don't get carried away."

"Changing your tune, are you?"

"Let's try a different subject. You said that you're doing things you've never done before. What kind of things?"

"Taking attendance, as an example."

"Impressive. Do you need special training or credentials to do that part of the job?"

"Aren't you cute? It's starting to sound like you're begging to sleep on the sofa tonight."

"Baby, don't be that way."

Aubrey said, "Don't baby me, you fool."

"I'm embarrassed for you. Well-educated people like you shouldn't have to revert to name-calling. It's so below the high status you've achieved in life by becoming my wife."

"Oh, brother, if this is status, I can't imagine how bad life is for people who don't have it."

"What are you saying?"

"Marrying you has been like falling into a deep chasm, and I can't figure out how to get out."

"It may not be much, but it's our chasm. Like I've always said, there's nothing like home sweet chasm." Aubrey could only shake her head. They laughed, stopped, faced each other, and shared a long, tender kiss.

CHAPTER 15

It was Friday morning. The FBI's first night of surveillance proved uneventful. Jefferson shared the news with Hector, and his partner said, "The killer has always struck on a Tuesday, Wednesday, or Thursday night. I wonder why he didn't take anybody out this week."

"He shot DuKane this week. Maybe that was enough for him. Next week will be much more telling. I'd suspect that he'll kill again next week, or at least attempt to. What did you come up with yesterday in identifying the skeleton?"

"The last owner of record for the house was a man named Alphonso Burton. It turns out that he served in the army. They had dental records for him and were able to give us a positive identification."

"What else did you find out about the guy?"

"It took a little digging, but it appears he was single. I found out that he was an only child. His parents are both deceased. I couldn't find any other relatives. He owned the house since 2001. It appears as though it has been vacant since 2005. That's also the year the coroner estimated that Burton died. He couldn't be more specific than that for time of death."

"What did Burton do for a living?"

"He didn't do anything. Apparently, when his parents passed away, they left him very wealthy. His mother had her own commercial real estate business, where she had done very well for herself. Besides brokering, she bought and sold properties. Her husband managed the properties.

They died within two years of each other and left Burton with close to twelve million dollars and several valuable properties. He sold most of the properties and was living the good life as best I can tell."

Jefferson's brow creased. "It didn't end too well. Were you able to find his remaining money?"

"He still has money invested in a variety of accounts. It appears that his corpse is still rich. Of course, nobody would reveal who the beneficiaries are for each of his accounts. I need to file the paperwork to secure a court order to force each company to share that information with us. I'll put that in motion today. I also plan to canvass the neighborhood to see what the neighbors can tell us."

"I don't see why I can't join you. There's not much more I can do for now with the Vigilante case. It appears that I have a clear schedule until at least next Tuesday. Let's take a ride."

The detectives arrived in the neighborhood a short time later. The street was lined with big beautiful trees. The homes were older but stately looking. It was a desirable neighborhood.

The detectives went to one of the houses directly next door to Burton's. Hector rang the doorbell but got no response. They moved on to the house on the other side. They could hear someone approaching the door and saw the peephole darken. A woman's voice called out, "What do you need?"

Hector raised his badge up so that the woman could see it through the peephole. "Hello, ma'am, I'm Detective Hector, and this is my partner, Detective Jefferson. We wondered if you'd be good enough to answer some questions for us about the man who used to live next door." A few seconds went by while the woman gave thought to the situation before she unlocked and opened the door. She stepped out onto the front porch.

"What do you want to know?" she asked.

Hector took the lead. "Did you know Mr. Burton?"

The woman appeared to be in her mid-fifties. She looked like she took care of herself, still attractive at an age where some people begin to look washed-out. She seemed confident but friendly. "I've lived here for twenty-two years," she informed them. "I knew Alphonso. He seemed like a good guy."

"I assume you've heard what's happened to him?"

"I saw a body bag being carried out of the house. The story I heard was that the remains of a man were found inside. Were they Alphonso's?"

"I'm afraid they were," Hector confirmed. "Can you tell us when you saw him last?"

"I think it was during the summer of 2005. He was always friendly and courteous, but we hardly ever talked other than to say hello. When we crossed paths, I talked more to his live-in girlfriend than to him. It was almost like he was studying us as we talked. The conversations were always relatively brief." Hector and Jefferson glanced at each other. They had never considered that he had someone living with him once they determined that he wasn't married. This was good information to help move the investigation along.

Hector asked, "Did they both disappear at the same time?"

"To be honest, I never thought of it as disappearing. Bella, Alphonso's girlfriend, told me a few days before they left that they were going to move down to Florida. She said they were going to spend most of their time down there, with occasional trips back to Chicago. I assumed that's where they were. What surprised me was that they didn't have somebody care for the house. The yard got overgrown. That made it obvious that the house was vacant, and it was broken into numerous times. It was stripped, and little by little, fell apart until it became the mess you see today. The city tried to find Burton, but they had no luck. I told my husband that I couldn't believe Alphonso didn't have the house cared for. When he was here, he kept the property tiptop as best I could see. Now I see why he was so remiss."

"Do you have a last name for Bella?"

"No, I don't."

"Do you know anything about her: where she's from, what she did for work, any details?"

"They were private people. I seldom saw one without the other, so I didn't really get to know the woman. They seemed to be happy. I don't think either of them worked. I can't be sure. I was still a grammar school principal when they lived here, so I wasn't around a lot during the day. Bella seemed to like my daughter, and she talked to her a little more than she did me. Perhaps my daughter could give you more information."

"Is your daughter here?"

"She's at school. She's a freshman at University of Illinois here in the city. She'll be home around four today."

Hector handed the lady his card and said, "Would you please have your daughter call me when she gets home today?"

"Okay."

"Is there someone in the neighborhood you think might have more information on Burton or Bella?"

"Not really. As I said, they mostly stuck to themselves. We have a block party every summer. Almost everyone comes. It's a nice neighborhood. Alphonso never came before Bella moved in, and he never came afterward either."

Jefferson said, "I have another question for you. How long did Bella live here?

"She moved in August 5, 2003."

"How do you remember that?"

"That date was my husband and my twenty-fifth wedding anniversary. At the time, I thought it was an interesting coincidence. It was a major event in our lives while our neighbor was also experiencing a major event occurring in his."

Jefferson smiled and said, "A very belated happy anniversary to you. Do you know if Bella moved any furniture in, or did she have suitcases with her when she moved in?"

"I never saw either. My husband and I were leaving as they were arriving. Alphonso introduced us to Bella and told us that she was moving in. We told him it was our anniversary, and we all chuckled about it being a special day. We didn't see her move anything in. She may have before or after that."

"Can you describe Bella for us?" Hector asked.

"Do you mean a physical description or do you mean something like what kind of person she was?"

"Both."

"Well, she was about five feet, eight inches tall. She was white. She had dark brown hair. She was a big-boned woman. I don't mean she was overweight; she was just big. She was nice-looking. She seemed to be the outdoors type by the way she dressed. I'd see them leaving the house occasionally with fishing equipment. They biked a lot in decent weather.

As far as describing the kind of woman she was, I can't give you much. She seemed to be very happy initially but became more withdrawn as time went on. I didn't know if it was something I said or did or if it was something going on in her personal life. That's about all I know."

"Do you know if they had many friends?" Jefferson asked.

"I don't remember them having any visitors."

"What was Mr. Burton like?"

The woman described the neighbor to the detectives. "He was about six feet tall and thin. He was African American. He had a full head of hair that he wore relatively short. He seemed to be athletic. I remember he told me that he belonged to a gym and they worked out regularly. He was a very quiet man. He always seemed to be happy. Although he had a friendly demeanor, I always felt like he was being protective of himself and didn't want to let people in. Frankly, I always wondered what his secret was, and I'm sure he had one."

"You've been a big help," Hector said. "Thank you. Please remember to have your daughter call me." The detectives walked toward their car.

Hector was pleased with the progress they had made. "The pieces are starting to fall into place a little. When I picked up the journal and pen from the lab, they had identified who the writer was through her fingerprints. It appears that the writer went missing back in 2003. Her prints were in the system from back then. She was a woman named Bertha Brown. Last night, I got home a little late. I was worn out, but I thought I'd skim through the beginning of the journal. It was written by a woman who claimed she was being held captive in the house. I didn't know what to think. Based on talking to the neighbor, it appears that Bella was Bertha, and that she may have actually been a prisoner in that house. I put the journal down because I knew if I got into it, I wouldn't get to sleep. I would be over-stimulated. Tonight, I'll go home right after we finish our day and dig in. I wonder if the woman is still alive, or if she was killed too."

"Hopefully the journal has lots of answers for us," Jefferson told him. "Rather than interviewing other neighbors, let's wait until you get through the journal. If a woman was held captive, we need to know if it was the woman the neighbor believed to be Burton's girlfriend, or another woman entirely? It's all very intriguing."

Hector agreed, started the car, and headed back to the station.

CHAPTER 16

Dirk Trout called Jefferson as the detectives were on their way back. He wanted them to investigate a possible homicide. A maid had uncovered a body at a local hotel when she went to clean the room. She knocked several times while calling out "Maid Service." There was no response. She used her pass key to open the door. It wasn't double locked, and she was able to go in. She saw a man lying on the bed. He looked lifeless, so she had called, "Hello, sir." As she waited for a response, she looked around the room. She noticed several prescription bottles lying on the floor, as well as two water glasses. There was still no response. She exited the room, closed the door, and found her manager. The manager made the call to the police. When the call was reported to Trout, he called Jefferson because he was the next up to catch a case. Trout reasoned that Jefferson didn't really have the time to take on another major case, and he thought this one would be more routine than some others.

Hector had never experienced a homicide investigation at a hotel before. Jefferson shared what he thought they might find. "I've been called to hotels before, only to find the guest was sound asleep and not dead. So before we enter, we need to knock very loudly on the door. It's possible that the guy has awoken since the maid left the room, and we don't want to walk in and give him a heart attack."

"You sound like a guy who has experienced that."

"Guilty as charged, and it wasn't a good experience. I walked into a room expecting a dead body, and the guy was sitting on the edge of the bed, naked. It scared the hell out the poor guy and left me with an indelible memory, and not the good kind." Hector grinned from ear to ear, and Jefferson said, "You remind me of my wife. She seems to enjoy my pain." Both detectives smiled and Jefferson continued: "These are tough cases to work, especially if it appears to be a suicide."

"Why's that?" Hector asked.

"Because there's so much that needs to be understood. If it's a suicide, why did the guy kill himself? Without a reason, the death can be suspicious. In fact, even if there's a reason, we have to be sure that the death is really a suicide and not a homicide made to look like a suicide."

Hector said, "When I stay in a hotel room, I always use the dead bolt. I would think just about everybody does. Apparently, this guy didn't if the maid was able to get into the room. It might mean that somebody was with him when he died, and upon leaving, couldn't double lock the door from the outside."

"That's exactly right. The fact that the door wasn't double-locked makes this more suspicious. But it could also be that the guy wanted his body discovered before too long or that he knew he was going to die anyway so figured there wasn't a need to double lock the door."

When they arrived at the hotel, the manager was waiting for them at the front entrance. He seemed edgy as he introduced himself. He walked them back to the room where the body had been found. There was a man in a suit standing in front of the door. He introduced himself as the head of hotel security. Jefferson asked him if anybody had entered the room besides the maid. He assured them that nobody had. Jefferson said, "Thank you. After we've had a chance to examine the room, we'll want to talk to the maid. Please be sure that she doesn't leave before then." The man told the detectives that the woman was very upset. She was sitting with her manager in their lunch room. He would make sure that she waited there for them.

Jefferson knocked on the door. He was very serious about knocking loud. There was no response. He had the head of security unlock and open the door. The detectives put protective covers over their shoes and walked into the room. They closed the door behind themselves and stood just inside the doorway, taking in the whole scene. The man was lying in the bed in a fetal position. He was dressed in only boxer shorts. He was facing them, and from his coloring, he appeared to be dead. They observed that his chest was still, no movement. They had no doubt that he was gone.

Jefferson continued to take in the room. "I don't see any blood or evidence of foul play. I think, for now, we can guess that the guy really did kill himself or died of natural causes." The man appeared to be about forty years old. It was hard to get a feel for height and weight, but he didn't appear to be a big man. He had a full head of curly red hair. He looked to be somewhat overweight but not obese.

"What do we do next?" Hector asked.

"We call the crime lab guys and the medical examiner and wait to hear what they discover. The less we move around in the room, the better. We don't want to tamper with the scene. The crime lab guys will be responsible for finding and analyzing evidence, and the medical examiner with determine cause of death."

"Don't you think that we could take a look at the bottles on the floor and see what the guy may have ingested?"

"We could do that, but there is no guarantee that the bottles contain what the labels indicate. Again, we'll depend on the medical examiner to tell us that. He'll also be able to tell us how much was ingested, if any."

"This is my first suicide, assuming it is a suicide. What's our role?" Hector asked.

"We leave the crime scene to the lab guys. They'll let us know if they uncover a note anywhere on the scene. We can get the man's identity from the hotel. The crime scene guys will be responsible for verifying identity, including contacting the next of kin to confirm a positive identification. We really have limited obligations until the other folks come to their conclusions. If they determine that it most likely is a suicide, but need more information, such as a possible motive, it will be up to us to dig for one. If they rule that the death is a homicide, then we obviously will do an investigation, as we would in any murder case."

"It sounds like we're off the hook on this one."

Jefferson nodded. "You're mostly right. The responsible thing on our part would be to dig into the guy's background and see if there is anything that might make his death suspicious. The lab guys are almost always correct in their assessments, but nobody is one hundred percent. We could find that somebody had a strong motive for wanting this guy dead. If the death is deemed a suicide and we don't find anything, then we can put this one to bed with a good conscience."

After the team from the lab arrived, the detectives talked to the maid. She was still shook up. She told them that she'd cleaned the room the day before and the man wasn't in the room at that time. They asked what time that had been, and she told them it was sometime mid-morning. She had nothing to offer that could help them other than that, so they headed back to the station. Once arriving, they spent the rest of the day doing a variety of chores relating to other cases. They didn't start doing any work on the possible suicide victim. They wanted positive identification before they invested time in this case.

• • • •

After dinner that night, Jefferson and Aubrey took Bossy for their walk. Aubrey asked how DuKane was doing. Jefferson said, "He continues to make progress. It appears that he'll be moved from critical care sometime this weekend if his progress continues."

"That's a relief. Have you made any progress in the Vigilante Killer case?"

"Not really. I think next week could be our week."

"What are you working on for now?" Jefferson told Aubrey about the skeleton that had been uncovered. She said, "That sounds creepy. Since when do you work on cold cases?"

"I don't."

"It sure sounds like a cold case. I mean, the remains are a skeleton. Obviously, the death is not fresh."

"You're correct, the skeleton does not represent a recent death, but the police have never investigated this death before. Cold cases involve those that have been investigated but not solved."

"Okay, I get it. Didn't anybody miss this guy? How could he be dead so long that the only remains are a skeleton and nobody reported him missing?"

"Apparently, he had no close family. It's a little too early to know, but he may have been antisocial, maybe even a psychopath. There was a journal found at the scene. The writer said that she was being held captive. The neighbor told us that the girlfriend lived with the guy for around two years. We don't know if she was the writer or if it was another woman. We also don't know what happened to the girlfriend or the possible other woman, if there is one. Hector is going to read the journal this weekend, and hopefully, it will give us some answers."

"Even for you, this case is weird."

Jefferson gave Aubrey a sideways glance and said, "What do you mean, even for me?"

"Don't be touchy, Mister. I just mean that you've had some strange cases through the years."

"Are you saying that I attract strange cases?"

"I'm not saying it, but if the shoe fits … if you know what I mean."

"Wow. Now all of the strange things people do are being blamed on me. The only strange thing I've ever done was marry you."

"Are you kidding? That was the sanest thing you've ever done, and the luckiest."

"You continue to surprise me with your modesty."

Aubrey smiled. "It's not my fault that I'm such a prize. It's just the way God made me."

"I wonder if he wanted to take a mulligan after making you."

"You may be bigger than me, but you're not big enough to get away with that one. It's going to cost you."

"Baby, you know that I love you."

"Don't baby me, Pal, you talked yourself into this one."

Jefferson looked over at Aubrey. She returned the look. They stared at each other as they continued to walk. Each began smiling at the other, until they both broke into laughter. Jefferson grabbed Aubrey's hand, and they walked hand in hand until they arrived home. Jefferson thought to himself that Aubrey was right. Marrying her was the luckiest thing that ever happened to him.

CHAPTER 17

On Monday morning, Hector couldn't wait to see Jefferson. On Friday night, he had started reading the journal from the basement of the dead man's home. He had a hard time putting it down. He ended up getting to sleep late. By nine thirty Saturday morning, he was back at it and continued reading, except for a few quick breaks. He read until just after eleven thirty that morning. He had a lot to share with Jefferson.

As soon as Hector arrived at work, he got a cup of coffee and sat at his desk across from Jefferson. "The lady is our killer," he announced. Jefferson looked at Hector quizzically. Hector realized that Jefferson had no idea what he was talking about. "I read the journal this weekend. At the end, the woman admits that she killed Alphonso Burton, aka the skeleton. Not only that, but she apparently is Bertha, the missing woman. The beginning of her story is dated the same day Bertha went missing."

"That might make things a little easier. Now we just have to find Bella/Bertha. Was the journal meaningless rambles, or does it tell some sort of a story?"

"It tells the story of her life under the control of Burton."

"Please, fill me in."

"This isn't going to be a short story, but I'll try to stick to the major points. I don't know if I should call Bella a victim or a killer—probably both. She was abducted coming out of her gym after working out. She had showered and dressed and was going to do a little shopping before returning home. She knew Burton. He had a membership at the same gym. She had talked to him from time to time. It was casual conversation, although she admits that it was, as she described it, flirty. On August 5, 2003, Burton approached her."

"Isn't that the date that the neighbor told us that Bella moved into the house?"

"Indeed, it is. To go on with the story, Burton asked Bella if she wanted to go for a cup of coffee. She declined. He told her that he had a gun in his gym bag and would use if she didn't cooperate. He told her to get into the passenger seat of his van. She hesitated, but then he started reaching into the bag. She did as he said. Once in the van, he told her that he knew she liked him as much as he liked her. He said they needed to be together, and he didn't want to lose time waiting for her to divorce her husband. She told him that she wasn't interested and wanted to go home."

"She can't be blamed for this guy's actions, but it sounds like Bella might have been a little too flirty with Burton for her own good."

"As you'll hear, this guy was a sicko. While they sat there, Burton told Bella that she was moving into his home. She objected. He told her that he could see that she was conflicted, but he knew that she really wanted to be with him, deep down. She objected again. He told her that he knew she'd eventually come around, but for now, he was laying down the law. He declared that as of then, she was officially his live-in girlfriend. She didn't know what to do. Up to this point, she was more nervous than scared. But Burton said something that changed all of that. He told her that if she ever tried to escape or tried to reach out to somebody for help, he would kill her twin daughters. Not only that, but he would make sure that they suffered before they died. She had never talked about her family to Burton. In that moment, she realized that he must have been spying on her. She was overtaken with fear for her children and agreed to do whatever he wanted."

Jefferson shook his head. "If she escaped, she could have called the police, and we could've protected her family until the guy was captured. I wonder if that was her plan."

"It didn't sound like she had a plan initially. She seemed to accept her situation," Hector said.

"The neighbor told us that she met Bella the day that she moved in. According to the timeline, that's also the day Bella had been abducted.

The neighbor said that they all chuckled because it was a special day for all of them. If a woman was just abducted, you would think that she would be uptight and withdrawn, as opposed to chuckling with a new neighbor. Maybe we should revisit the neighbor and try to get some clarification. At least we now know why the communication was so limited. Burton couldn't risk having the wrong thing said. Perhaps the neighbor wasn't very observant. She seemed nice enough, but talkative. Some talkative people aren't especially good at reading other people."

"That's true," Hector said. "I'm trying to come to terms with why Bella seemed to accept her situation without too much of a struggle. I don't have kids yet, but I'd think that if she was trying to safeguard her children, she'd do whatever it takes. So, on some level, it makes sense." Hector continued his story. "Bella said that the gym bag was sitting on the middle console. She thought about going for the gun, but she said he was an athletic guy, and she wasn't sure of herself and decided not to. She talked about arriving at the guy's house. She didn't make any mention of meeting the neighbors. Burton brought her into the house and down to the basement. His gym bag was hanging from his shoulder. He put his hand around her arm and pulled her into him. She tried to pull away, but he was too strong. He tried to kiss her. He put his lips on hers, but she didn't respond. He got angry and slapped her across the face. It stung, but she showed no emotion. She wasn't going to give him the satisfaction. It was at that moment she knew how she was going to act for the remainder of her captivity. She'd be docile and emotionless. She knew that would leave Burton with little satisfaction, and she hoped that he'd want to move on."

"Wasn't she afraid that if he did choose to move on that he might kill her? He couldn't let her go at this point. The damage was already done."

"She recognized that she could be killed, but she didn't see any other options. She was repulsed by the guy, and she knew she could never show him any affection, or even fake it. He captured her and was able to keep her because she needed to protect her kids. But he couldn't make her react in any way that would give him satisfaction. There was going to be no crying or pleading with him. That wasn't going to happen. After the slap, Burton just stared at Bella for a few seconds. Then, he told her that he understood. He knew that she was just playing coy. He apologized for the slap. She didn't acknowledge the apology. He pulled her over to a cot. It was made of heavy steel. On it sat handcuffs. Burton cuffed the woman to the cot. He said that he had to get rid of her car. She had her purse in her hand. He took it from her and emptied the contents onto the cot. He picked up her keys and her cell phone. He left everything else lying there. He told her that he would be back later. He reminded her that she shouldn't try anything that would get her daughters killed, and he left the basement.

"The woman was terrorized. Burton had her keys, giving him access to her house. If only she could warn her family, she thought. She looked around, trying to figure out a way to escape. Burton had left the lights on, so she was able to take everything in. The basement had a few windows, but they were too small to climb out of, even if she could get rid of the handcuffs. She saw a workbench and dragged the cot over to it to look for something to help her remove the handcuffs. There were no tools lying around. There were old kitchen cabinets hanging over the bench, but they were locked.

"Bella started to cry. She tried to stop. She needed to act before it was too late. She took a deep breath and looked around some more. She determined her only chance was to try to drag the cot up the stairs and then outside. It was an arduous process. She finally managed to get the cot on its side so that it would fit up the stairs. It was heavy, and she struggled, the cuff tugging on her wrist with each step. She began sweating. She got to the top of the stairs only to find that the door was locked. She banged on the door with her free hand. She banged some more and screamed as loud as she could. She screamed again and again, to no avail. The cot was pulling hard on her wrist. She was in pain. Her throat felt sore. She felt hopeless and helpless. It was the worst moment of her life to this point."

"You have to wonder if this woman was his first prisoner," Jefferson mused. "When we go back and talk to the neighbor, perhaps she can also tell us if Burton ever had any other live-in girlfriends."

Hector agreed, then continued recounting the contents of the journal. "Several hours later, Burton returned. He brought sandwiches down to the basement. The cot had apparently left scratches on the stairs because Burton figured out what Bella had done. He told her that this was her only warning. If she tried anything else, he would go after her daughters. He stared at her with rage in his eyes. He said something about trying to take care of her, but she needed to work with him. He took his sandwiches with him and left the basement. He didn't return until the next day."

Jefferson's phone rang. Dirk Trout was on the other end of the line. Trout was in the commander's office. They wanted Jefferson to come join them. Hector heard him say, "I'll be right there." Jefferson told Hector that he would be back as soon as he could, and he said, "Now it begins." He got himself prepared mentally to do battle with the commander. The man had agreed to back off. Jefferson wasn't about to let that change.

CHAPTER 18

The door to the commander's office was open. The commander motioned for Jefferson to take a seat next to Sergeant Trout when he came in. Once he was seated, the commander asked, "What's going on with the Vigilante Killer investigation?"

"With all due respect, Commander, I'm sending you daily updates. You have the most recent report."

"I've seen your reports. Let me remind you that this case has the highest visibility of any currently going on in the city. Why isn't the task force more actively working this case?"

"There's nothing to work. We're as current as we can be. As you know, we have two cops who are under surveillance by the FBI. Until the killer strikes or tries to strike again, we've nowhere to go. Every crime scene has been checked out with a fine-tooth comb. Our patrol guys are talking to people in neighborhoods where shootings have taken place. No new witnesses have turned up. Without more evidence or information, we're at a standstill. Anything else that we do is wasting man hours."

"You're regarded as a top detective. Surely you can do better." The commander's voice was calm, but his eyes were shooting darts.

"Commander, I'm not going to go down that road with you. As far as I'm concerned, you can take me off of the case or you can respect my judgment and let me do the job the way I see fit. That's what we agreed to. Which way do you want to go?"

There was a long silence. The commander got up and started pacing. Jefferson couldn't help but think of a bulldog as DuKane had labeled him, while watching the man go back and forth like a caged animal. Jefferson was surprised that he felt totally at ease. The commander's bluster was not affecting him. He looked over at Trout. The sergeant, as usual, was studying his hands. A smile crossed Jefferson's face.

As they sat in silence, Jefferson realized that the commander was waiting for him to speak. In these tense moments, the rule seemed to be that the first one to speak loses. Jefferson knew that he could outlast the commander. Trout was another story. In front of the commander, Trout was consistently silent.

After a good minute or so, the commander did speak. "If I don't see progress soon, we're going to have a new agreement, and you won't like it. Do you understand?"

"I understand that you have a lot of pressure on you. I'm sorry about that. I suggest that you work it off at the gym and not at the station. It's counterproductive to take it out on the men who work under you. The guy we're after is very good at what he does. He's either an insider himself or he's getting inside information. We should know a lot more in the next week or two, and then things should pick up in terms of this investigation. That's the best I can do. If you think somebody else can do better, I'm all for the change. Otherwise, I've got other cases I'm working, and I need to get back to them." Jefferson surprised himself with his continued resistance to the commander's demeaning management style. The things he said were true, but he had never thought he would have that kind of discussion with any commander, let alone The Bulldog. He waited for the commander to blow a gasket. It didn't happen. He just stopped pacing and glared at him. After a short while, he told Jefferson to get back to work. Jefferson walked out feeling good about his performance.

When he got back to his desk, Hector asked, "Was that about the Vigilante case?"

"Of course it was."

"I thought the commander was going to back off."

"He was and he is; he just hasn't totally come to grips with it. But he will."

"Are you upset?'

"I thought I would be if he started up with me, but I was more amused than upset. It surprised me."

"How was Trout?"

"He was his usual self in front of the commander, no more than a fly on the wall. I wouldn't know how to handle it if he ever took a position. The man might as well be a statue. I think I'm more disappointed in him than I am in the commander. Despite whatever the commander's motivation is, at least he's passionate about something." Both men sat silently for a moment as if reflecting on the situation. Jefferson broke the silence and asked, "Anything new here?"

"I have a couple of things for you. I didn't get a chance to tell you earlier, but I got a call as I was driving home last Friday night. It was from the daughter of the neighbor in our skeleton case. She said that she couldn't ever remember seeing Bella alone. She always seemed to be with Burton. At one time, Bella told the girl that she reminded her of her twin daughters, who were about the same age. When she asked Bella where her daughters were, Bella told her that they were with their father. The girl thought it was unusual. She imagined that Bella would have shared custody at least, but apparently she didn't. She said Bella was always really nice to her. I asked her if Burton was nice also. She told me he was nice but never had anything to say."

"Did the girl ever say whether she saw Burton without Bella?"

"Great minds think alike. I asked her that question. She told me that Burton often left the house without Bella, and she saw him doing yardwork from time to time. I also asked her what their relationship was like. She said that they weren't lovey-dovey, but they seemed normal. I didn't learn anything else that is going to help us."

Hector changed subjects. "While you were with the commander, I heard from the medical examiner. Everything points to a suicide with the guy found at the hotel. There was a handwritten note found under the body. In the last year, the guy lost his job and his wife. He took full responsibility for both. He had served time in Afghanistan. He saw several of his buddies killed in the conflict over there. One of them dived on top of an explosive and was torn apart. It saved our guy's life. No matter how hard he tried, he couldn't get over it. He felt that it should've been him who died. He was constantly depressed, and he no longer fit into society, according to the note. He decided to join his buddies."

Jefferson scowled. "We need to quit sending our young people to war. My own son will soon be old enough to go to war. Frankly, I don't know how parents can take knowing that their son or daughter is fighting in a foreign country. It's totally unacceptable to me. We need to be more selective as to where we send troops and *why* we send troops. If they're not killed or gravely wounded while fighting, too many of them come home and commit suicide. Over twenty veterans commit suicide every day. These people are someone's sons or daughters, and in many cases, someone's parent. It's wrong."

The detectives drifted into silence again. Jefferson reflected on how sad the world could be. The department was having tremendous pressure placed on it because a handful of gangsters had been killed. Meanwhile, more veterans commit suicide each day than the serial killer had shot during his entire spree. Yet, the local killings were big-time headlines, and you rarely read anything about the poor veterans. Jefferson's heart was heavy with the reality of the misplaced priorities.

Hector interrupted Jefferson's reflections. "For what it's worth, there was no sign of foul play in the guy's death. The medical examiner said that it was an overdose that killed him. He took a combination of sedatives, antidepressants, and pain medications, all in extra large doses. He left nothing to chance."

"But don't you wonder?" Jefferson asked. "He didn't double lock the door. Did he want someone to find him before he died? Was it a cry for help?"

"Marcus, you are ever the optimist. Based on the quantity of drugs he took, I think he really wanted to die, and we can only hope that he's in a better place."

"Amen."

CHAPTER 19

In an effort to shake himself out of his depressing thoughts, Jefferson turned to Hector. "I have other work that needs to be done this afternoon, but let's see how much further we can get in your recap of what you read in the journal."

Hector nodded and started in anew. "I thought the first day of the woman's capture was important enough to share as much as I could. I'll just try to give you an overview from this point forward."

"That sounds good. Do you know where Bella got the journal and pen she used?"

"Yes. She had both in her purse. When she tried to escape and realized that she couldn't, the contents of her purse were scattered on the floor. She gathered them up and put them back into the purse, except for the blank notebook and pen. She hid those under the workbench. She said that she was afraid that Burton might take her purse and the contents. She wanted to keep the notebook and pen to document her experience as a way to vent her anger and frustration and to help her cope. She hoped that he hadn't noticed the notebook and pen when he confiscated her keys and phone. He did take her purse the following day."

"Did she say why she had the pad in her purse?"

"No. I know you haven't seen the pad, but it's actually a four by six spiral notebook with a little holster for a pen. Bella never mentioned why she had this blank notebook."

"Jerome, why do you think she didn't use the pen to stab Burton instead of the glass?"

"I can only guess. Perhaps she didn't think she could actually kill him or disable him enough with the pen. Certainly, the glass is a lot sharper." Jefferson nodded as if to say he agreed with that theory.

Hector continued. "Bella seldom left the basement in the first month. Burton brought meals to her. She had to ask to use the bathroom, and then Burton would bring her upstairs and accompany her inside. He gave her no privacy. She said it was embarrassing, and she felt like a dog whose owner controlled when she went potty."

Jefferson looked pained as he listened. Hector continued with Bella's story. "Bella told of being raped over and over during the first month. Burton hit her from time to time. He never beat her severely, but he hurt her. She didn't fight back, or ask him to stop, and she seldom cried. As she had said before, she always tried to stay devoid of emotion. She believed that Burton knew that he wasn't doing any serious damage and that was intentional on his part. She said that he was just letting her know that he was in charge and could do whatever he wanted. It made her crazy that he was right. She was at his mercy. He was stronger than her, and he held all of the cards. From what I read, he continued to rape her for the entire time she was held captive. The beatings became much less frequent, but they became more brutal. At one point, she thought she had a concussion."

"What set the guy off when he beat her?"

"Initially, I think it was just to show Bella that he could do whatever he chose to do. Later, he took her out into public. If Burton got the impression anything was awry, he beat her when they returned home. Those beatings were more severe because he wanted her to pay for her sins, so to speak."

"Did she give any examples of a time he beat her?"

"Bella noted a lot of incidents. As an example, when they got home from the gym, he beat her for trying to make eye contact with a trainer who walked by her while she was walking on a treadmill."

"It's hard to believe that he brought her to a gym."

"He bought a family membership to a club on the north side of the city, a good forty-five minutes away from the house. Apparently, Bella lived, prior to the abduction, in Hyde Park on the south side. He didn't want someone to recognize her."

"Doesn't that seem like a big gamble for Burton to take? The city is large, but people move from neighborhood to neighborhood all the time."

"Bella talked about that. She said when Burton first started taking her to the gym, she hoped that someone would recognize her. But she had lived in Omaha all of her life prior to the family moving to Chicago just a few months before the abduction. The only people who knew her in the city were a few neighbors. Burton was taking a chance, but the odds of her being recognized were very small."

"Why did she move to Chicago?"

"Her husband was a banker. He was offered a position heading up the Chicago Division for a large international banking company. She didn't mention which company, but it sounds like they were doing very well financially, as you can imagine."

"I can't understand why Bella didn't reach out to somebody for help when they were out in public," Jefferson said.

"She discussed that. She often thought about it. She said that she knew Burton was crazy, and she believed that he would really torture and kill her daughters if she called out for help."

Jefferson had a quizzical look on his face. "If she screamed while at the gym and got people's attention, I would think Burton would have to run. If he did, with a phone call, she could get help from us to protect her family. It just doesn't seem like it would be that much of a gamble."

"I can't argue with that. For what it's worth, she said that Burton always carried a small gun with him whenever they left the house. She said that he hid it under his sweat suit when they went to the gym. We also can't negate the fear factor. Fear is a big deal, especially when it comes to the welfare of one's family."

Jefferson responded with, "I'm sure."

"To pick it back up, things improved somewhat over time. Besides taking Bella to the gym, Burton often took her when he was running errands. He took her on bike rides, fishing, and occasionally out for a meal. She didn't know if it was to soften her up, because he trusted her more, or if he wanted to give her the opportunity to mess up so he could beat on her. She continued to show little emotion, even when he was forcing sex on her."

"Burton had to get frustrated with that."

"According to Bella, when things were going okay, Burton talked to her like she was his girlfriend. He would try to be romantic. She told him that she had no interest. He felt that she was just playing hard to get. He was convinced that she loved him and someday she would slip up and it'd come out. She called him delusional, among other things."

Jefferson asked, "Did she call him that to his face or just write it?"

"As best I can tell, she said as little as possible at the beginning of the ordeal but became more assertive as time went on. She said something about living in constant fear, but after a while, she talked back to him to test her limits with the guy. She talked about crossing the line a few times and paying for it."

"Did she say how she paid for it?"

"Yes, with a beating."

Hector's phone rang. It was the medical examiner. He had a positive identification on the guy who had committed suicide. His ex-wife had identified the man. Hector asked, "Is she still there?"

"No, but I can give you her contact information if you want to talk to her."

Hector told him he did and took down the information.

CHAPTER 20

When Hector called the ex-wife of the suicide victim, she answered on the third ring. She had a quizzical sound in her voice. Hector surmised that she was trying to figure out who was calling her from an unfamiliar number. He introduced himself and told her that he was sorry about the death of her ex. He asked her if she had time to talk to him for a few minutes. Her ex-husband's name was Will Franklin. She had kept his last name after the divorce. She said, "After identifying Will's body, I called in to work. There's no way I could be productive today. So, yes, I have time. How can I help?"

"Let me apologize up front, but I have to ask some personal questions, if that's okay."

"Go ahead."

"Why did you and Mr. Franklin get divorced?"

"Before he went to war, he was a positive, upbeat guy. He had lots of friends. He was outgoing and easy to be with. I couldn't help but to fall in love with him. He was everything that I ever dreamed of. He came home after several tours in Afghanistan a changed man. He still had a good heart, but it was a very heavy heart. Emotionally, he was broken. He was constantly depressed and sullen. He didn't want to be social. He lost interest in everything. I know that he still loved me, but he could no longer express it. It was like he felt guilty for having good things in his life. He was being treated and was on several medications, but nothing ever changed." Ms. Franklin grew silent.

Hector assumed that she was trying to get control of her emotions. He said, "That must have been very sad for you."

"It was. I divorced him because it was breaking my heart to see him that way day after day. I tried different things. I tried to give him more affection. I gave him more space. I'd push him into taking me out. I'd make his favorite meals and rent the kinds of movies he used to like. I tried different activities with him, taking bike rides, visiting a beach, or going to festivals. Often, he begged out. When he agreed to them, he did it to appease me, and he showed no joy. I divorced him because life was becoming a constant downer with him. I needed to escape before it was too late. Besides, I thought that it might be the jolt he needed to find himself. Unfortunately, he accepted it with little emotion."

"I'm really sorry about that. It must have made you feel terrible. It sounds like you never quit loving him."

"I never have. My friends tried to get me to start dating after the divorce, but I wasn't ready for someone else. My feelings for Will were too strong. If he started recovering, I would've gladly remarried him. It wasn't to be. I don't know what I'm going to do now."

"I know this isn't a good thing to say right now, but maybe his passing will give you closure to that part of your life and you'll be able to start writing a new chapter." Hector waited for a response, but there wasn't one. He said, "I have a few more questions."

The woman said, "Okay."

"When a man is fighting demons that he brings home from war, he can get aggressive or be abrasive. Do you think Will made any enemies upon his return?"

"No, he was more withdrawn and hollow as opposed to angry. All of the fight was gone from him. If I couldn't stir him up, I can't imagine anybody else could."

"Can you think of any reason someone would want to kill Mr. Franklin?"

"Why? Don't you think it was a suicide?"

"Unfortunately, we do think it was a suicide, but we want to be as sure as we can be. He deserves that after giving so much for our country."

"Thank you for that. As far as I could tell, if people felt anything for Will, it was sorrow, not anger. His lack of emotion may have been frustrating at times for others. I know it was for me, but anger, I just don't see it."

"I just have one other question. Did Will form any habits, such as gambling, drugs, or anything that would have him dealing with unsavory characters?"

"He was dependent on his medications. They allowed him some means of escape. But when we were married, he spent his time doing one of three things. He was at work, he was at therapy, or he was home. When he was home, he slept a lot. He had little energy. I never saw any signs of the things you are asking about."

"Again, I'm sorry for your loss. Thank you for sharing with me. I don't think anything is going to develop to change the medical examiner's explanation for the cause of death, but if it does, I'll contact you."

"I'd appreciate that. Thank you."

Jefferson had heard the entire conversation with Ms. Franklin. "You handled that call really well. You showed great respect and empathy. I'm proud of you." Hector smiled, even though he felt like a little kid who had just pleased his mother. He understood why Jefferson made the comment and tried to take it in the spirit it was intended. Hector had the reputation of being the bull in the china shop. He was rough around the edges, so it was noteworthy that he had been so careful with the widow.

"What are you thinking now about Will Franklin's death?"

"I think we got it right. It was a suicide. I guess we need to move on."

Jefferson responded, "I'm in agreement. The only other thing we should do is call his last employer to be sure that he didn't have any issues with coworkers." Hector thought about it and nodded.

"I'll call Ms. Franklin back and ask for the information regarding his employment." It occurred to him that Jefferson was subtly telling him he should have asked for that information while he had the woman on the phone. It made him anxious. Even as gently as Jefferson communicated the message, Hector didn't like being corrected. It was hard for him to take criticism.

Once he had the information he needed, Hector called the last employer. He found that there were no problems between Will and other employees. He had been an electrician. He worked for a small family-owned company that dealt mainly with homeowners as opposed to other companies. For the most part, he worked alone, and his dealings were mostly with homeowners in their homes. The company never got complaints about him or his work. The reason they let him go was because of excessive absenteeism. One of the owners of the company said that Will was taking one to two days off per week. They knew he was in a bad place, but they needed dependable help. The owner said it was hard letting Will go, but that Will had understood and seemed to take it in stride. He didn't show much emotion. That was consistent with what his ex-wife had to say about him. Hector thanked the man and said goodbye.

Hector shared what he learned with Jefferson. They agreed that the case should be closed. Suicide had been the right determination.

CHAPTER 21

On Tuesday evening, Jefferson was feeling tired. He and Aubrey usually went to bed right after the ten o'clock news, but he was planning to crash closer to nine thirty. He was watching television with Aubrey when his cell phone began ringing. He answered the phone. It was his counterpart with the FBI, agent Pete Berz. One of the two cops the FBI had surveillance teams monitoring had left his house. Jefferson got up and started walking around as he talked. He perked up with the news. He asked, "Which cop are we talking about?"

"It's Officer Waul." Ernie Waul was the bald, bearded cop. He was divorced, with one child. Jefferson and Hector hadn't done a great deal of background work on either of the two cops under suspicion to this point. What they did know was that Waul had served in the armed forces as a sniper. He had an exemplary record with the Chicago Police. He had been an officer for close to five years.

Jefferson asked, "Do you have a tail on him?"

"We only have one car following the guy. I'm not confident that we can keep eyes on him. If the killer strikes tonight, while Waul is out of sight, we'll put a GPS Tracker on his car. We'll also assign a multi-car team to keep him in sight."

"I have a couple of requests. First, can you get someone to cover his home so that we can document when he returns. Secondly, if you go to the tracker, I'd appreciate it if you would get a warrant to do so."

Berz said, "I'll send someone to his house as soon as we get off the phone. In terms of the tracker, a warrant isn't required at this point."

"I know that it isn't required, but the legality of not having a warrant is under heavy debate. I don't want to gamble that we won't have issues going to court without the warrant. If we get one, no matter how the debate comes out, we're golden."

Berz responded, "Okay; we should have no trouble obtaining one if the killer actually strikes tonight."

"Thanks, Pete. Was Waul carrying a bag when he left his house?"

"No, but he might have one in his trunk."

"Please let me know of any developments. This could be the big break we're looking for, although I've been hoping it wouldn't be a cop doing the shooting." Berz agreed, and the men hung up.

Jefferson was no longer feeling tired. His adrenaline had kicked in. He found himself alert and ready to go. Unfortunately, there was nowhere to go and nothing he could do. He called Hector and told him the news. As he talked to Hector, the noise in the background was making it hard for Jefferson to hear. Hector apologized for the noise and explained that he was with friends at a club but that he understood what Jefferson was telling him. He asked Jefferson to call him back if there was any more news.

Jefferson walked back into the family room and shared his news with Aubrey. Even she was energized when she heard about what was going on. She asked Jefferson what he was going to do. He said, "There's nothing I can do but wait. I don't think I'm going to be able to sleep now. I'm about halfway through reading *The Autobiography of Benvenuto Cellini*. I guess I'll put a big dent into the second half of the book." Aubrey gave Jefferson a wry smile. She was always surprised by the books her husband read. His reading tastes were so eclectic. About the only thing he didn't read were murder mystery novels. He said he got his share of that at work.

At two thirty in the morning, Jefferson was sound asleep in his favorite recliner in the family room. He hadn't intended to sleep, but the reading did the trick. It relaxed him and took his mind off of work, and he dozed off, never having the chance to turn off the lamp. Just as he had fallen into a deeper sleep, his phone, which was sitting on the end table, began to vibrate. He couldn't understand the noise he was hearing in the middle of his dream. But suddenly, he opened his eyes and found himself awake.

He looked over at his phone and then at the clock on the wall. He now had his bearings and assumed the call was about the Vigilante Killer.

"Hello, Marcus. This is Sergeant Trout. I just got a call. The Vigilante Killer has struck again. He got his N. He killed Nelson Raymand with one shot to the middle of the forehead. Apparently, Raymand was on his street approaching his apartment building when the killer struck. Our guys just got on the scene fifteen minutes ago. It appears that there were no witnesses."

Jefferson told Trout about his earlier conversation with the FBI agent. He waited for a response. Almost sounding detached, Trout said, "That sounds like it has possibilities." Jefferson couldn't help but notice the lack of emotion or excitement in Trout's voice. Jefferson wondered if the guy had to practice to sound like a robot. He hung up, wrote a note for Aubrey, and headed out the door. He debated calling Hector and decided it wasn't necessary. Jefferson didn't expect the crime scene to turn up anything useful. He opted to go it alone and let Hector get some sleep.

On the way to the scene, he called the FBI agent. He woke the agent up. He apologized. He asked the agent to check with his person parked on Waul's street to see what time the cop arrived home. The agent said that he would do so and call Jefferson back.

By the time Jefferson arrived at the crime scene, there were six police cars, an ambulance, and a fire truck lighting up the street. Several neighbors were either out in the street taking in the activity or looking out their windows. Jefferson was able to identify the officer in charge and began talking with him. No clues had been found. It was just like all of the other killings. Jefferson asked the officer who had called in the shooting. The officer told him it was a neighbor. The woman had been asleep but woke up to use the bathroom. She heard a noise that sounded like a car backfiring. Carefully, she peeked out of the front window of her apartment. She saw the body in the street and called the police. "I talked to her. She said she didn't see anyone until the police cars started arriving."

"Do you believe that she didn't see anything?" Jefferson asked.

"There's no reason to doubt her. She didn't sound particularly scared. She's an older lady, and she's seen plenty of violence. She seemed to take it all in stride."

"What time did she call it in?"

"She called at nine minutes after two."

Jefferson thanked the officer. He walked over to the building that had been identified as the one used by the killer. Officers had already been through it, but Jefferson wanted to take it in himself. He walked all around the building. It was a vacant four-flat. He walked through each apartment, not really expecting to find anything. It was clear which window the shot came from. It had a tennis ball-sized hole drilled into the plywood covering it. The round piece of wood was lying on the floor in a small pile of sawdust. There were no shells left behind. In fact, nothing else was found.

When Jefferson returned to the street, the medical examiner had concluded his initial examination. He felt confident saying that the death was indeed the result of the gunshot wound to the head. There were no surprises, nor were there any pieces of new information to add to what the police already knew. Jefferson headed for home. It was now five thirty, and he still hadn't heard back from the FBI agent. He called him. When Berz answered, Jefferson asked, "What time did Waul return home this morning?"

"The reason I haven't called you is because Waul still hasn't arrived home. We have no idea where he is."

"That's peculiar. Maybe he's out celebrating his victory."

"I'm sure the killer isn't going to be celebrating," Berz replied. "I don't think you're going to find him to be the celebrating type. When this all gets settled, it will be interesting to see where he actually went."

"I didn't really think Waul, if it is him, would be celebrating."

"What do you mean if it is him? Don't you think he's your guy?"

"It sure looks that way, but we'll give him the benefit of the doubt."

"I'll get the warrant to get a tracker on Waul's car," Berz said. "We'll get a full surveillance team on him, although, from the pattern you've described to me, we shouldn't expect him to kill again until next Wednesday or Thursday. What do you plan to do?"

"We'll take a much deeper dive into Waul's background and try to understand a motive, if he is our killer. I still think that if it's Waul, he has an insider from my station feeding him information. We'll look for connections he might have to our people. I understand how someone based out of my station can get information from within. But for someone in another station to be so plugged in without help doesn't seem possible. Let's keep in touch. Hopefully we can wrap this up in the next week or so."

CHAPTER 22

After going home to freshen up, Jefferson went to the station. Hector had already been there for an hour. He and Jefferson had talked by phone and each knew what he had to do on this Wednesday. Hector was making good progress, and he filled Jefferson in on what he had discovered on their abduction-murder case so far that morning.

"On the day Bella was abducted, three people were reported missing in the city, one woman and two teenagers. The name of the woman who went missing that day is Bertha Brown, not Bella. There is a picture of Bertha Brown in her missing person file. We can show it to the neighbor and find out if Bertha is Bella. When Bertha went missing, two detectives were assigned to the case the next morning. I haven't had time to go through the case file in depth yet. I plan to do that next. However, I can tell you that the woman was never found. Her disappearance has become a cold case. The detectives on the case theorized that the woman was killed. They suspected the husband but never came up with anything concrete. Here's the part where I know I'll get your attention. One of the detectives on the case was none other than Dirk Trout."

Jefferson recoiled in surprise. "Are you serious?"

"I'm absolutely serious."

"Perhaps you won't have to dig too deep into the case file," Jefferson said. "Maybe Trout can give us the information we need. I need to fill him in on where things are with the Vigilante Killer anyway. Let's go see if he's available."

Jefferson knocked on Trout's office door and was told to come in. He and Hector walked in and took seats across from Trout. He just stared at them and waited for one of them to say something. Hector said, "We wanted to see if you remember working a missing person case. A woman by the name of Bertha Brown."

Trout raised his eyebrows. "I remember the case well. It was the last case I worked prior to being promoted to sergeant. Why are you asking?"

Hector answered. "We think she might be Bella, the woman who was being held captive by Alphonso Burton."

Trout had to think about what was being said. After a long and silent fifteen seconds, he asked, "Why do you think that?"

"Because Bertha was the only woman reported missing on the same day that Bella was abducted. From a quick look at the case file, it appears that a body wasn't ever found. I'm betting the two women are one and the same."

Trout rubbed his chin. "That's interesting. I wonder where she is now, or if she's even alive."

"We'll do our best to find out," Jefferson said. "We can go over the case file in depth later on, but for now, can you give us an overview of the case?"

Trout said, "I can fill Hector in. You need to get a report in to the commander and me about last night's killing with a plan for moving forward. The commander already yanked my chain this morning. Hector can share my information with you later." Jefferson was frustrated but didn't show it, and he got up and headed to his desk.

Once Jefferson had left, Trout started telling the story to Hector. "I remember the case very well because it was my last case. It's kind of haunted me. I never liked leaving my old desk with an open case."

Hector was somewhat surprised. In sharing that little bit of information, Trout showed the most emotion Hector had ever seen from him.

Trout continued. "Bertha had left her house in the morning. She told her husband that she was going to the hospital, where she did volunteer work. She worked half days. When she wasn't home around dinnertime, her husband called her on her cell phone. The call went right to voice mail. He left a message. An hour later, when he hadn't heard back, he began to worry. He left several other messages, but she never returned the calls, nor did she arrive at home. He called us. He was asked to come into the station to file a report, and he did. My partner and I were assigned the case the next morning.

"My partner called the husband. Mr. Brown seemed frantic. He said that he was at home, and we agreed to come to his house to meet with him. We could have had him come back to the station, but we wanted to get a feel for the lay of the land, so to speak."

Hector asked, "What was he like?"

"He was a big guy, maybe six feet four inches tall, and he was heavyset. He wasn't particularly good-looking, but he was real bright. He was a banker but had an engineer's personality. Everything was serious with him, and he wasted no words. He was very purposeful. He seemed genuinely concerned, but we were suspicious of him."

"Was there any specific reason you were suspicious?"

"Yes. He ran the Chicago Operation for a big banking company. I could see him being a forceful leader. He seemed to have drive and determination. His size projected strength. But at home, we discovered that Bertha was the boss. In fact, she ruled the roost with a heavy hand. She could be verbally abusive to him and humiliate him in front of his daughters and others. It didn't sound like they had a great marriage. This added to our suspicion."

"If the guy was genuinely upset that his wife was missing, perhaps she was treating him like he wanted to be treated," Hector suggested. "I've read that some men who are all-powerful at work enjoy when their spouse takes control at home. I guess it helps them to get some relief from the constant pressure of having to be in charge."

"We considered that, but we still found ourselves wondering if he had anything to do with her disappearance. Things heated up when we checked with the hospital to see when Bertha left work. We went to Human Resources. They had no record of her volunteering there. We were told that everybody who worked at the hospital as a paid employee or as a volunteer needed to be vetted through Human Resources before being offered a position. Official badges were mandatory for every employee to wear when in the hospital. Bertha Brown was never issued a badge, nor had she been hired."

"Did you think the husband was lying to you or was Bertha lying to him?"

"He was a bright guy. We didn't believe he was lying to us. He would've figured out that we would check with the hospital. We concluded that she was lying to him. Her daughters had just graduated from high school, and both had full-time summer jobs. He was at work. She didn't have to account for her time. We never made sense of why she needed to lie."

"Was there any other reason you suspected the husband?"

"Yes. After our trip to the hospital, we returned to his house. He and his daughters were all home. They were upset and were waiting together, hoping to hear from Bertha or from us. He said something about none of them being able to go on with their lives until she was found. When we told them about our visit to the hospital, they all seemed surprised. We told Mr. Brown that we wanted to talk to each of his daughters alone. He got very defensive. He said that he didn't want us talking to his daughters or himself without a lawyer. He implied that he realized that the family was always under suspicion in cases like theirs, and he didn't want things to go sideways on them. At that point, we hadn't implied guilt on anyone's part, nor had we started asking the tough questions. We were surprised by his reaction. We became more suspicious of him and started wondering if the daughters were in on whatever went down."

"How did you find out about Mr. Brown and Bertha's marital situation?"

"One of the daughters. They were eighteen years old at the time. One of them called us and made an appointment. She was old enough to make the decision to meet with us without a lawyer present. She told us that the last time she saw her mother, they had an argument, which I guess wasn't uncommon. The last thing she said to her mother was that she hated her. She was feeling a lot of guilt and needed to bare her soul. She gave us all of the dirt. She had heard her mother talking to her father. I guess Bertha was threatening divorce, and her father was very upset. The daughter wasn't totally concerned at the time because she often thought her parents would be better off divorced. Theirs wasn't a loving relationship. The girl went on to say that she hadn't seen her father that upset ever before and that his feelings on the matter caught her off guard even more than the threat of divorce."

"Did the daughter imply that the father had something to do with the disappearance of her mother?"

"No, just the opposite. In spite of the way her mother treated her father, she knew that he loved her. She said that he might be a hard-charging businessman but he was a pussy cat at home."

Trout's phone rang. He could see that it was from the commander. He picked up the phone and said, "Hello?" After a silence on his part, he said, "Yes, I see." There was a long delay, and he said, "I'll be right there." He hung up and told Hector that he had to go, but he could pick up the story later. Hector nodded and returned to his desk.

CHAPTER 23

Jefferson was busy at work, researching the background of the suspected Vigilante Killer. The human resource department was most helpful. Jefferson implied to the HR rep, without actually saying it, that the department was checking out Officer Ernie Waul's background because he was being considered for another position within the department. He didn't want to do harm to Waul's reputation without proof of wrongdoing on his part. Jefferson found out that Waul came to the police department as a decorated soldier. Before hiring him, the department did check into his background. What was discovered was all very positive. Not only was Waul a good soldier, he showed no signs of struggling to adjust when he came home.

As a police officer, Waul's performance was strong. He demonstrated maturity and good judgment. He was well-trusted within the department and highly regarded. He was the kind of officer who showed great promise and could be expected to rise through the ranks quickly, if that's what he wanted.

After reviewing his findings, Jefferson told Hector, "From what I can tell, we could end up working for him. His record is spotless."

"Where does that leave us?" Hector wondered out loud.

"It leaves me hoping that he isn't our guy. But he is our only suspect right now. The other suspect that the FBI has been watching didn't leave his house last night. Whoever the sniper is, we know he's pretty smart. If it's Waul, the smart thing for him to do would be to perform as an ideal cop to avoid suspicion. We can't count him out at this time. I need to get more background on his personal life, to see if there is anything there that might throw new light on the situation. I'll keep working on it. It's going to be a little tricky because I don't want to contact somebody and then have them inform Waul that we're checking on him. The person I spoke to in the HR department is going to share more information with me, but she had to get to a meeting. It's just about time for me to call her back. What are you going to do?"

"I'm going to go through the case file on Bertha Brown. Once I do that, I think it's time that we try to find her." Jefferson nodded in agreement, and the detectives went to work.

Jefferson called the woman in HR and was able to connect with her. She told him that Waul was divorced and was paying child support for his son. Every payday, a portion of Waul's earnings were transferred directly to the ex-wife's account. The HR representative was able to give Jefferson the woman's name and a phone number. Jefferson had all that he needed from HR. He thanked the woman and got off the phone. He thought that Waul might have his son on weekends, limiting his opportunities to strike. At least this piece fit with the schedule the Vigilante Killer kept.

Jefferson went through the roster from Waul's station. He was looking for someone within that station who might somehow be connected to his own station, but nothing jumped out at him. Next, he contacted the Deputy Chief for the Department of Education and Training. Jefferson and the woman were acquaintances. The department is Chicago's version of a police academy. All new recruits do their initial training there. The deputy chief gave Jefferson the contact information for the training officer who would be most familiar with Ernie Waul. He was able to make a live connection with the officer. The man had only good things to say about Waul. Jefferson asked the officer to e-mail him the roster from Waul's training class. The man agreed and said he could do it right away.

Within two minutes, the e-mail arrived. Jefferson opened the attachment. He looked through the list of names. The list was in alphabetical order. As he got near the end of the list, one name caused him to recoil. The name was Daniel Trout. Jefferson had heard that Sergeant Trout's son was a cop, but he had never met him. Jefferson looked up at the ceiling, staring as if all that he wanted to know was up there. Hector noticed and asked, "What's up?"

"You're not going to believe this one. Waul went through the education and training program with Daniel Trout, who I'm guessing is Dirk's son."

"Holy shit!"

The two men sat in silence for several seconds. Hector finally broke it. "Maybe that's why Trout seems so remote whenever the Vigilante Killer is discussed. Is it possible that he and his son are working with Waul?"

"We have a long way to go to try to connect those dots, but I think we have to explore all possibilities. It could be that Trout simply shares everything with his son. After all, they're both in the same business. The sergeant could be innocently sharing, not realizing his son's involvement." Again, the two detectives sat silently, thinking through the possibilities. Jefferson said, "Trout knows that we're looking at Waul. If he knows Waul, for him not to say anything to us about it is very strange. When I told him that we had two cops we were putting under surveillance, he didn't show any emotion or the slightest sign of recognition, even though I gave him Waul's name. I don't like it."

"It's possible that the sergeant doesn't know Waul," Hector pointed out. "Do we go to the commander with this?"

"No, we keep this to ourselves until we've had a chance to investigate. We need to concentrate on determining why Waul and Daniel Trout would want to be vigilantes. I don't know anything about Daniel Trout, but everything I've uncovered regarding Waul leads me to believe he isn't our guy. I'll start out by contacting the officer I talked to with the education and training division. Let's see what he can tell us about the relationship between our two guys."

Jefferson's call went to the officer's voice mail box. He asked the man to call him back. After that, Jefferson did a lot of digging He talked to several people who helped him put some of the pieces together. He told them that he was a writer for the in-house police newsletter and that he was writing an article on Officer Waul. He said that Waul didn't know that he would be recognized in a future edition and asked the people to keep the secret. He didn't want to ruin the surprise. Jefferson didn't like to lie, but he didn't have much choice. Men were being killed. It had to stop. He hoped that his investigation stayed hushed, although he knew he was risking Waul hearing something. He didn't have other options.

Waul hadn't grown up in the Chicago Area. He was originally from Dubuque, Iowa, and had grown up on a farm. Jefferson assumed that he was a hunter when he was growing up and that was how he became familiar and deadly with a rifle. Waul lived there until he went away to college. He had attended Indiana State University, where he met his future wife. She was from Indianapolis. They moved to Chicago after graduation. It wasn't home for either of them, but it was within driving distance of both of their homes. There was no indication that Waul had any particular issue with gangs.

Jefferson also checked on Waul's ex-wife to see if there were gang issues within her family. He contacted the Indianapolis Police. There was no record of the ex-wife or family members being in a gang or having issues with a gang. Jefferson realized that at some point, he might need to dig deeper into the ex-wife's family, but for now, he didn't want to risk someone in the family contacting Waul. He would let it go.

Jefferson wanted to call the ex-wife. He was sure that she would be a great source for information. Nobody else seemed to have anything bad to say about Waul. His guess was that she might. He was weighing the pros and cons when his phone rang. It was the call he was waiting for. It was the officer from the training department. Jefferson asked, "Do you remember Daniel Trout?"

"Yes. You asked me about Ernie Waul before. The two of them were the best of friends. They connected right from the start. They were inseparable, it seemed."

"You had great things to say about Officer Waul. What can you tell me about Officer Trout?"

"He did a good job while he was here. My impression was that he would turn out to be a decent cop, but he wasn't as promising as Waul. Waul was special. Trout was above average. His father is a sergeant."

Jefferson almost said that he reported to Sergeant Trout but thought better of it. If he told the officer that he reported to Trout then the man would ask him why he didn't go to Sergeant Trout for information. He couldn't get into that. He let it go. He asked, "Do you remember if either of the two guys had a problem with gangs or gang activity to a larger extent than the rest of us?"

"I know Waul was from Iowa. I'm pretty sure that his small town didn't have a big gang problem. I don't remember anything that struck me as unusual with either of the trainees. They seemed to be well-balanced kids." Jefferson thanked the man for the callback and got off the phone.

When Jefferson hung up, Hector asked him if he was ready to compare notes. He said he was, and the two detectives started talking.

CHAPTER 24

After Jefferson reviewed his findings with Hector, Jerome began to share what he uncovered in the case file of the missing woman. He said, "It appears that Sergeant Trout and his partner did a thorough investigation. From reading the file, they suspected the husband had something to do with the woman's disappearance, but they never found any concrete evidence. They also believed that the daughters might have had a hand in things. Apparently, Mrs. Brown was very demanding. She wanted what she wanted when she wanted it. She was self-centered."

"That doesn't seem like a reason for the girls to want their mother to disappear," Jefferson said.

"The girls, Caron and Carla, are identical twins. But their personalities are very different. Caron has a pleasant personality, while Carla is more like her mother. She can be charming, but she has a nasty edge to her at times. From what I read, Carla and the mother frequently butted heads. Bertha had a temper, and she and Carla actually came to blows once, slapping each other and screaming. Caron seemed to mostly get along with Bertha, but she had a stronger bond with her twin. Carla had the stronger personality, as you can imagine. She tended to be the alpha. As the leader, she could get her sister to do whatever she wanted, it seemed. Trout and his partner were suspicious of the girls, although the husband remained the prime suspect."

"Was anybody outside of the family under suspicion?" Jefferson asked.

"No. Trout and the other detective interviewed family members, friends, and the husband's business associates. Nobody popped out as a person of interest."

"Did they get any feedback relating to Bertha's relationship with her husband?"

"The recurring theme was that Bertha ran the show at home. Many people seemed to know that Bertha was never that good to her husband. But the husband apparently loved her. As far as people knew, the relationship hadn't soured before Bertha disappeared. It never seemed to be a warm and tender one in the first place."

"If Bertha is Bella and she was abducted at the gym, was her car found there after she disappeared?" Jefferson asked.

"No, her car was found later at O'Hare, in a long-term parking lot. The investigators thought that she might have left town. They discovered that there wasn't an airline ticket issued in her name. They believed that unless she had fake ID cards made, she didn't fly out of town. The fake credentials remained a possibility, but nothing they found suggested that happened. They never crossed it off of the list, but they couldn't prove anything, and they moved on."

"Did Bertha work?"

"Before they moved to Chicago, she ran a claims department for an insurance company. The detectives talked to several people she worked for and some who worked for her. They confirmed that she was a strong personality with a bad temper. She was good at her job, but was not particularly popular. Behind her back, she was referred to as Big Bertha, but not because of her size. It was because she moved heaven and earth when she wanted something. One woman told them that you didn't get in Big Bertha's way. By the way, she is big woman, not necessarily heavy, but tall and large-boned. Bertha no longer worked after the move to Chicago."

"Did Trout ever figure out why Bertha had told her family that she was volunteering at a hospital?" Jefferson asked.

"They never found anything conclusive, but they were fairly certain that she was having an affair. She was away from home at least one day almost every weekend doing her volunteer work. At least, that's what she told her family. The detectives didn't discover where she really was when she left her home. Other than a possible affair, nothing else made sense to them."

"That's what hit me when you told me about the fake volunteering. The woman who was being held captive, Bella, she said she knew her captor from a gym. Did Trout talk about doing any investigative work at the gym?"

"Indeed, he did. The case file included interviews with a trainer who worked with Bertha, one on one, and a woman who led an exercise class Bertha participated in. The detectives also talked to several people who were in her class. Nobody noticed anything unusual. Bertha didn't seem to have any special connections as far as the other people noticed. Trout and his partner didn't suspect that Bertha had been abducted, so they never checked on backgrounds of the people at the gym."

Jefferson said, "That makes sense. I wouldn't have suspected it either."

Hector picked up his story. "I did check with the gym. Alphonso Burton belonged to the same gym. They were able to give me the name of Bertha's personal trainer. He has moved on and opened his own facility. I was able to hunt him down. He remembers Bertha and said Burton was a longtime member of the gym and he knew him too. He said that he could remember seeing Bertha and Burton talking on different occasions. He never thought anything of it. He saw nothing to suggest that their relationship was anything more than friends."

"That doesn't prove anything, but at least we now can put Burton and Bertha together. Did you read anything else that seems useful?"

"Not really. I think the next thing that we need to do is bring the picture of Bertha from the case file to Burton's neighbor so she can verify whether Bertha and Bella are the same person."

Jefferson agreed. "Let's do that first thing in the morning. It's been a long day. Anytime we sit on our butts all day, it beats the heck out of me. I'm ready to go home."

Hector smiled. He was ready too.

• • • •

The next morning, during the drive to revisit Burton's neighbor, Jefferson had a question for Hector. "Assuming Bertha was having an affair, do you think it could have been with Burton?"

"I've been wondering the same thing. It certainly is possible, but in her journal, she said that she knew Burton from her gym. She never implied that they were having a relationship. In fact, my impression was that he was almost a stranger."

"Another possibility is that she was having an affair with a different man. Burton could've figured it out and decided that he wanted her. In that scenario, Burton could assume that she wasn't happy at home and she might appear to be open to him."

Hector thought about it for a minute before he replied. "Bella said in her journal that Burton talked about her divorcing her husband and marrying him. The scenario you described might explain why he thought she would be open to leaving her husband for him."

"Or the two of them may have been having an affair and talked about her leaving her husband. It doesn't make sense that Burton would keep her captive if they were having a relationship."

Hector responded, "It sure would be a strange way to woo a woman. Even I wouldn't stoop to that level." Jefferson chuckled. With that, Hector pulled in front of the neighbor's house. The detectives got out of the car and headed to the front door.

CHAPTER 25

Just before climbing the stairs leading up to the front door of Burton's neighbor, Jefferson's cell phone rang. He pulled it out of his pocket and saw that it was the commander. Initially, he assumed that the commander was getting restless, especially with the latest shooting occurring just two days earlier. He was ready to ignore the call, but then it hit him. The commander usually called him on his office phone, and his habit was to leave a message if Jefferson didn't answer. Something must be up.

"Hello, Commander," Jefferson answered. "What's up?"

"I've got real bad news. DuKane passed away."

Jefferson's jaw dropped. It had been nine days since DuKane had been shot. He was stabilized and making good progress. Jefferson had believed that DuKane might even be going home within a week. He looked over at Hector and whispered, "DuKane." He didn't have to say anything else. From the look on Jefferson's face and his reaction to what the commander must have said to him, it didn't take a detective to figure out what must have happened.

"Jefferson, are you there?"

"I'm here, Commander. What happened? We were led to believe that he was out of the woods."

"Everything was going good, but he had an ischemic stroke. A blood clot from his chest area traveled to his brain. He was dead almost instantly, with no warning. They tried to revive him but weren't able to."

"Oh my God, his poor family must be devastated. I just talked to his wife yesterday. She told me that he was well enough for visitors. He was putting pressure on her to let me visit. He was hungry for information on our investigation. I was hoping to get to the hospital tonight. Poor Ginny. Did you talk to her?"

"I spoke to his wife, but it was a very quick conversation. It was apparent that she didn't want to talk. She wasn't prepared for him to die after the progress he'd been making. The only other thing I can tell you is that he died in the early hours of the morning, and no family members were there at the time."

Jefferson knew there was nothing for him to do, but he needed to make the effort for his own sake. "Commander, is there anything I can do?"

"Yes. Bring in the bastard who killed DuKane." There was a long silence. Jefferson had things he could say, but he realized that this was one time the commander was right on.

"I'm going to do my very best. I can guarantee that."

"Good, we'll get in touch with you concerning the funeral arrangements."

The commander abruptly hung up. Jefferson put his phone away and looked at Hector. Hector was visibly upset. No words were spoken between the partners, but there was a lot of communication going on. Their faces, especially their eyes, said it all. Jefferson gently grabbed Hector's upper arm and started walking back to their car. Hector knew that they were leaving, and he was relieved that they were. He was no longer in the mood to care about a man whose skeleton was found two years after he was killed.

• • • •

After they heard about DuKane, Jefferson and Hector did very little meaningful work before the funeral. The death took a toll on them. DuKane had been such a good man. It was so hard to believe.

The funeral took place the following Monday. There was a short church service, with thousands standing outside the church listening to the proceedings on loudspeaker. It was a silent, respectful crowd. In attendance were many dignitaries, including the governor, the mayor, and, of course, the police superintendent. After the church service, there was a short trip to the cemetery just blocks away. During the procession, the streets along the route were lined with police officers who saluted as the hearse passed by.

Jefferson and Hector attended the funeral together. Before the graveside service began, Jefferson spotted Vicky Soderheim. She looked lost. He went over to her and gave her a hug. She held on for dear life. The two of them and Hector moved to a spot where they could observe the proceedings. Jefferson put an arm around Soderheim's shoulder. He wondered what she was feeling. She could be feeling grief, sorrow, regret, guilt, fear or any number of other things. Whatever it was, she wasn't holding up well. She had the saddest puppy dog eyes. They were red and puffy. As they stood there, he could feel her shake. Jefferson knew that she wasn't going to get over this anytime soon, and possibly never would. She was going to need help, beyond anything he could offer.

At the funeral, the police commissioner and the mayor both made passionate speeches about DuKane. The commissioner reviewed the highlights of DuKane's career. It had people laughing and crying. It was a great eulogy. DuKane's wife and kids were in bad shape. They chose not to speak at the service because they couldn't. They were too broken up. DuKane's brother spoke for the family. He had to stop several times and regain his composure. There wasn't a dry eye when he was finished. It was apparent that DuKane had been much more than a police officer.

Mrs. DuKane had contacted Bill Small and asked him to say a few words at the funeral. When it was his turn, he walked to the front and faced the other mourners. He tried to talk three different times. He was trying to hold back the tears, but was unsuccessful. He couldn't get the words to come out. He managed to choke out the word sorry and walked over to Mrs. DuKane and gave her a long hug. If it wasn't such a sad affair, the image of Small hugging Mrs. DuKane would have been an amusing sight. He was such a huge man, and she was a tiny woman. The contrast was striking.

Jefferson had known DuKane for a long time, even though they had worked at different stations for most of their careers. He was very emotional as well, so he could understand how Small was feeling. Bill stepped away from Mrs. DuKane as Jefferson watched him. The big man wasn't taking it well at all. He looked defeated, with tears streaming down his face, but he made no noise. That was the same reaction Jefferson was having. He wondered why they couldn't just let themselves cry, but he knew that he couldn't.

Hector didn't have any history with DuKane. His first encounter with the detective was after he and Jefferson were transferred to the same station as DuKane. He immediately liked the man, and he quickly gained a respect for his integrity and character. It was the first funeral for another cop that Hector had attended. He was surprised at how emotional it was for him. He knew the sadness he was feeling wasn't going to disappear quickly.

After the graveside service and the eulogies concluded, Jefferson and Hector took Soderheim out for a cup of coffee. It was one thirty in the afternoon, and none of them had eaten lunch, but nobody was in the mood to eat, particularly Soderheim. "That was a nice funeral, if there's such a thing," she said. "I'm so glad Fred's family got to see and hear how much he was loved and respected."

"As cops, we don't always get respect," Jefferson said, "but when one of us dies in the line of duty, Chicago comes out in support of their finest. I'm not sure if we always deserve it, but Fred DuKane certainly did. But no matter how good the service, it doesn't make it any easier."

Soderheim hung her head and asked, "How is his family going to make it without him?"

"Financially, they'll be fine," Jefferson responded. "His widow will receive his full pension. There is something called the 100 Club. They're a nonprofit organization that helps families of fallen police officers, firefighters, and paramedics. They will support DuKane's children through college. Emotionally is another story. I have no idea how they get through the pain, or if they do. How are you doing, Vicky?"

"I won't lie to you. I'm a mess. I'm going to take a leave, I think. I know I can't be effective right now, and I don't want to put someone else at risk by not doing my job right."

"That's a good idea. But we want you to come back when you're ready. We need officers like you, who do what has to be done. You have a bright future."

"Thanks. I think I'll be back, but for now, I just need to work through all of the things I'm feeling."

Jefferson nodded and took a drink of his coffee.

CHAPTER 26

Jefferson never went back to the station after the funeral on Monday. He spent a few hours with Hector and Soderheim and then returned home. He actually got home before Aubrey. He took Bossy for a long walk. She was excited. She seldom got afternoon walks, and she seemed to have an extra bounce in her step. She was just what Jefferson needed for what ailed him. She always made the world a little better place.

The walk gave him time to reflect on recent events and about his family. He realized that when working, he got so into what he was doing, he seldom took the time to appreciate what he had. On this day, he was truly appreciating his family.

That night, after dinner, he spent a lot of time just talking to Aubrey. They took Bossy on another long walk. During their walks, they mostly just teased each other and had fun. Today, though, Jefferson wanted to have a more serious talk. He was in a reflective mood and just needed someone to listen. Aubrey was a perceptive lady. She could read her husband, and she worked at just listening without judgment or giving advice. The bottom line was that Jefferson was upset with the death of DuKane, and he was nervous about his own safety. Aubrey wanted to tell him to beg off of the case, but she knew that wasn't what he wanted to hear. It certainly was what she would have preferred, but it was part of his work, and she understood what that meant in the life of a police officer. And this was about him and what he needed. She knew he would stay on this case, and so did he. DuKane's murderer had to be caught.

"Tomorrow is going to be a very difficult day. I'm sure that the mayor was unmerciful with the commander about solving this case after the funeral and the public spotlight it brought on the department. I already picture the scene tomorrow. The commander will call me to his office. When I get there, the comatose Sergeant Trout will be staring at his hands, and the commander will begin the barrage. He'll have forgotten about his commitment to let me do my job without harassment. We'll get into it because I refuse to just sit there and take it. I want nothing more than to solve this case as soon as possible. He must know that." Aubrey just nodded her head. She felt bad for her husband, but there were no words that would comfort him. He just needed to vent.

• • • •

On Tuesday, Jefferson got to the station early. He wasn't going to give the commander any more fuel to add to the fire. He hoped to find some little piece that had been overlooked to gain further insight into the case. At least that way, he would have something to offer the commander. He reviewed the case file that DuKane had been maintaining. DuKane had uncovered a pattern for the killer. That was big. If he could only find one other thing, it might be just enough to break the case wide open. He spent hours on it but had no luck.

When Hector arrived at work, he suggested that they make the return visit to Alphonso Burton's neighbor. "Let's wait until later," Jefferson said. "I'm expecting the commander to call me at any minute to read me the riot act. I don't want to leave here now and have that hanging over my head all day. Let me get that over with first."

Neither detective accomplished anything for the rest of the morning. They both kept busy, but mostly doing paperwork, not detective work. It was hard to focus. There was still a large cloud hanging over them with the loss of DuKane. Jefferson kept waiting for the call from the commander, but it never came. He didn't know if he should be relieved or if this was just a delay in the inevitable. Perhaps the commander actually realized that there weren't many productive things to be done until the killer struck again. They were anticipating Officer Ernie Waul would make his next move on Wednesday or Thursday night. If he did, Jefferson felt confident that he wouldn't get away with it ever again.

Later in the afternoon, Jefferson said, "I'm tired of waiting. I'm ready to move. Let's go see the neighbor." Hector enthusiastically agreed.

As Hector was driving, he started a conversation. "For the last few days, I've been dealing with a personal issue. It seemed to loom so large. But DuKane's death put things into perspective. What his family is dealing with is huge. What I was dealing with is insignificant."

Jefferson considered this before he responded, "Certainly, a death pretty much trumps most things, especially when it occurred like DuKane's. But our everyday problems are not insignificant. If they're causing you anguish, they're significant. Fortunately, in time, many things work themselves out. Do you want to share your issue or would you prefer not to? Sometimes it helps just to get things off your chest."

"It's going to seem kind of silly. I've been dating this gal for a few months now. I've developed feelings for her. I know that she is getting serious with me, although we have avoided putting too much into words. I think we've been trying to take it slow. Well, at least, I know that I have."

"That doesn't sound like a problem to me."

"I haven't gotten to the problem yet. I was out with a few friends one night last week. We were at a club. I was having a good time. I spotted a girl I went to high school with. She was one of the most popular girls in the school. I, like most of the guys, had a crush on her back then. She was, and still is, beautiful. It's painful to say this, but she was out of my league. As I was staring at her, she looked over at me, and our eyes locked for a second. I looked away. I was sure that she didn't know that I existed in high school. I assumed that she didn't even know that I was someone she went to school with, that there was no way she would ever recognize me. I thought of going up to her, but I didn't want to embarrass myself."

"That doesn't sound like the Jerome Hector I know."

"You're right. I have gained confidence in myself since then, but seeing her put me back in high school mode, with all the doubts of a teenage boy. It was weird. I felt someone tugging at my sleeve. I turned and it was her. She called me by name and gave me a big hug like we were long-lost friends. We spent the next hour together. It felt like she was flirting with me. I didn't know if it was my imagination or if it was for real. But then she said that she had to go. She gave me her card. She's an account executive with an advertising agency here in Chicago. She asked me to give her a call sometime because she'd love to get together again.

"I went home that night, and I was feeling really good. But then I couldn't sleep. I kept thinking about the woman I'm already dating. I kept wrestling with myself. Do I keep dating my current girlfriend and forget about my high school crush? Or do I quit dating my current and concentrate on my new friend? Or do I try to have relationships with both?"

"I can see the dilemma. What did you decide?"

"That's the issue. I can't decide. I'm pretty sure I can't date both women. These days, when you're dating someone, they expect to be with you on most Saturday nights. How do I keep both women feeling special?"

"Jerome, you're not engaged. Can't you just tell both of them that you're dating more than one woman?"

"Wow, apparently, you've been married forever. No woman is going to tolerate that. The only way to date more than one woman is to sneak around. I don't want to be that guy. I have to make a decision."

"Okay, I have one other dumb idea. Why don't you take out the new lady a few times to see how the women compare, and then make a decision?"

"Marcus, these aren't cars that you take for a test drive before you decide which one to buy. I'm trying to be a good guy, something that you helped me to better understand. I can't believe that it's you making these crazy suggestions. For someone who seems to care about people, your solutions don't reflect it. I'm starting to wonder how you ever landed Aubrey."

"I landed her with good looks and charm. I'm just trying to think like a today kind of guy. It's a different world than when I was dating. We didn't go to a website looking for our next date. We also didn't date seven different people every week because the Internet makes so many more people available."

"When you date someone exclusively for a couple of months, it's different than dating several people every week. Surely you get that."

"I get it. What are you going to do?"

"Like I said before, DuKane's death puts things into perspective. My issue isn't that big of a deal. Either woman will do fine without me. They both have so much to offer. I never thought that I'd be in a position of having to choose from two women who are both too good for me. I'm going to have to give it more thought."

Jefferson nodded. For some reason, he found the situation amusing, but there was no way he was going to share that with Hector.

CHAPTER 27

As they pulled in front of the home next to Alphonso Burton's, Jefferson had a flashback to what had occurred the last time they had arrived at the neighbor's house. He swallowed hard and tried to put it out of his mind. He looked around and took in the neighborhood. It was a well-kept neighborhood for the most part, with the exception of Burton's abandoned home. There were stately trees lining both sides of the street. His thoughts drifted to Alphonso Burton, and that reminded him that bad people can live in any setting.

As the detectives arrived at the front door, Hector rang the bell. They could hear someone stirring inside. A female voice called out, "Who is it?"

They could see the peephole was darkened, and they knew someone was looking out at them. Hector wondered why the neighbor didn't recognize them. He said, "It's Detectives Jefferson and Hector. We'd like to talk to you." He held his identification in front of the peephole. The door opened. Hector saw why the woman didn't recognize them. It wasn't the woman they had met with before. It was a much younger woman, probably the daughter. Hector had talked to her on the phone but hadn't met her in person. "It's good to meet you face-to-face," Hector said. "I have a few more questions for you. I want to show you a picture." He pulled out the picture of Bertha Brown. He asked, "Do you recognize this lady?"

The daughter, Glenda, said, "Of course, that's Bella."

"Are you absolutely positive?"

"Yes."

Jefferson asked, "Did Mr. Burton have other girlfriends as far as you know, before Bella moved in with him?"

"Not that I am aware of. He seemed to get serious with Bella very quickly."

"Why do you say that?" Jefferson asked.

"Well, it seemed like he had only been dating Bella for, like, a month when she moved in." The detectives looked at each other.

"Are you saying that you saw Burton with Bella prior to her moving in?" Jefferson asked, to confirm.

"Yes."

"Did you see her here or someplace else?" Jefferson asked next.

"I saw them together here several times before she moved in. As I think about it, I actually saw them going into a gym together when I was doing some shopping. I was going to say hello, but they seemed to be so wrapped up in each other, I didn't bother them."

Jefferson asked Glenda if she remembered the name of the gym or where it was located. She remembered both and shared it with the detectives.

"After Bella moved in, did she seem happy to you?" Hector asked.

"Honestly, they seemed like a married couple. I never got a sense of whether they were happy together or not. The relationship seemed normal to me."

"Thank you," Hector said with another look toward his partner. "We may reach out to you again, but for now, you've been a great help."

The detectives headed back to their car. Hector said, "This case has just gotten very interesting. In her journal, Bella, or should I say Bertha, gave no indication that she and Burton had a relationship prior to the abduction. She indicated that he was just an acquaintance. If they were having an affair, did he actually abduct her, or was she with him by choice?"

"As in most cases, the more you know, the more you need to know," Jefferson responded. "I wonder if her lies about volunteering were just a ruse to get her out of the house to spend time with Burton. Why would he abduct her if they were seeing each other already? If she wasn't abducted, why was she writing about it in a journal? That piece is especially curious to me."

"That still leaves one big question. Is she still alive?" Hector added.

Jefferson shot back, "And if she's alive, where is she?"

"I also wonder if she did actually kill Burton or if the journal is one hundred percent bogus. If she was being held against her will, I could see her killing him. If that wasn't the case, why would she kill him? She didn't kill her husband when she left him, assuming that she wasn't abducted."

Jefferson's brow furrowed. "If Bertha isn't alive, we may never get the answers that we need. We have to try to find her. I say we try to locate her family, for starters. If she was abducted, it makes sense that she would return to them. But then I have to ask, why didn't she call the police and report the situation, including her stabbing of Burton?"

"Let's assume Bertha is alive and we can find her. I think we'd be better served if we had a theory before we start talking to her. Certainly, our conversation would be different if we thought she was a victim and not a perpetrator. I'd like to have some inkling one way or another."

"How do you propose that we do that?"

"I think we can go back and try to talk to other neighbors," Hector suggested. "Maybe someone knows Bertha and Burton better than Glenda and her mother did. Maybe even Glenda's father might be able to give us something new. I think we should also go to the gym where Glenda spotted them. If we dig, we might learn a few things to set us in the right direction."

"That makes good sense to me. Why don't you call Glenda and see if her dad's home? If he is, we can go back over there. If he isn't, we can head to the gym and go back one night this week when we'll be more likely to catch other people at home too."

Hector called Glenda. Her dad was at work, but she told him that he usually got home by six most nights. The detectives drove to the gym. Although they had to wait fifteen minutes for his class to end, they got the opportunity to talk to the owner of the club. After introductions, Hector asked the man if he remembered someone by the name of Alphonso Burton. The trainer responded, "Yes. Alphonso was a client of mine at one time."

Hector said, "Did you also work with a woman by the name of Bertha?"

The trainer looked at Hector curiously. Then he asked, "Do you mean Bella?"

"I'm sorry, I did mean Bella."

The trainer gave him a funny look as he said, "As I'm sure that you know, they lived together. I trained Bella too."

"What can you tell us about them as a couple?" Jefferson asked.

"They seemed to have a nice relationship. They were both into fitness and health. This seemed like a happy place for them. They worked hard. Bella seemed especially driven. They pushed each other. It's not that common for couples to spend so much time together at the gym. Couples usually drift to separate activities when they're here together. Bella and Alphonso did a lot of the same things. They even spotted for each other when they lifted weights. What more can I tell you?"

Hector asked, "Did you ever get the feeling that they were having a problem?"

"I'm not sure I understand the question, but I never noticed any tension in their relationship."

"You indicated that they mostly worked out together," Jefferson said. "Did they ever work in separate areas of the gym or were they always near to each other?"

"They mostly stayed together, as far as I remember. They did shower here at times after a workout, and obviously, they used separate locker rooms. Other than that, they mostly were a pair. I always thought it was cool that they could work so well together and had fitness as a common interest."

"Do you know why they quit coming to the gym?" Hector asked.

"That was kind of strange. The last time I saw them, I was talking to Alphonso about fishing. I was just getting into it. He was an avid fisherman. I don't even remember why, but he offered to bring me some back issues of *Field and Stream* magazine. I guess he had every issue going back several years. I told him that I would appreciate that. He said that he would be back in two days and would bring them with him. He never came back. I haven't heard from or seen either of them since then."

Jefferson asked, "Do you remember when that was?"

"No, but they had scheduled a session with me that last day that I saw them. That's why we had the opportunity to talk about fishing. I can look it up and see when that last appointment was with them."

"We would appreciate that," Jefferson said.

The trainer took the detectives back to his office and went to work with his keyboard and mouse. After a minute, he said, "It was December 2, 2005."

Jefferson thanked the man. He and Hector headed to their car. As they were walking, Hector said, "Bertha's journal didn't give dates for many of the entries, but she did date some of them. As best I can tell, that's right about the time she claimed to have stabbed Burton. The pieces are falling into place. If they showered in separate locker rooms, it sure seems like Burton gave her every opportunity to escape or seek help. It's hard for me to believe that she was so scared of him that she didn't do either. I feel strongly that she wasn't abducted. I'm ready to try to find her."

Jefferson thought about it for a while, then said, "You're right."

CHAPTER 28

When the detectives arrived back at their station, they decided to call it a day. Bertha Brown would have to wait. They assumed that the Vigilante Killer would be striking either Wednesday or Thursday, leading to a very long day for them. There was no emergency dictating they stay, so they didn't.

After a nice dinner, Jefferson and Aubrey took Bossy for a walk. It was a pleasant night, and Bossy seemed even more enthusiastic than usual, frequently pulling Jefferson along. When it was hot out, Bossy was content marching along at a causal pace. When it wasn't hot, she was raring to go and kept Jefferson hopping.

Jefferson asked Aubrey how her day was at the school. She said, "I had a strange one today. About ten minutes into a study hall, a boy came up to my desk and asked for a hall pass to visit the restroom."

"That is strange, needing a hall pass to go to the bathroom."

Aubrey gave him a look and shot back, "No, fool, that's not the strange part. That's standard procedure. The strange part is that he never came back. He left his backpack sitting at his seat in study hall."

"What did you say to aggravate him so badly that he refused to return?"

"Please. I was sweet, like I always am."

"That only happens when you want something."

"What are you saying? Are you accusing me of being someone who uses people?"

Jefferson thought about it for a while. "No, you're really good with other people. You only use and abuse me."

"That's not my fault. Bad guys have bad things happen to them."

"Now you're saying I'm a bad guy?"

"You have a bad mouth. It gets you in trouble with me all the time."

"I guess this means the honeymoon is over."

"That ship sailed a long time ago, Buster. Let me get back to my story. After the boy was gone for ten minutes, I started worrying about him. I have never had anything like that happen before. On one hand, I wanted to go look for the student. But on the other hand, I had a library full of other students, and I was responsible for them. I decided to call the dean of boys. When he answered, I spoke as quietly as I could and told him what happened. He said that he'd search for the boy and get back to me."

"What did he say when he got back to you?" asked Jefferson.

"I didn't hear back from him until almost the end of the period. He told me that he never found the student. He went MIA."

"Does that happen often with students?"

"I never heard of that happening before at this school."

"What kind of kid is this boy?"

"I have no idea. I don't really get much opportunity to interact with the students. I have them for a study hall, not an academic class, where there would be interactions. I would describe him as average, although I don't really know what that means."

"Is he the kind of kid you would expect to be bullied?"

"He is an average-sized boy and average looking. There's nothing that jumps out at me. Although I don't see it very much, bullying is relatively common, unfortunately."

"Did the dean contact his parents?"

"I'd guess he did. I never heard anything more. I went to the dean's office after school to ask about the boy, but the dean wasn't there. Neither was his assistant. I'm left hanging. I hope everything is okay."

"I can't imagine that the boy was kidnapped while at school. I would guess that he was being bullied and took off to avoid an issue."

Aubrey gave that some thought and then just nodded.

Bossy kept pulling, even after they got back to their house. She didn't want the walk to end. It wasn't easy, but Jefferson prevailed. He got Bossy into the house, but she looked at him as if to say, *I'm disappointed in you.* He gave her a treat to try to make up for his apparent indiscretion. That always cured Bossy's woes and made him feel less guilty.

The couple settled in front of the television. He read the newspaper while glancing up at the television from time to time. She was tired and looked at the television but wasn't all that interested.

Around nine p.m., Jefferson got a phone call from FBI Agent, Pete Berz. Ernie Waul had left his house. Jefferson thought about it for a little bit and then said, "I didn't expect anything until tomorrow night or Thursday. Do you think he's breaking his pattern?"

"I don't know, but he was carrying a briefcase and a duffle bag. We have three different cars coordinating our efforts to keep eyes on him. If he does make a move tonight, we'll nab him. I'll call you when I have something to report."

"Please do, no matter what time it is." After getting off the phone, he told Aubrey about what was happening. He said, "Keep your fingers crossed. Hopefully this whole thing will end tonight."

Aubrey didn't need any convincing to wish the same. She was scared for her husband's safety, and she wanted nothing more than to have the killer caught.

About a half hour later, the FBI agent called Jefferson again. He said, "We followed Waul. He parked his car and carried his bags into an apartment building."

Feeling his heart rate increase, Jefferson said, "It sounds like he's positioning himself to strike."

"I don't think so."

"Why not?"

"Because he went into an occupied building, not an abandoned one. The killer has never used an occupied building before. There is no reason to expect that he'd do that now."

"Perhaps his next victim doesn't have any abandoned buildings within shooting range of his home. Maybe Waul is improvising."

"You gave us the list of gang members whose names begin with O and their addresses. None of them live on this block, or anywhere within shooting distance. I have one of my support guys researching to see if Waul has a connection to anyone who lives in the building that he entered. I'll let you know what we find or if anything changes."

Just before ten p.m., Berz called back. "Marcus, Waul has a sister who lives in the building he's visiting. She is a single mother. Ten minutes after he entered the building, a young woman left. We think it might have been his sister. Our best guess is that Waul is babysitting for her. The bags might be because he plans to spend the night at her apartment. That might explain why he never came home last Tuesday night. Maybe he sits for his sister from time to time."

"Do you have any idea what the sister does or where she goes?"

"We were able to determine that she's a nurse. She works one of the evening shifts at Rush University Medical Center. As I said, we're guessing the woman we saw leaving the building is his sister. We plan to keep Waul under surveillance for a few more hours. If he isn't babysitting, there's still a chance he plans to strike tonight."

"I would appreciate that. Until he either does strike or someone else does, he remains our lead suspect."

The agent came back with, "You mean your only suspect."

"Ouch, that hurts," said Jefferson. "I've never worked a case with fewer leads than this one. As much as it pains me, I'm praying that Waul is our man and that he strikes soon, so we can put an end to this case."

"If Waul is your guy, maybe he slept at his sister's last Tuesday. That would explain why he didn't come home. But, it begs the question, why would he sleep at his sister's after murdering someone?"

"Perhaps he's trying to keep his humanity. He sees himself as doing a good thing as a vigilante. But he also knows that there's something wrong in what he's doing. Being with his sister and her child might keep him feeling better about life, maybe cleaner."

"That works for me as much as any other explanation. I don't have a clue. As I said earlier, we'll see this through. We'll stay on him until this plays out. Let's see what happens tonight and in the next two nights."

"You're right. Thanks for your continued support. Let's stay in touch."

CHAPTER 29

On Wednesday, around mid-morning, Detectives Jefferson and Hector met with Sergeant Dirk Trout in his office. Although Jefferson had already filed a report for both Trout and the commander, he recapped his conversation from the preceding night with the FBI agent. Trout said, "That's like no news. It certainly doesn't clear Waul of suspicion." He stared at Jefferson, waiting for more, but there was nothing else.

Hector decided that it might be a good time to change the subject. He told Trout that he and Jefferson were going to track down Bertha Brown and bring her in for questioning. Hector explained that they had reason to believe Bertha's story about being held captive was fabricated.

Trout looked confused as he said, "From what you told me, Brown acted in self-defense." Hector sensed that Trout was being a little protective of the woman. He could understand Trout feeling a kinship with Mrs. Brown from having worked her missing person's case.

Hector chose to answer, while Jefferson kept quiet. "This is the way we see it, Sergeant: It's self-defense when it's a matter of life or death. The scene she described in her journal didn't sound like she was in a fight for her life. She had other options, but she made the choice to kill him anyway. The killing wasn't provoked because of the threat on her own life. At different times in the journal, she alluded to being scared for her life, but none of Burton's actions seemed to be life-threatening. When she had the opportunity to escape, get help, or call the police, she did nothing."

"How did she have the opportunity to take any of those actions?"

"Their trainer told us that Burton and Brown showered from time to time before leaving the gym. They obviously used different locker rooms. Brown had lots of different opportunities to take action if she wanted."

"I thought you told me that she didn't try to escape because she feared for her family."

"You're right. I did tell you that, because that's what it said in the journal. But it just doesn't wash. One call to the police while Burton was showering and it would've been all over for the guy. To top things off, the neighbor girl told us that she saw Burton and Brown together at his house and entering a gym prior to the abduction. We think we're building a solid case. The jury can decide if it's murder or self-defense, if we get to take this case to trial."

Trout asked, "Do you know where to find Brown?"

Hector replied, "We do. The DMV records show that she has a vehicle registered to her and her husband at the address where she lived prior to her disappearance. From the date, it appears that they bought that vehicle shortly after she went free. From other information, such as credit card charges and so forth, we're fairly certain that she is living back with her husband."

"Go get her," Trout urged.

The detectives left Trout's office, picked up a few items at their desks, and headed to their car. They started toward the Browns' residence.

As Hector drove, he asked Jefferson, "Do you think Brown was really abducted?"

"It's possible. They could've been having an affair. Burton wanted her to leave her husband and she wasn't willing. He came from money. Maybe he was raised to believe he could have whatever he wanted. The guy could've been a little warped and decided he would have her one way or another."

"I'm having trouble with that theory," Hector said. "She didn't appear to be under duress to others. How does someone who is being held captive appear to be stress free? And as we agreed, she had plenty of opportunities to get help or get away."

Jefferson thought about it for a while. "I agree, but I ask myself why she took the time to write the journal portraying herself as a captive if that wasn't the case. There is no good answer to that, unless she really was being held captive."

It was Hector's turn to ponder the situation. After searching for an answer, he came up empty. "I just don't know. I'm still suspicious. I also wonder why she didn't call the police after she killed Burton. If her story is true, and she thought that she acted in self-defense, calling us would have made sense. It's almost like she wanted to hide the incident from us, but she left her journal at the scene, admitting that she killed him. I find it strange that she made that entry after killing the guy. A normal person would get out of there as quick as she could. Who kills somebody and stops to write in a journal?"

Jefferson said, "I find it strange that she left the journal at the scene. I could see running out of the house immediately after stabbing Burton and forgetting the journal. But to kill him, write in the journal, and then leave it there just doesn't add up for me."

They pulled up to the house. It was a beautiful large brownstone. The front yard had a wrought-iron fence around it. The detectives opened the gate and walked toward the stairs leading to the front door. Jefferson said, "This should be an interesting adventure."

• • • •

Hector rang the doorbell. The front door had a large glass pane. It was covered with a sheer curtain. The detectives couldn't see through it, but they could see the figure of someone approaching the door. A voice called out, "Who is it?"

Hector responded, announcing both himself and Jefferson. A woman pulled the edge of the sheer curtain back and peeked through the glass. Hector held up his identification. The woman let go of the curtain. They could see that she hadn't moved, but she didn't open the door. They stood quietly, waiting to see what she was going to do. Hector put a hand on his gun but didn't pull it from its holster. After about fifteen seconds, he said in a commanding voice, "Please open the door." They could hear the deadbolt sliding open, and slowly, the door swung open.

Hector asked, "Are you Bertha Brown?" He knew who she was because he recognized her from her picture.

The woman looked from Hector to Jefferson and back to Hector again. She answered, "Yes. What can I do for you?"

"We're here to talk to you about Alphonso Burton," Hector said.

"I figured that I'd hear from the police eventually. I'm kind of surprised that it didn't happen sooner." She was very calm and under control. She said, "All I can tell you is that Burton was a very bad man who robbed me of two years of my life. I have nothing else to say without my lawyer present."

Hector replied, "Then you leave us no choice. You're under arrest for the murder of Alphonso Burton." He read Bertha her rights. The woman was taken aback. She didn't expect to be arrested. She looked back and forth from detective to detective. This time, the look was not quizzical, but laced with disdain. The detectives let Mrs. Brown get her keys, lock her front door, and accompany them to their car without handcuffs. Thirty-five minutes later they arrived at the station.

Brown was allowed to make a call after she was booked. She called her husband. They had always had an attorney, but he wasn't a criminal attorney. After she returned home, they both knew that this day might come and she might need a criminal attorney. They had researched attorneys and met with several. They explained to prospective attorneys that they couldn't get into the details, but they thought they might need legal counsel at some point. There might be a murder charge brought against Mrs. Brown at some point in the future. They landed on Anthony Cavitello. He had a great reputation, and he seemed intrigued by their story. He pushed them hard to tell him more. They explained that it would be better for him if they didn't share details at that point. They were impressed with how aggressive he came after them for more information.

Bertha's husband, Charles Brown, called Mr. Cavitello after Bertha had called him. He told Cavitello that Bertha had been arrested on suspicion of murder. Cavitello wanted more information. Charles told him that Bertha was sitting in a cell. He wanted the lawyer to get right to the station. Bertha could give him the story once he arrived. The lawyer had an appointment that he needed to keep, but he agreed to get there right after it. After the call, Charles Brown immediately headed to the station. He wanted to get there quickly in support of his wife.

It was just after two thirty p.m. when Mr. Brown arrived. He asked to see his wife but was denied access to her. Cavitello had told Brown that he wouldn't be able to get to the station until sometime after four. Brown was anxious. He knew that his wife was innocent, but he also knew the circumstances surrounding the case were strange, and he wasn't confident in things turning out as they should.

When Hector came out to the lobby and introduced himself to Brown, he invited the man to come back to what he called a conference room to talk to the detectives. Brown gladly accepted. He was sure that he could reason with the detectives.

CHAPTER 30

The Vigilante Killer arrived at the pancake shop a little after seven a.m. His companion was already there, sipping on his second cup of coffee. The two men gave each other a half-hug and sat down. It was Wednesday morning. The killer was planning to strike again that evening. He wanted to find out if there was anything happening that he needed to be aware of that could compromise his mission. But first, the two men made small talk. They knew each other well and could probably talk all day and never get to the killer's purpose for the meeting. But, after a half hour, after their order was taken and the food was served, the killer, in a low voice, asked, "Are there going to be any issues tonight that I should be aware of?"

The companion answered, "I don't know of anything that's going on. As I told you the last time we talked, Jefferson is not routinely meeting with the task force. The only ones who really know what's going on other than him are his partner and the brass. I think they're still looking at a cop by the name of Ernie Waul as a person of interest. He was a sniper just like you when he was in the service. The last time I heard anything, the FBI was keeping tabs on the guy. I'm sure it will become apparent soon that he isn't the guy they're looking for. I don't know if they've come across any other leads in recent days."

The killer said, "I'm thinking that I might put a scare into Jefferson. Maybe if he feels threatened, he might back off a little or at least start working more with the task force."

"That's not going to happen. The last time you tried to scare a cop, you killed him. I'm very angry that you shot at DuKane, even if killing him was an accident. When you talked me into this, you were only going to eliminate the bad guys. You're not going to put another good guy at risk."

"Don't worry. I'll be more careful. I'll shoot over his head. It'll be enough to scare him, but even if he moves suddenly like DuKane did, the shot will still miss him."

"No. If you take another shot anywhere near another cop, you'll be on your own. Jefferson's got a job to do. Like DuKane, he's a good man, a family man. You keep doing what you're doing, you'll risk being captured. I want you to quit now, before something bad happens to you."

"I can't quit. Who else is going to stand up to these gangs? They have taken over neighborhoods, people's lives, and caused nothing but pain and grief to so many innocent people. I won't quit."

"Unless the task force starts meeting regularly, I can't provide the kind of information you need to stay ahead of Jefferson. He will catch you. If he catches you, there's every reason to believe he'll catch me too. There are days that I almost hope that happens. I really wish we never started any of this. The revenge factor was a motivator, but it no longer provides me with any satisfaction. I'm just feeling empty and sad. I never saw my life coming to this. This was a mistake. What can I do to make you stop taking lives?"

"I don't want to get caught, mainly because I don't want to jeopardize your freedom. But I feel like what I'm doing is more important than you and I. That's why I have to keep going. I'm going to give Jefferson a scare whether you think it's right or not. It's important to give the guy a reason not to get too aggressive in pursuing me. It's for your safety and mine."

The companion sat silently for a few seconds. He looked the killer in the eyes and said, "You're being a fool. If you take a shot at Jefferson, all hell will break loose. Even if Jefferson takes a step back, the rest of the department won't. The biggest manhunt in Chicago history will take place. It's a stupid plan."

"It doesn't matter how many people are looking for me; if they don't know who they're looking for, they won't find me. I've been very careful. I just have to turn it up a notch."

"Now you're being a stubborn ass. I'm just done. You're on your own from now on. I'm going to put my life in order because you're going to get caught, and we're both going away. This isn't how I planned my life. If you quit now, we can both go on with our lives, and nobody will be the wiser. Each hit puts you in more danger."

"This is just like being at war. Every assignment is dangerous. But with good planning and execution, no assignment has to be any more dangerous than the last one."

The companion shook his head and said, "Unlike war, you're gaining more enemies day by day. The army against you is getting larger and larger. I would expect that the FBI is going to get involved soon if you're not caught." In a louder voice, the companion said, "It's time to quit!" They both realized that the comment had to have been heard by other people in the restaurant. They looked around and saw people looking back at them. They both put their heads down and sat silently for several minutes.

The companion looked up. He said, "Let's not rush into anything. Don't take any action tonight. Let's allow things to sit overnight at least. We can sleep on all of this and see where we're at tomorrow. I don't want to quit on you, but I don't think I can go on, especially with you talking about taking another shot at a cop. Will you promise me that you won't do anything until we talk again tomorrow?"

The Vigilante Killer gave thought to what was said. After reflecting, he said, "I don't see anything changing, but I'll hold off until we talk tomorrow." The killer rose. He laid down a tip and picked up the check from the table. The companion rose. They shared another half-hug. The killer said, "It was good to see you. I'll call you tomorrow morning." He walked toward the front of the restaurant.

The companion sat back down. He started thinking about what he wanted to do. What the killer was doing was a good thing. He was eliminating people who were very dangerous. These lowlifes were drawing younger kids into their webs and making killers out of them. It was a horrible situation. There was a need for more to be done than the cops were able to do. There was no question that the Vigilante Killer was doing a valuable service for the community. The companion didn't like the idea initially. In fact, he and the killer argued back and forth for several weeks before he had agreed to help. DuKane's shooting and death changed things. It went against everything the companion stood for. He thought long and hard about turning himself in and revealing the identity of the killer. It would ruin his own life, but he didn't feel like he had that much to live for anyway. It bothered him that the Vigilante Killer would be put away for life, but it beat seeing him killed. There seemed to be no good answer if the killer refused to stop what he was doing. The companion needed to give it more thought.

CHAPTER 31

When Hector and Charles Brown arrived at the interview room, Jefferson was already there. Hector introduced the men to each other. The room felt like a basement. It had no windows. It was dark, drab, and had a very cold feeling to it. There was a piece of glass in a frame on one wall. Brown correctly assumed that it was a two-way mirror. The men sat at a dark gray metal table with four folding chairs. They weren't much to look at, but they weren't all that uncomfortable. Hector offered to get Brown a cup of coffee or a soda. Brown said that he didn't need anything.

Going on the defensive right away, Brown said, "I can't believe that with all Bertha's been through, you're charging her with murder. Don't you know that this sicko was holding her prisoner?"

"Then you know that she killed a man?" Hector said.

"I know the whole story," Brown responded. "Apparently you don't, or you wouldn't have arrested Bertha."

Leaning back in his chair, Jefferson said, "Why don't you tell us her story as you know it, so we can better understand what really happened."

This was the opportunity Brown was hoping for. He wanted to lay out Bertha's case. He was sure that once the detectives understood what happened, they'd see that Bertha did the only thing that she could have in order to get her life back. He told the detectives the story of Bertha's abduction. It matched up perfectly to what Bertha had written in her journal. The detectives reacted as if they were learning of this for the first time. They seemed to be sympathetic and somewhat surprised. This encouraged Brown to continue.

He described the torture and multiple rapes of his wife. Tears streamed down his face as he described what his wife endured. Several times, he had to stop to compose himself. Jefferson told him to take his time and relax. He said, "We're so sorry for all that your wife had to go through."

Brown finished the story by explaining how his wife stabbed Burton. She took Burton's car and drove home. He ended his story there.

"It must have been a shock to you when she walked through the doorway," Hector said.

"I was at work when she returned home for the first time in two years. She didn't try to contact me. She wanted our first contact to be in person and not by phone. When I arrived home from work, I was shocked to see her. At first, I wondered if I was dreaming. I never expected to see her again. When I realized that it was really her, we hugged like neither was ever going to let go. We cried, we kissed, and we continued to hug each other. It was the most emotional moment of my life, even more so than the birth of our twins."

Smiling at Mr. Brown, Hector said, "That's an amazing story. It sounds like her story would make for a great movie with a happy ending. We have some procedural questions we'd like to ask you, if you don't mind."

Brown was feeling good. The detectives were getting it. Maybe they wouldn't even need a lawyer now, he hoped. "What do you want to know?"

"Let's start with Burton's car. What happened to it?" Hector had started with what he considered a softball question, to keep Brown talking and in a comfort zone.

"The next day, I followed my wife to a small industrial building. I guess Burton owned the building and leased it to some company. He had access to parts of the building and the parking lot. We dropped the car off in the lot and left it there."

Nodding, Hector asked, "How was your wife's health when she returned home?"

"Physically, she was good. Burton fed her, and he took her to the gym to work out. She maintained physical health. Mentally, she was a wreck. I think she was in shock initially, and in short order, I believe she was suffering from post-traumatic stress disorder. She went through several months being depressed and not functioning well. I wanted her to see a doctor, but she refused. As the weeks went by, she improved little by little. For the last year and a half she has been better, thank God. I don't think that she'll ever be one hundred percent."

Hector was ready to start getting down to the things the detectives really wanted to know. "Why didn't either you or your wife contact the police once she was safely home?"

"We talked about it briefly. She was a mess at that time. She wasn't up to dealing with the police. She had just endured a horrible two years, and she was at the end of her wits. She needed a chance to get back to her life, a time to recover from the horrible ordeal. The last thing she needed was the extra anxiety that dealing with the police would bring. As she recovered, we decided it was too late, and we let it go. Frankly, I wanted her to get as much distance from the experience as possible. Bringing the police in would only take her back there. That's why I'm so concerned right now. Bertha is healthier now, but I believe that she's still fragile."

"We looked over your wife's missing person file. It said that the day she went missing, she was supposedly doing volunteer work at a hospital. But when they looked into it, they were told that she didn't volunteer at that hospital. Did you ever get an explanation from your wife?" Jefferson asked.

"Yes. She said that she never checked in with human resources but just showed up and helped where she could. She didn't work through HR because she didn't want to be tied to any specific schedule. Apparently, people knew her there, and she had no trouble helping out or moving around the hospital. She told me that if the investigators interviewed people around the hospital other than HR, they would have discovered that she was a regular."

Hector couldn't help himself. He asked sarcastically, "And you believed that?"

Brown looked irritated. To this point, the conversation had been friendly. He responded, "Of course I believe Bertha. What are you trying to say?"

"I'm not *trying* to say anything. I'm saying that in this day and age, nobody is allowed to work in a hospital without being vetted by the hospital. Any supervisor who utilized a non-approved volunteer would be fired immediately." Hector knew that this would create a breakdown in his relationship with Brown, but he also knew it could help to create some doubt in his mind about his wife. Jefferson understood immediately what Hector was doing, and he sat back and let him continue. Brown didn't respond.

"How do you think we tied your wife to the murder of Alphonso Burton?" Hector asked.

"First of all, it wasn't murder. It was self-defense. I have no idea how you found out about Bertha being Burton's prisoner."

Hector was amused at how Brown turned the question around. Instead of positioning Bertha as a murderer, he positioned her as a victim. Hector had to give him credit for being a bright man. He said, "Then you didn't know about your wife's journal?"

"I don't know anything about a journal."

"She kept a journal during the duration of her captivity. She took the time to put a final entry into the journal before leaving Burton's house. She described the act of killing him."

"That's crazy. I don't believe that. If there was a journal, where did you get it?"

"You used the word crazy. Here's the crazy part. After taking the time to make the final entry, she left the journal behind, as if she wanted us to find it. Why would she do that?"

"I told you that she was in shock when she got home. I'm sure she wasn't acting rationally. She had gone through two years of hell, and it culminated with her stabbing her captor. That certainly affected her ability to think clearly."

Hector was ready to go for the big one. He said, "We think that Bertha was having an affair with Burton and made the decision to run off with him. They lived together happily for a few years, until something went wrong. To be honest, we don't know what set Bertha off. There was no indication at the crime scene that Burton's death was a case of self-defense." He stared coldly at Brown and waited for a reply.

Brown glared back at Hector. His look said that he wasn't buying into any of this. Although it had become apparent that Brown believed his wife's story, Hector was sure that he had provided him with enough information to initiate an interesting discussion between the two of them the next time they saw one another. Hector only wished he could be a fly on the wall during that discussion.

"I'm done talking to you. I'd like to go back to the lobby to wait for Bertha's attorney."

Jefferson escorted Brown back to the lobby area. He said, "Thanks for talking to us. Good luck."

Brown didn't respond.

CHAPTER 32

Bertha Brown and her attorney, Anthony Cavitello, talked for over an hour. Bertha's husband wasn't granted permission to sit in on their meeting. The detectives wanted him to sit and stew. They presumed that he'd give thought to what they had told him. They hoped he would become more and more upset with each minute that passed. When Bertha finally did get home, if he was upset enough, it could lead to serious issues between the couple. Ultimately, they wanted Bertha to become frazzled. People tend to make mistakes when they're upset. They needed for Bertha to help them build their case. It was close to six o'clock by the time the detectives sat down with Bertha and her attorney in the interview room.

Sergeant Trout sat on the other side of the glass watching the proceedings. He was particularly interested in this case. Generally, Trout showed little interest in most cases, but he had a history with Bertha Brown despite the fact that he'd never met her.

The meeting was being recorded, and before it moved forward, Hector read Brown her rights, even though she had already hired a lawyer and he was in the room. The attorney thought it was overkill.

Jefferson said, "We'd like to hear your explanation of why you murdered Alphonso Burton."

Cavitello spoke up before Brown had a chance. "My client admits to killing Burton, but she didn't murder him." He then looked at Bertha and nodded his head yes, as if to say she could speak now.

Bertha Brown told her story. It was very much like the story in the journal. She had been taken captive by Burton. He kept her as a prisoner for about two years. He raped her and abused her frequently. He kept her locked up in his basement for much of the time. He kept control of her when she wasn't locked up by creating a fear for her family's well-being.

Mrs. Brown explained how and why the killing took place. She said, "When Burton went out without me, I was handcuffed to the heavy cot in the basement with the door at the top of the stairs locked. When we were both at home, I spent some of my time by his side in the upper floors of the house. He never let me out of his sight when I wasn't in the basement." Jefferson made note of that. Later, he would ask her if she meant never let her out of his sight at home or did she mean anywhere.

"As time went on, Burton occasionally didn't handcuff me when he left me in the basement. It didn't happen often. It seemed that when he was happy with me, he let me go without handcuffs. The problem was that I never understood what was making him happy and what wasn't. My demeanor never changed. I always did whatever he told me to. As you can see, the man wasn't only crazy, but he was weird too."

Brown continued her explanation. "Near the end of the ordeal, I could see that Burton was changing. It was like he was losing interest in me. At first, I was feeling good about that. He started talking about how he could do much better if he replaced me. I was thinking that he just wanted to make me jealous. But then he inferred that he was working at finding my replacement. I asked him if that meant he would let me go. His answer was something like, I should figure that one out myself. I realized that if he did replace me, he would have to kill me. I knew who he was and where he lived. He couldn't risk setting me free. I knew at that point, I would have to act.

"One day, the day that I stabbed him, he left the house without handcuffing me. I looked around to try to figure out what I could use to hurt him badly enough to escape. Everything that might be useful seemed to be locked up in cabinets. It occurred to me that the glass from the window might be my best chance. I dragged the cot over to the window and climbed on top of it. I was wearing a T-shirt. I removed it and used it to punch the window, breaking the glass. The space was too small for me to fit through the window or I would've run. The glass was sitting on

141

the ground outside of the window frame. I was able to reach the pieces of glass. I carefully picked up a large piece. I pushed the cot back to where it belonged and waited for Burton, while building up my nerve to do what I had to do to save my life.

"Later, when Burton got home, he came down to the basement. I didn't want to try to stab him when he was looking directly at me and could see me coming. I knew he could overpower me. As he approached me sitting on the cot, I got up and started walking toward the window. He looked at me like he was trying to figure out what I was doing, but he followed me. As we got close, I told him to look up at the window. I told him that it had somehow been broken. He looked up at it, and then I did it. I stabbed him. He stood there, looking shocked. I stabbed him again and again before he could react. He fell, and that was the end of my hell. What else could I do? What would you have done?" Bertha looked at Jefferson and then at Hector.

Blowing out a puff of air, Jefferson said, "That's one hell of a story. Nonetheless, you can see why we're charging you with murder. You admit to killing the man. It will be up to the judge at the preliminary hearing to determine whether he believes it's murder or self-defense."

Looking affronted, Cavitello said, "You're seriously going to schedule a preliminary hearing after all Mrs. Brown has been through?"

"We've been in touch with the attorney general's office, and that's what they want to do," Jefferson replied. "It's their call. We do have a few questions for you, Mrs. Brown." Neither Bertha nor the attorney responded, so Jefferson asked a question. "Why didn't you call the police after you escaped?"

"I was in no shape to deal with the police. My husband will tell you, I was a mess. It took months for me to even think about living again. I still have sleepless nights after that ordeal."

"As you probably guessed, we found your journal at the scene. You took the time to write one final entry, but then left the journal there. Why would you do that?"

"I did it for today."

"What does that mean?"

"I'm sure that when I went missing, you collected my DNA. My DNA is all over Burton's house. I knew that, eventually, you'd find me. The journal was left as evidence as to what I went through. If I gave you the journal after you put the pieces together, you might not have thought it was authentic. But now, you have to realize it is. I mean, who would make up a story like this? You know I went missing. The journal explains that, and it explains why I had to do what I did to survive."

Jefferson changed direction with his next question. "Earlier, you told us that Burton never let you out of his sight. Did you mean when you were allowed to be out of the basement in his home, or did you mean ever?"

"He never let me out of his sight anytime I was out of the basement."

"What about if you were out and you had to use the bathroom?"

"The man was crazy. He would make me hold it until we got home."

Hector felt like it was time to get to it. He said, "We have reason to believe that you were having an affair with Burton prior to your story of the abduction."

Shocked but trying to hide it, Cavitello said, "Why would you think that?"

"Your client was seen with Burton at his house several times prior to going missing, and they were also seen going into a gym together, looking a lot like sweethearts. They were more than acquaintances, contradicting what Mrs. Brown had written in her journal. She was gone from home often, supposedly doing volunteer work at a hospital, but they have no record of her working there. To me, that suggests that she was sneaking around, like somebody might do if they were having an affair."

Cavitello looked at his client, then back at Hector. "I need to talk to Mrs. Brown to understand what this is all about. Why don't you take a break, turn off the recording devices, and let us talk for a few minutes."

The detectives agreed. Cavitello could have shut the interview down, so they were happy to give him the time he requested. They hoped that when they returned, he would let them continue.

CHAPTER 33

After the detectives left the interview room, an annoyed Anthony Cavitello said to his client, "Do you want to tell me what the hell is going on?" Bertha Brown didn't answer. She put her head down, avoiding eye contact. This only caused Cavitello to feel angrier. "You told me that Alphonso Burton was only an acquaintance, someone you had seen occasionally at your gym. If you've been to his house, you're more than acquaintances. Were you having an affair with him?" Again, there was no response. Cavitello yelled, "Damn it, if you want me to defend you, then you need to tell me the whole story and not just the parts that are comfortable to talk about. Surprises aren't good for you or me, and it's especially bad when the prosecution knows more than I do. What's it going to be? Come clean or I'm leaving." It was a statement and not a question, and it was delivered adamantly. Now Cavitello fell silent.

Bertha looked up. There were tears in her eyes. He stared back at her with anything but sympathy. He was visibly upset. She said, "I did spend some time with Burton, but it didn't mean anything."

"In other words, you did have an affair?"

"Yes," Bertha confirmed.

"Damn you, you should have told me this before we met with the detectives. I never would've let you talk to them if I'd known about the affair. I was under the impression that we could have a friendly discussion with them and make this thing go away. Now it's clear that it isn't going to go away. If we don't agree to carry on the conversation, they will take it as a silent admission to guilt. If we do talk to them at this point, nothing good is going to come of it. We are between a rock and a hard place now, playing defense instead of offense. Damn, damn, damn. Why didn't you tell me about the affair before?"

"Obviously, having the affair was stupid of me. It cost me two years of my life. I didn't want to lose my husband and the respect of my daughters. I thought I could keep the affair to myself."

"Where's that gotten you? Now you can waste some more of your life in prison."

"I'm innocent. You're a good lawyer. You'll win this case."

"Listen, Mrs. Brown, I'm not sure I'll represent you at this point. Tell me the whole story, the real story. Don't leave anything out."

Bertha waited a few seconds. She swallowed hard and said, "Okay. The only part I left out before was about the affair. Burton and I were seeing each other for several months. I realized how stupid I was being. I love my husband. He's provided well for our family. He's a good father. I can't tell you why, but I was starting to feel unfulfilled. I believed that there was more to life. About that time, I met Burton. He wooed me. He just caught me at a vulnerable point in my life. I tried to break it off with him after I came to my senses. He wouldn't hear of it. I quit taking his calls, but I'd see him at the gym. He pressured me. The last time I went to that gym, he was there. He got nasty, threatening to tell my husband about us. It scared me, but I held my ground. I decided that I was going to quit that gym and find another one. When I went to leave, he was in the parking lot. The rest of the story is just how I told it to you the first time. He abducted me. Nobody should have to go through what he put me through."

Cavitello just stared at Bertha after she told her story. He was trying to figure out if he could believe her or not. "How can I believe this story? How do I know that you didn't leave your husband for Burton, then something went wrong in the relationship? Maybe you fabricated this story to gain your husband's sympathy and to cover up the truth."

"I can see why you have your doubts. It was stupid of me not to tell you the whole story. I think the journal proves my story. Certainly, if I ran off with Burton, I wouldn't be planning for it to last two years and then to return home. That would be unheard of. Yet, I kept the journal for the two years, describing what he put me through. Why would I do that if I was with him voluntarily? And why would I put the effort into making up that story if it wasn't true? What would my purpose be to make these things up during that time? It would make no sense at all, would it?"

Cavitello studied her. She had a valid point, but he still wondered if he could trust her. "I'll stay on, but if anything else comes out as a surprise to me, I'm through. Are we clear?"

"Yes, we're clear. My husband doesn't have to know, does he?"

"I'm not a marriage counselor. Frankly, I don't care if he finds out or not. My concern is keeping you out of prison. Your relationship with him is your business, not mine." Cavitello may have been a good lawyer, but even in the best of times, he wasn't touchy-feely. He was still very irritated with Bertha, and he wasn't trying to hide it. He asked, "Is there anything else that I should know about? We can't afford any more surprises."

"You have the whole story."

"I'm assuming that the hospital volunteering thing is crap. You were using it as an excuse to be away from home to see Burton?"

"Yes."

"Okay, I'm going to invite the cops back in. I want you to tell them about your affair. At this point, we're better off conceding it. Tell them exactly what you told me. Then, before they ask, tell them the truth about the volunteering thing. If we tell them what they can already prove, it shouldn't weaken our case, but will give us some credibility. After you finish explaining those things to them, I will officially end the interview."

"Okay. Will I have to spend the night in jail?"

"Yes, you will be kept in a holding cell. The earliest we can get a preliminary hearing will be tomorrow. If the judge decides that there is enough to establish probable cause, he'll set bail, and we'll go from there. I'm fairly sure that the bail will be reasonable. We should be able to get you home tomorrow, unless something I don't know about surfaces." Cavitello stared at Bertha to see her reaction. She looked irritated but said nothing.

• • • •

The detectives returned to the interview room. Cavitello said, "Mrs. Brown is ready to answer your question about her relationship with Alphonso

Burton." He looked at Bertha and said, "Go ahead and tell the detectives about the relationship." Bertha repeated the same story she had shared with Cavitello. She also confessed that the volunteer work was fabricated to help her get out of the house to spend time with Burton.

Cavitello said, "Let me summarize the situation as I see it. Mrs. Brown had an affair. It was wrong, and it was a mistake. It cost her dearly. As a captive, she feared for her family's lives, and then, late in her captivity, she feared for her own life. It took a great deal of courage, but she did the only thing she could do. The journal is certainly evidence of that. I haven't seen the journal yet, but my client tells me that it describes her horrific experience graphically. Is that correct?"

Hector held his gaze as he responded, "Yes, it paints a picture of captivity, torture, and rape. Your client seems to have a talent for fabricating. It's hard to believe her. The thing that continues to bother us is that Mrs. Brown never tried to escape. She told us earlier that Burton never left her side. However, we found out that there were times when they were at their gym and they would shower in separate shower rooms after working out. She had every opportunity to escape or to try to solicit help. She didn't. It sure appears that killing Burton wasn't her only option."

Bertha broke in and said, "If you read my journal, you know that I was afraid for my family's safety if I escaped. I really saw no other option." Tears ran down her face.

Cavitello took over. "Gentlemen, I really don't see how you have a case. I think the best thing for everybody is that we drop this and let this poor woman try to get on with her life."

The comment brought a smirk to Hector's face. He said, "We didn't bring Mrs. Brown in for questioning. We've charged her with murder, with the district attorney's blessings. The DA's office thinks that we have a solid case. Let me summarize key facts for you. Your client confessed to killing Burton in her journal. We only found one set of fingerprints on the journal, and they belong to your client, giving authenticity to who wrote it. Your client has admitted to us that she stabbed Burton. Her DNA is the only DNA on the murder weapon other than Burton's. Your client has lied to us at least twice, that we know of. She lied about her affair. She lied about never being away from Burton. She lied to her family about volunteering. I'm confident that the prosecutor won't have any issues discrediting anything Mrs. Burton says or has written. She murdered Burton. There were other options. I'm not a lawyer, but it seems to me that your best play might be to make some sort of deal with the District Attorney's Office. We're not going to retract the charge for murder. I think the DA is considering charging your client with first-degree murder, actually. She could go away for a long time."

Cavitello was irritated but stayed calm. It seemed to him that Hector was being smug. He didn't like it. He knew that this case was going to be a challenge, but that didn't deter him. He wasn't sure if he really wanted to defend Brown, but Hector's attitude got his adrenaline flowing, and he was going to help Bertha. *Let's see how smug you are after I beat your asses in court,* he thought. He said, "Gentlemen, I think we're done here. We tried to cooperate with you, but you already have your minds made up. We'll take our chances with a jury. I'd like to talk to my client for a little longer before I leave, if you'd be kind enough to turn off your recorders and give us some privacy."

The detectives left the room. They joined Trout in the observation room. Trout said, "I can't believe the lawyer let her talk to us. That was a mistake on his part. Nonetheless, this whole case will hinge on whether the jury buys into her story. We can prove she has been dishonest, but that doesn't prove her story isn't the truth. The journal adds credibility to the whole thing. That's what worries me. You need to dig more. We're close, but I'm not confident that we're there. I want more."

Both detectives were surprised at how Trout was actually showing some life, even some emotion. Hector thought that Trout was probably pissed at the woman for creating the situation that put him in a position not to be able to solve his last case as a detective.

"Okay, Boss," Jefferson agreed. "We'll put more work into this case. Let's start by following the money. We'll go after Burton's finances during the period he and Brown were together. I don't know what we're looking for, but my guess is that we'll find something that will help us."

CHAPTER 34

On Wednesday night, Jefferson got home later than usual. It was close to eight. Bossy met him at the door. After making a fuss over seeing him, she bawled him out in her own way for being late. She knew that meant there would be no long walk in her immediate future. Jefferson had to laugh because Bossy sounded like she was actually trying to say words. He was sure none of them would be very nice.

Aubrey warmed up the leftovers from dinner. Jefferson went to his kids' bedrooms and said hello to each of them. They were both studying, and he didn't want to distract them, so it was a quick hello with a kiss on their cheeks and back into the kitchen.

He and Aubrey sat and talked as Jefferson ate his dinner. He asked Aubrey how her day was. "It was okay. I finally got information on the kid who left my study hall to use the restroom and never returned."

"Was I right? Was it something you said to the poor kid?"

"Aren't you funny?" she replied. "I'm innocent of all charges."

"So tell me, what did happen to him?"

"He wants to be a rock star. From what's being said at school, he has real talent. He and a friend have performed locally as a duet. They decided to take their act to Nashville. I guess the friend stayed home the day that they left, pretending to not feel well. The friend's mother has a part-time job, working afternoons. After she left for work, the kid texted my student, saying that he was coming to pick him up. The other kid has his own car.

I guess these kids had been planning this for weeks. They had talked to their parents about leaving school to begin their music careers. Neither set of parents would allow it. Once my student got the text, he asked to go to the restroom. End of story."

"How did the parents find out?"

"That evening, the kids both called home and explained what they did. Needless to say, the parents weren't pleased. My student's parents called the police. But there was nothing the police could do. The boy wasn't missing. He apparently wasn't in danger. Here's the thing. The kid is already eighteen. For some reason, the parents held him back a year from school, so he is about a year older than most of his classmates. Because he's eighteen, it means that he can quit school and leave home if he chooses to do so."

"I hope you were good to the kid while he was in your study hall."

Aubrey asked, "Why do you say that?"

"Maybe if he has good memories of you, we can score some tickets once he hits the big time."

"Of course I was good to him. You know that I'm known for my sweetness. My guess is that he'll credit me with helping him to become rich and famous. He'll say something about owing it all to his high school study hall teacher, Mrs. Jefferson."

"The sad part is that you actually believe it. You're so delusional."

"Jealousy will get you nowhere."

"I can see this is going nowhere. Do you have anything else to share with me about your day?"

"The best thing that happened today is that I found a book that had been missing."

Jefferson responded, "Well, that's good news. Where was the book found?"

"It had been put on the wrong shelf."

"I imagine that happens often."

"Why do you think that?"

"I know when I go to the library, I'm not always as careful as I should be to replace a book exactly where I found it," Jefferson admitted.

"That's awful! You're married to a librarian. Where's the respect? It's like a cop's wife being a pick-pocket. It goes against every principle of humanity."

Jefferson smiled and said, "I'll try to do better."

Aubrey was ready to move on. "What's new with you?" she asked.

Jefferson filled Aubrey in on what had transpired with the skeleton case. He had been sharing the story with her as it developed. She was very interested in hearing the newest information. When he finished the story, she asked, "Do you really think she ran off with the guy and then killed him?"

"I do. You know all about evil women."

"What's that supposed to mean?"

"I refuse to talk without my attorney present."

"That's smart on your part. If you think this woman ran off with your victim, do you think the journal is a fake? Do you think she planned to kill him right from the start and wrote it to provide herself with something like a self-defense motive?"

"I can tell we have been together a long time. You are almost like a junior detective. I believe that is one of two possibilities."

"Why would she run off with the guy, knowing that she was going to kill him, and then spend two years with him?"

"It doesn't make sense to me either, but if that's the case, we're missing a piece. We need to uncover more information, and we will if it's there," Jefferson said.

"You said there are two possibilities. What's the second one?"

"The second one is that she wrote the journal after she killed him."

"Do you think she stayed at the house with the dead body in the basement until she had the journal completely written?"

"That's a possibility, but I think if she did write the journal after killing the guy, she did it after she returned home to her family."

"Then you're saying she returned to the scene of the crime after she had the chance to write the journal and dropped it off at the guy's house?"

"That's what I'm saying."

"Why would she do that?"

"If that's what happened, she probably did it to help cover up what really happened."

"What do you think really happened?"

"If I had to guess at this point, I would say that she had an affair with the victim and decided to leave her family. I don't know why she just disappeared as opposed to telling her husband that she was leaving. I know that she is a sneaky woman, and she seems to like to do sneaky things. So she just sneaked out. Or it could be that she wasn't sure that the new relationship would last, and she wanted to leave the door open to returning home someday. Faking the abduction could've been her plan all along. If that's the case, it apparently worked, because she is back home, and her husband seems thrilled to have her. Following that scenario, she could've been working on the journal all along, just in case things didn't work out with the boyfriend."

"That's certainly an interesting theory. Do you think you can prove it?"

"We only have to prove that she murdered the guy and it wasn't self-defense. My alternate theory is that she never planned to return home. But somewhere along the way, she missed her girls, or the relationship soured. She told her boyfriend that she was going to end it. He threatened to expose their relationship to her husband. She made the decision to kill him. After doing that, she went home and wrote the journal."

"Unless someone can verify she wrote the journal at home, how can you prove that?"

"I don't know that we can."

"What are your chances of getting a conviction?"

"The District Attorney's Office is not one hundred percent, but they think we're close. We have one other thing going for us. The woman's attorney is a guy named Cavitello. While he was meeting with her, we did some research on the guy. He has a terrific reputation. There's a catch. Apparently, our suspect didn't do her homework. Cavitello had a guy working with him who was an ex-attorney who got disbarred. He was considered a great lawyer when he practiced. After getting disbarred, he joined Cavitello as an advisor. He controlled Cavitello like a puppet. He was definitely the brains behind the law office. He and Cavitello had a falling out, and he left the practice recently. From what we've seen so far, Cavitello isn't too bright. He let us interview his client, and there were too many things he didn't know that can come back and bite them. I'm sure we can depend on him to make a few more blunders."

"As always, Detective Jefferson will get his woman. How are things going with the Vigilante Killer?"

"Now you're starting to remind me of the commander, with all of your questions about that case. That's not a good thing. Just like I told him, we think the perpetrator will strike either tonight or tomorrow night. If it's who we think it is, we'll have him."

"You don't know how much I hope that happens. After what happened to Fred DuKane, I can't wait for this case to be solved."

"So you love me after all."

"If anything happened to you, Bossy would miss you. It's all about keeping Bossy happy." Aubrey gave Jefferson a big smile. He returned an even bigger one. He adored Aubrey.

CHAPTER 35

Jefferson was hoping for a call on Wednesday evening, telling him the Vigilante Killer had struck again and was caught, but it didn't happen. When the alarm went off Thursday morning, he was disappointed that it was not his cell phone waking him up. He took Bossy for a mile-long walk, showered, ate breakfast, and headed to the station.

Hector arrived ten minutes after Jefferson did. The detectives made some small talk and got busy doing research into Alphonso Burton. Hector worked at investigating the man's finances. Jefferson looked into his background, what he did for a living before retiring at a very early age, and trying to understand what kind of man he had been.

As Jefferson checked into Burton's background, he couldn't find any run-ins with the law. He researched where Burton's parents lived when he was growing up. That led him to uncovering where Burton went to high school. In talking to the principal, he found that there weren't a lot of teachers still at the school from Burton's days. By checking records, the principal was able to identify a current teacher whom Burton had a class with as a student. Jefferson asked the principal to have the teacher, Mrs. Kale, call him at her earliest convenience. During the teacher's lunch break, she phoned Jefferson. She was an English teacher. At first, she couldn't place Burton, but she had a collection of yearbooks from each year that she was at the school. She kept them on bookshelves in her classroom.

She pulled down the book from what would have been Burton's senior year. Upon seeing his graduation picture, she immediately recognized him.

"Now I remember him," she said. "I don't have a lot to tell you. As best I remember, he was a good student. I tend to remember those students who showed great promise or those who were problem students. He was neither. He seemed to get along well with the other students. I'm not positive about this, but I believe that he wasn't that creative but he had a fundamentally sound grasp of our language and how to use it. He communicated well. Why are you asking about him?"

"I'm sorry to have to tell you this, but he passed away, and we're doing routine checks into his background."

"I'm so sorry to hear that. It's always so shocking for me to hear of the passing of my former students. I knew them as young adults. It doesn't seem right. Why would you be doing a background check unless he died of a suspicious cause?"

"Mrs. Kale, his death has raised some suspicion, but I can't go into details."

"How horrible. It's become such a crazy world."

"Tell me about it," Jefferson replied.

"I just remembered something else about Alphonso. Between classes, I went out in the hallway one day. We're encouraged to visit the hallway between classes. The students tend to behave better when teachers are present. On that day, as I stepped out in the hallway, I saw Burton kissing another student from my class. I didn't know that they were an item and was surprised because there was no sign of a relationship during class hours. I went up to them to remind them that kissing wasn't allowed in school. They both apologized, and that was the end of it. The girl seemed okay with everything when class began. I couldn't help but notice, Burton didn't make eye contact with me that whole hour. The next day, things were back to normal. It's funny how I forgot all about that till now."

"Do you remember the girl's name?"

"No, but I think I can pick her picture out of the yearbook if I can find it. Give me two or three minutes." Within a minute, Mrs. Kale returned to the phone. "The girl's name is Stevie Brooks."

Jefferson thanked the teacher and said goodbye. He did a search for Stevie Brooks. He found a Stevie Brooks Anton. She was the right age to have been the woman he was looking for. He was able to reach her on her cell phone. He asked her if she went to high school with Alphonso Burton. She said that she had. Jefferson told her that he'd like to ask her some questions about Burton. She told him that she didn't have time right then. She was at work and was headed to a meeting. He asked her where she worked. It was only about twenty minutes from the station. Jefferson made an appointment to meet Stevie at her office in a little over an hour. He could've talked to her on the phone, but he preferred to be able to watch people he interviewed, to look for the non-verbal communication from them. Besides, he hated sitting at the desk all day. He wanted to get out. He told Hector about the appointment and invited him to come along. Hector was delighted to have a reason to get up and out. They immediately left the station and headed to a coffee shop to enjoy a cup together before meeting with the woman.

As they drove to the coffee shop, Jefferson shared what he had uncovered. "It seems our Mr. Burton was a real Don Juan. He was caught kissing a girl in the hallway at school. That appears to be the worst thing he'd ever done." Jefferson gave Hector all of the details. He told him that they would be seeing Stevie Brooks Anton, the girl Burton was caught kissing.

Once they each had a cup of coffee, Hector filled Jefferson in on his own findings. He had called the company where Bertha and her husband had dropped off Burton's car. The company leased the facility from Burton. A representative told Hector the name of an accountant to whom he sent the monthly lease payment. The accountant worked for Burton. The accountant was also their contact person for any business related to their lease. It seemed that the accountant was responsible for managing all of Burton's holdings.

"What holdings?" Jefferson asked.

"He owned that manufacturing facility and several other money-making properties. The accountant has been responsible for managing the properties, collecting proceeds, paying bills, maintaining the properties, and of course, paying the corresponding taxes."

"Did you talk to the accountant?"

"I did. That's how I found out he was the go-to guy. This is interesting. The accountant knew Bella. He told me that Burton and Bella seemed to really be in love with each other."

"Didn't the accountant notice that Burton has been missing, and didn't he find it strange that Burton was not drawing any funds to live on?" Jefferson asked suspiciously.

"I discovered that the accountant has power of attorney for Burton. Burton had no family left. Burton wanted someone to be able to do the things that needed to be done if he became incapacitated. The accountant has been running Burton's little empire, including signing his tax forms, using his power of attorney."

"That still doesn't answer my question. Didn't the accountant notice Burton disappeared?"

"I saved the best for last. Bella called the accountant just about the time we surmise Burton was killed. She told him that she and Burton were going to move to Florida. She said Burton wanted him to run everything as he had been doing. She also told him to continue to invest Burton's profits. She said she was wealthy and that she would be taking care of their financial needs while they lived in Florida. Here's the best part: She told him not to expect to hear from Burton for several years. He found that really strange, but Burton had a different lifestyle than anybody else he knew. He accepted it."

Jefferson looked doubtful. "Why would the accountant accept that coming from Bella? It would seem to me that he would want to check this out with Burton."

"That's exactly what I thought," Hector said. "I ran it by the accountant. He said that he did think it was strange, but not because Bella delivered the message. She had become a main contact for him. He thought it was strange that Burton wasn't going to draw any of his funds. He accepted it because Burton was so unpredictable."

"Do you think the accountant is an accomplice?" Jefferson asked. "It's hard to believe that he was comfortable with not hearing from Burton for years."

"It's a possibility," Hector said. "When I called him and started asking questions, he sounded totally relaxed and friendly, though. He was curious why I was asking the questions. When I told him Burton had been killed, even over the phone, I could hear that he was stunned. After that, he sounded more upset than he did anxious. He gave me the impression that he really cared for Burton. I guess he was the family accountant before Burton's parents died, and he knew Burton when he was just a boy. The man was clearly shook up. I don't think he was involved in Burton's death. But I do think it's strange that he accepted the whole Florida story. I do believe that the accountant is going to help us to nail her."

Jefferson said, "Although it doesn't sound like Bella was being held captive, a good attorney will negate the accountant's testimony. He'll ask if it was possible that Burton made Bella call the accountant. Of course, the answer will be yes."

"Why would Burton have her call the accountant, telling him no funds would be needed? If they were moving, they still needed money. It's also strange that she told the accountant not to expect to hear from Burton for years. To me, it's setting up as a premeditated murder and proves this is not a case of self-defense.

"You make a lot of good points."

"I can check to see if they had booked a flight to Florida around the time Burton was killed," Hector added. "If they hadn't booked a flight, it would prove that they hadn't actually scheduled the move."

Shaking his head, Jefferson said, "If a flight was booked, it would help validate Bertha's story, but if a flight hadn't been booked, it doesn't prove that they weren't planning the trip. She can claim that they were going to drive. Let's check it out so that there are no surprises later." Hector nodded in agreement, and Jefferson continued, "We have a lot of evidence that indicates that Bella committed murder, but we can't prove that it wasn't in self-defense. We need one more significant piece to get us over the hump. We also have to be prepared for the defense to make Burton look like a monster. We need to continue to dig into his background to be prepared to deal with whatever they throw at the jury."

"When we look at the evidence, we have no doubt that Bella did the crime. It seems like a jury would see it that way too," Hector asserted.

"You're right," Jefferson agreed, "but if there's a shadow of doubt, she'll walk. Did the accountant have anything else?"

"Yes. He told me that Burton's estate is worth upwards of ten million dollars. The surprising part to me is that Bertha didn't try to take any of his fortune. The accountant is Burton's trustee. He said that Burton was leaving all of his assets to children's charities. I guess he wasn't such a big ogre. Maybe Bella turned on Burton because he wouldn't name her as his beneficiary."

"We'll never know. It wouldn't seem that she needed money. Her husband's no slacker himself. I'm sure she has all of the money she needs."

"That's probably true. I have one other thing of interest. Burton and Brown did some traveling when they were together. They went to Hawaii several times, and to Florida. She traveled as Mrs. Burton. That means she either had to have a driver's license or passport with the name Bella Burton on it. I'm not sure how she managed that, but I'm guessing it was a phony. I could find no record of them ever marrying."

Jefferson nodded his head yes and then said, "I'd have to believe it's hard to travel with someone against their will through an airport. Certainly, Burton couldn't have a weapon on his body. The travel doesn't prove anything but it makes the captive story seem that much less likely. Our case is shaping up, but we still need to find that one other piece."

The detectives got up and headed to their car. It was time to go see Stevie Brooks Anton.

CHAPTER 36

They arrived a few minutes early and headed into Stevie Brooks Anton's office building. Anton worked as a partner in a small accounting firm. She was a CPA.

The detectives took the elevator to the seventh floor and headed to the door leading to the reception area. Although the building was older, it had recently been updated. It still maintained a classical ambiance while having the feel of a newer building. The reception area was done in marble and wood, with two leather sofas facing each other and a coffee table in between for the comfort of waiting guests. The coffee table had an array of magazines neatly lying across it. Jefferson and Hector were asked to take a seat and were told that Ms. Anton would come for them soon. Jefferson glanced around, while Hector picked up a magazine and started paging through it. In a short while, Ms. Anton arrived. She introduced herself and invited the men back to her office. She was an attractive, tall woman. In a way, she reminded Jefferson of Bertha Brown. She carried herself like someone who was confident and in control.

She asked them if they wanted something to drink. They didn't. She said, "You wanted to talk to me about Alphonso Burton?"

Hector took the lead, saying, "Yes, we do. We talked to an ex-teacher of yours, a Mrs. Kale. She told us that you were friends with Burton. Is that correct?"

"I guess you could say that. How did Mrs. Kale know that?"

"She told us that she caught you and Burton kissing in the hallway."

Anton looked up as if she were trying to find something on the ceiling and then a smile came to her face. When she finally spoke, she said, "I forgot all about that. It's really surprising Mrs. Kale remembered. I didn't think it was that big of a deal."

"Were you and Burton dating?"

"Not really. We ran into each other at a party. We were just kids. We knew each other from school, but we mostly just exchanged hellos. We spent a lot of time together at the party, though, and by the end of the night, we were making out, nothing heavy, just kissing. The next Monday, we saw each other outside Mrs. Kale's class. As I remember, we spotted each other and both smiled. He came up to me and planted a kiss on my lips, and we got caught. That was about it."

"Did you date after that?"

"No. He asked me out, but in the light of day, I realized that I wasn't really interested. I can't tell you why, but something about him made me feel uncomfortable. Maybe it was that kiss at school. It seemed a little forward and maybe presumptuous on his part. He hounded me for a while, but the more he did, the more I knew that he wasn't right for me."

"Can you be more specific when you say he hounded you?" Hector said.

"This was before cell phones were so readily available. He used to call my home a lot. At first, I talked to him, but after a while, I quit taking his calls. In fact, at one point, my dad told him not to call anymore because it was upsetting me. He was never scary, just overbearing. After my dad talked to him, he called much less frequently, but he always tried to talk to me at school."

"What kind of things did he have to say?"

"He told me how much he liked me. He said that he always had a crush on me. He would tell me about all of the fun things we could do together. He seemed to have a lot of money, and I think he believed that would be attractive to me."

"Did he ever threaten you?"

"No, he never made any threats. We didn't hear much about stalking in those days, but I did feel like he was stalking me. He talked to my friends about me, and he'd find out where I was going to be and show up there, until I urged my friends not to share my information with him."

"How did things end?"

"He backed off little by little, until I actually started dating someone regularly. Then he kind of disappeared. I think it finally sunk in that I wasn't playing hard to get. I just wasn't interested."

"Have you seen Burton since graduating from high school?"

"No, I haven't. I wondered what happened to him. Now let me ask you, why are we discussing him? Is he in some kind of trouble?"

"I'm afraid that he's dead, and the circumstances require us to investigate."

Ms. Anton looked back at the ceiling. She was trying to process what she just heard. "That's horrible. I'm sorry to hear that. But I have to say, for some reason, I'm not surprised. Like I said, there was just something about him that was different, and I think whatever it was might make people uneasy. I think of people my age as being too young to die. I guess we all feel that way."

"You're right. Before we go, is there anybody else you would recommend that we talk to for better insight into Burton?"

Anton thought for a while and then said, "He had a friend, Benton Wever. I knew Benton well because we went through grammar school together. I believe he and Alphonso were the best of friends. I actually always thought that it was strange because they were quite different. Benton was laid-back. Everybody liked him."

"Do you know where we can reach him?"

"I'm pretty sure that he still lives in the city. I ran into him in the last year or two, and he did at that time." "Thanks. You've been a big help." Jefferson thanked her as well, speaking for the first time, and then the detectives headed to their car.

Jefferson was the first to speak once they were alone. "That was interesting. From what we heard, Burton wasn't a monster, but he had some issues."

"Maybe he wasn't a monster yet back in high school, but it sounded like he was headed in the wrong direction. Even so, I still believe that Bertha Brown was with him by her own choosing. I hope we learn what the dynamics of the relationship were. It's got to be an interesting story."

"Speaking of relationships, have you worked out your own issue?"

"Which one?" Hector asked.

Jefferson laughed and said, "Oh yeah, I forgot who I'm talking to. I'm referring to the many adventures of your love life. Did you figure out what to do between your girlfriend and your ex-classmate?"

Hector smiled. "I think I have. I talked to my mom about the situation."

"Your mom?" Jefferson blurted out in an astonished voice.

"Yeah, my mom is the smartest person I know, and she's real. All that she cares about is my best interest. I don't have a wife to turn to when I want a sounding board like you do."

"You never will have a wife like me if you keep running to Mom when you get in over your head."

"Hey, take it easy," Hector said. "You're supposed to have my back, not stab me in it."

"Like you once said to me, when you really need me, I'll be there. So, what did you and your mom decide?"

"We didn't decide anything. I talk to my mom, but I do make my own decisions. My mom asked me how I felt about my girlfriend, as you call her. I told her that I loved her. She asked me how I felt about the other woman. I told her that she was always someone I had a crush on and that I was very intrigued by the possibilities of what the relationship could be."

Jefferson interrupted. "Is that your way of telling your mom that you're turned on?" He laughed.

"I'll ignore that comment. My mom asked me how I believed these two women felt about me. I told her that I was sure my girlfriend loved me too. I'm not sure if the ex-classmate really sees a future with me or if she just sees someone to hang with for a while. Lord knows she's had her share of boyfriends."

"Did your mom give you advice?"

"She did. She said lust never lasts. Even in the best of situations, it's temporary. It'll diminish. There're no guarantees that love will last, but it has the potential to grow and grow. She said, given the chance, invest in love."

"Your mom is a smart lady. Is it all right if I call her when I need advice?" Jefferson asked.

"You already have Aubrey, who, apparently, is much smarter than you are. You leave my mom out of your sordid affairs."

CHAPTER 37

It was close to five o'clock when the detectives walked back into the station. They headed straight to Sergeant Trout's office. As usual, the door was closed and the blinds were down. Jefferson knocked on the door. Trout yelled out, "Come in."

As they entered, Trout gave them his famous blank stare. Jefferson wanted to tap him on his head and say, "Is anybody home?" He thought better of it. He filled Trout in on their conversation with Stevie Brooks Anton.

When he was done, Trout said, "Interesting; anything else?"

"No," Jefferson replied. The detectives waited for Trout to ask more questions. He didn't. They stared at him, and he looked at the wall behind them with a blank stare. Without another word, they got up from their chairs and headed out the door. As they were walking back to their desks, Jefferson said, "Once again, I find it interesting that he never asks about or makes comments relating to the Vigilante Case. You'd think it would be on his mind constantly, with the commander so intense on the case being solved quickly."

"To be honest with you, it concerns me," Hector agreed. "We suspected that Trout's son might be feeding information to Ernie Waul, if Waul is our shooter. We know that Trout's son and Waul had become close. I'd guess that Trout knows Waul. Maybe he's the one conspiring with Waul and not his son. I can't understand why he would be so low-key and show so little interest in nailing the killer. With it being such a high priority of the entire department, I'd expect more push from Trout, or at least a little interest."

"I can't imagine that Waul's name never comes up when Trout is talking to his son. It blows my mind that Trout never acknowledges that he knows Waul, or at least knows of him. In terms of Trout's lack of interest, I'm in agreement with you that it's strange. It's like he doesn't want the case solved. Another possibility is that his son is the conspirator and he knows it, so he isn't going to do anything to endanger his son."

"I can't imagine that, but it makes sense," Hector said. "It might explain why Trout seems to be in a daze most of the time. He has a real dilemma, with no good way to end it."

"Tonight's the night," said Jefferson. "The killer hasn't struck yet this week, and it's Thursday. Hopefully this all comes to an end this evening." Hector nodded and started packing up to go home. Jefferson planned to send an e-mail to the commander, keeping him current, before heading out too.

Bill Small, Fred DuKane's ex-partner, walked over to Jefferson. He asked, "Is there any progress in finding DuKane's killer?"

"Things are kind of at a standstill right now, but we think this might be the night that things happen. I'll keep you in the loop if anything significant occurs."

"Do you have any new suspects?" Small asked.

"No. We're still concentrating on the small list of names that we put together."

Small wished Jefferson luck and walked away. Jefferson completed his work and headed home.

• • • •

Jefferson and Aubrey went to bed around ten thirty that night. He told her, "I'm expecting a call sometime this evening alerting me of the capture of the Vigilante Killer." Aubrey thought, *Thank God.* They kissed and went to sleep.

Jefferson had a hard time falling asleep, but once he did, he slept soundly. When the alarm went off the next morning, he was surprised that he hadn't received a call. He turned off the alarm and checked his cell phone to see if he had somehow missed it. He hadn't. He was disappointed. He got up and sat on the side of the bed with his face in his hands. He wondered why the killer strike.

Aubrey continued to lie in bed, watching her husband. When he put his phone down, she assumed that he had checked it for a missed call and there wasn't one. She was probably more upset then he was. She remained silent until she felt she was calm enough to speak without emotion. Then she said, "Do you think that it all went down and they just haven't gotten around to calling you yet?"

"There's not a chance of that. Nothing happened last night."

"What do you make of it?" Aubrey asked.

"Two possibilities come to mind. One is that Ernie Waul is our guy. Whoever is conspiring with him warned him of our plan. He stayed home so that he wouldn't get caught. You can't catch a guy doing a crime if he doesn't do the crime."

"What's the other option?"

"Maybe Waul isn't our killer, but the real killer knows that Waul is our main suspect. If the real killer struck last night, we would know Waul isn't our guy. The killer likes that we suspect someone else. By the killer not striking last night, Waul remains our most viable suspect."

"That only makes sense if the killer doesn't plan to strike again. If he makes another move, you'll figure out that Waul isn't the guy."

"That's partially true. The killer seems to know our every move. The FBI won't keep teams of agents on Waul forever. The killer might have decided to wait it out before getting back into action."

"What are you planning to do?" Aubrey asked.

"Right now, we're at a standstill. I would bet this is the day that the commander shows his true colors again. It's going to get ugly, and frankly, I understand it. I know that the mayor is still all over the commander. I'm surprised that the commander hasn't been his old self much sooner than this. I wish I knew how to make something happen quickly."

"I get all that, but the question remains, what do you plan to do?"

"Your voice is much sweeter, but now you're starting to sound like the commander."

"Yes, but my motive is much different. I'm much more worried about my husband than I am about the case being solved."

With a smirk, Jefferson responded, "See, you do love me."

Aubrey appreciated that her husband wanted to be playful, and she was normally all for it. She just wasn't in the mood right now. She was worried both about the killer trying something with her husband and about the commander abusing him. She said, "Marcus, for the third time, what are you planning to do?"

Jefferson realized that Aubrey was concerned. He got serious again and said, "I think we need to concentrate on finding who the conspirator is. I'm going to take a shower and get down to the station. It's time for us to solve this case. All I can tell you for now is that I'll be even more focused." He wished he had more to offer, but he didn't. Jefferson showered, grabbed a cup of coffee to bring with him, and headed to work.

● ● ● ●

He was one of the first people to arrive at the station. He started putting some notes down on paper. It occurred to him that a good place to start would be a motive as it related to the conspirator. He needed to check into both Trout and his son to see if there was something in their background that would provide motivation for wanting gang members dead. He would do the same thing with the other members of his task force. Based on the killer's actions, the man seemed to know what the police were doing at all times. It made sense that the conspirator was in a position to know everything. The only people in the know were the commander, Trout, and the task force.

The commander wasn't in yet. Jefferson sent him a text message, telling him that he would like to meet with him, one on one, at his earliest convenience. He thought that he would be proactive because he was sure the commander would call him into his office as soon as he got to work, anyway. Jefferson wanted to tell the commander what he was planning to do. He didn't want Trout to know. The only other person he would tell would be Hector.

Forty minutes later, the commander walked up to his desk and said, "Let's go to my office." He didn't look as nasty as Jefferson expected, but he was probably saving it for when they were behind closed doors. They walked silently to the office, and the commander motioned for Jefferson to sit. The commander listened intently as he laid out his plan. When Jefferson shared that he would be checking into Trout and his son, the commander's expression didn't change. It was like he wasn't surprised. There was a silence, spent with the commander staring so hard at Jefferson it was like he was trying to see through him. It was discomforting, but Jefferson didn't flinch. The commander finally nodded his head slightly.

Jefferson asked, "Do you have any other ideas for me?" The commander continued his death stare and shook his head no. Jefferson said, "Okay," and slowly got up, waiting for the other man to tell him to sit back down, but it never happened. He walked out of the office and back to his desk.

Hector was sitting at his desk by the time Jefferson got back. He looked up and noticed Jefferson had a strange look on his face. "Were you in with the commander?" he asked.

"I was," Jefferson replied.

Hector wanted to know if Jefferson was all right. He said that he was. Jefferson said, "Let's go get a cup of coffee and talk about the case."

CHAPTER 38

Over a cup of coffee and a croissant, Jefferson recapped his meeting with the commander for Hector. Hector was surprised and asked, "The commander never said a word after you got to his office? That's not the way the commander deals with things."

"I couldn't believe it myself. I kept waiting for the explosion to take place, but it didn't."

"Do you think he's taking lessons from Trout?" asked Hector.

"Definitely not; his look said volumes. He was as intense as ever. Honestly, I wanted to look away, kind of like Trout does when in front of the commander, but I wasn't going to back down or show any weakness. I think he was looking for me to crack. It was strange."

"Apparently, he's okay with your plan. If I know one thing, it's that he wouldn't hold back if he wasn't satisfied. When things don't meet his expectations, he screams. When they do, perhaps he shuts up."

"Maybe that's it, or maybe he's actually just trying to live up to his commitment to me. Either way works for me."

"How do you suggest we proceed?"

"When we get back to the station, I'm going to dig into the backgrounds of Trout, his son, and the other task force members. I may need your help at times. Meanwhile, I was hoping that you'd find Alphonso Burton's friend that Stevie Brooks Anton told us about. We need to contact him and see what he can tell us about Burton."

"The guy's name is Benton Wever," Hector said. "Do you want me to set up a meeting with him, or is it okay if I conduct an interview over the phone?"

"I think doing it over the phone is fine, unless you think we should meet with him after you start talking to him."

Suddenly, a loud noise startled the detectives, and a mirror behind the counter of the coffee shop came crashing down in hundreds of pieces. Without thinking, Jefferson shouted loudly, "Everybody get down." There were only a handful of customers in the shop, and all but one of them hit the ground. The man who remained seated looked around at everybody else, trying to understand what was happening. Hector quickly crawled over to the man and pulled him down to the floor. The man didn't resist, but from the look on his face, he still had no idea what was happening.

Jefferson crawled over to the front window. He spotted a bullet hole high up on the glass, just as he had suspected he would. The window was intact, with some minor cracking, moving away from the hole.

Jefferson and Hector made eye contact. Jefferson motioned for Hector to look up and notice the bullet hole. Hector did. There was a solid wall under the window, shielding Jefferson, who was on all fours. He lifted his head to peer out of the window. Two pedestrians were looking around. They were apparently trying to figure out where the noise came from. Other than that, traffic was moving, and nothing seemed abnormal. Jefferson didn't see anyone who looked to be the possible shooter. He looked around the shop and said, "My partner and I are cops. Is anybody hurt?"

One of the customers said, "I'm okay." Nobody else replied.

The man behind the counter had ducked down when the shot was fired. He called out, "Do you want me to call 9-1-1?"

Jefferson said, "We'll take care of that." He called for backup. He peeked out into the street again. Nobody else in the shop moved, except Hector, who had joined Jefferson and was scanning the street. He looked at the four-story building across the street. His thoughts had immediately gone to the Vigilante Killer. The building across the street wasn't vacant. On the street level were three retail stores. It appeared that the other floors were either apartments or business offices. There were no signs indicating business activity in the building. He made the assumption that the building contained apartments. He looked from window to window, trying to see signs of a shooter. He couldn't spot anything.

Sirens were screaming out as several squad cars arrived. Before long, eight cops entered the shop. Jefferson and Hector stood up, and the other customers followed suit. Jefferson said to the cops collectively, "Please keep these people here until we get back. We're going to check the building across the street, and then we'll want to talk to everyone for a few minutes." He pointed to two of the cops and said, "I'd appreciate it if you two would come with us." He pointed to two of the others. "Why don't you two get out on the street and see if there are any witnesses who saw something. I'm sure the shooter is in the wind, but maybe he was spotted."

The detectives and the two uniformed officers crossed the street. They approached the building from where they guessed the shot was fired. There was a door into each retail shop, and there was one other door that led into a hallway. They could see both a stairway and an elevator through the window. The door was locked. There were doorbells for six apartments. Jefferson rang the first one, but there was no answer. He rang the second and third and still got no answer. On the fourth ring, a woman's voice asked, "Who's there?" Jefferson introduced himself and told her he needed to talk to her. She said okay and told him that she would be right down. Apparently, she didn't want to buzz him in because she didn't know if he was legitimate or not. In less than a minute, she was looking through the window at the four men. Two were in uniform. She opened the door.

Jefferson said, "We're sorry to bother you, but did you hear a loud noise a few minutes ago?" The woman had, and she asked him what it was. He told her that a rifle had been fired, and he believed it came from her building. He told her that he wanted to do a search of the building. She stepped aside and let the men in. They walked the corridors on each floor. They knocked on each door. They were unable to get into four of the apartments, but they did get into the woman's apartment and one other. Neither the woman nor the man in the other apartment had seen anything. Jefferson said to Hector, "I think we're wasting our time. I don't even think we should put the effort into trying to get into the other apartments. Let's go back to the coffee shop and talk to the other people."

They did, but nothing they heard indicated that the other people might be targets. They collected personal information from each person and from the clerk. They found the bullet, bagged it, and took it with them. It sure looked like a bullet from the Vigilante Killer's rifle. They talked to the two cops who had tried to find a witness out on the street, but they had come up with nothing.

As they headed back to the station, they agreed that it had to be the Vigilante Killer. Hector said, "He's pissed that we're getting in his way."

Jefferson agreed. "It sure seems that way. Fortunately, it was just a warning shot. If he wanted us dead, we would be. We need to check on where Waul was at the time the shot was fired."

Hector said, "Wouldn't the surveillance teams have been on Waul?"

"No, it's too early in the day. They start their watch after he arrives home at the end of the workday. I'll call his sergeant and see what I can find out."

"Before you do that, how are you doing with all of this?"

"You want the truth?"

"That would be cool."

There was a long silence, and then Jefferson responded, "I'm scared. This guy killed DuKane. He knows who we are, but we don't know who he is. We're never safe, day or night. We thought he only acted at night, but this proves that he will work days too. How do we protect ourselves? Until we find him, we're at his mercy. If he fired the shot as a warning to frighten me, it worked. How are you feeling?"

"I'm anxious. I'm sorry to say this, but I would think that you're the target if he wants to shoot at another cop, but who knows. He might decide to shoot your partner to scare you off. I never signed up for this."

"That's for sure. I don't think I can tell Aubrey about this." Hector nodded in agreement. Jefferson said, "I've always told her everything. This is going to be tough. If she finds out later, it won't be good. Maybe I better tell her."

Hector responded, "Let's make it our priority to stay out of harm's way for the rest of the day and deal with that issue at the end of it."

Jefferson agreed, but then he started worrying about his family. It occurred to him that the killer might strike at his family to get to him. He found himself feeling both furious and wanting to cry. The men sat in silence for the rest of the drive back to the station.

CHAPTER 39

Once back at the station, Jefferson got a cup of coffee and sat down at his desk. Hector thought his partner looked pale but said nothing. Jefferson stared into space with a blank look on his face. He was scared and concerned, but there wasn't anything he could do about it. Even if he was accompanied around the clock by body guards, the killer could get to him if he wanted. He thought about his family again. He thought of sending them out of town, but his wife had a job, and the kids had school. It would be so unfair to send them off, and it would create bad feelings all around. His frustration turned to anger. He thought, *I have to nail this bastard, and I have to do it now.* He was going to go on the offensive. *That's it, you're mine,* he thought.

His first call was to Officer Ernie Waul's sergeant. The sergeant's name was Brian Conrad. The men had crossed paths a few different times, but they were no more than acquaintances. When Conrad answered the phone, Jefferson introduced himself. Conrad said, "Detective Jefferson, it's been a long time since we've run across each other. What can I do for you?"

Jefferson said, "I need to talk to you about something, but I need your word that it won't go anywhere else."

"Without knowing what's on your mind, it's hard to make that guarantee."

"We have suspicion that one of your men may be involved in something really bad."

"If you're right, don't you think my commander should know too?"

"He probably should, but there's a reason nobody else can know. As bad as this may sound, I'm taking a gamble in bringing you in on this. I wouldn't if I didn't need information from you."

Conrad sounded upset when he asked, "I have to ask what the risk would be by involving my commander?"

"Somebody is feeding our suspect information to help him, and that person has to be someone in the know. I sincerely doubt that it's your commander, but we can't take that chance. This is being handled on a strictly need-to-know basis."

"Wow, this is heavy, Brother. My inclination is to stay uninvolved, but if one of my guys has gone bad, I need to know it. I'll stay mute for as long as I can, but my commander can never know that you talked to me."

"That's a deal," Jefferson said and proceeded to share the story with Conrad. As he spoke, Conrad listened in silence. He couldn't believe what he was hearing.

When Jefferson finished his story, Conrad said, "I don't know where to start. Waul is the last man I would suspect of doing something so wrong. He's a good man, great character. He's one of those guys I never worry about. He does his job well, and he does it by the book. He follows rules. I'm sure you're wrong. All you really have is that your killer was probably a sniper in the service and Waul was a sniper. I know about your reputation. You're a good detective. You have to admit that this is a big stretch."

"Look, I don't want it to turn out that the Vigilante Killer is a cop, but it's a real possibility. The killer knows about our activities in trying to capture him at every turn."

"Well, I can guarantee you that I'll keep your secret because I wouldn't dare dirty Waul's name unless there was a lot more evidence. Why do you need my help?" Conrad asked.

"I just have a couple of questions for you. First, where is Waul today?"

"He has the day off. I have no idea what he was planning to do."

"Can you remember when he asked for the day off?"

"I'm not sure . . . Monday or Tuesday, I think. Why does that matter?"

Jefferson explained about the gunshot earlier in the day. He said, "The killer was sending me a message. This isn't something he would've planned for a long time in advance. If Waul had requested the day off two months ago, it would take some of the suspicion off of him. But for him to request the day off maybe two days ago and then somebody firing a warning shot at me today, it's suspicious."

"If your killer knows so much, maybe he knows that Waul is a suspect and that he asked for the day off. If the killer knew that, maybe he took the shot at you not so much as a warning, but to cast more suspicion on Waul."

After a moment, Jefferson replied, "To be honest, that hadn't occurred to me, but it's possible. Actually, I hope that theory is correct because I'm hoping not to get shot at again."

Conrad could hear Jefferson's tone of voice change as he mentioned getting shot at. He empathized with him. He realized that Jefferson had to be on edge. He said, "I'll help you in any way I can. I'm sure that when the truth comes out, Waul will be proven innocent. What else can I tell you?"

"Do you know if Waul ever had problems with gangs?"

"He's arrested gang members, but I can't remember anything that would set him off."

"Do you have any idea why Waul became a cop?" Jefferson asked next.

"As a matter of fact, I do. His dad was a cop, and so were his grandfather and uncle. Being a cop was kind of like the family business. It's all that he ever wanted to do. He's well suited for it. He cares about people, but he also cares about doing the right thing. Part of the reason he went into the service was that he thought it would make him a more viable candidate for the police force."

Jefferson asked, "Do you know if any of the other cops in his family had issues with gangs?"

"Look, Jefferson, we all have issues with gangs. They're our natural enemy. Waul never talked to me about any issue with any family members and gangs. I'm sure, like all of us, Waul would like to see gang members off the street, but he has no extra vendetta, as far as I can tell."

"Is Waul's dad or uncle still on the job?"

"His dad's retired, but his uncle is still at it."

"What does he do?"

"He's the chief of police for the Elmwood Park Police Department."

"How long has he been with the Elmwood Park Department?"

"I think his whole career."

"I have one other thing. If, in casual conversation with Waul, you can find out how he spent today, it might help. Although he can't know we're looking at him, it would be good to find out at this point if he has an alibi for today. It could help clear him."

"He'll be back tomorrow. I'll see if he wants to talk about his day off with me. I'll let you know what I find. Now that I'm somewhat involved, please keep me updated as things progress one way or another."

"I will. I'm sorry to bring this to you, but I appreciate your help and professionalism." The men hung up.

Jefferson added Waul's dad and uncle to the list of people he wanted to check out. Maybe something in one of their backgrounds might give a clue as to what set Waul off, if he was their man. Then Jefferson started thinking about what Conrad had said about the shooter taking a shot at Jefferson to make Waul look more suspicious. That would put Jefferson further from capturing the killer, but it sure would help him breathe a little easier.

CHAPTER 40

The Vigilante Killer met with his companion over dinner at an Italian restaurant. The restaurant had black-and-white pictures on the walls that looked like they were taken between 1900 and 1950. They were of individual people and groups of people standing and sitting in different locations that certainly looked like Italy. The tables were covered in plastic, red-and-white checkered tablecloths.

The waiter brought menus and took a drink order. In a short time, he returned with their drinks and brought them bread with a bottle of olive oil and a bowl of parmesan cheese. He took their dinner requests. They were now ready to talk.

They had asked to sit in a quiet corner so they could have as much privacy as possible in a reasonably busy restaurant. They spoke in hushed tones. The companion was livid, but he was careful not to raise his voice. He said, "I told you not to shoot at any more cops. What the hell is wrong with you?"

"There's nothing wrong with me. This was good for both of us."

"How could you shooting at another cop be good for anybody?"

"Look, you know Jefferson is a good detective. Eventually, if he's allowed to do his job, he's going to figure out that you're the inside guy. When that happens, we both go down. You don't deserve that. You should be recognized as a hero. After shooting in his direction, he's going to be on edge. He'll start having doubts about whether he really wants to get too close. He'll be afraid that I might lose it on him. I'm not done, either. If he doesn't back off, I'll let him know that his family isn't safe. I have a responsibility to protect our identities. I don't know any other way."

"When we first started cleaning up the streets of punks, the mission made perfect sense to me, and although I had a tough time deciding to help you, I could still feel okay with it," the companion said. "Everything changed when you killed DuKane. I'm really worried about you. I think you've gone off the deep end. The cops aren't your enemy. DuKane, Jefferson—you're talking about good men. I'm telling you right now, if you make another move against another cop or their family members, I will turn myself in and give it all up. I didn't agree to going after cops."

The killer was silent for a few seconds. When he spoke, he stared intently at his companion. "Cops are trying to stop me from doing the right thing. I have the gangs running scared. From information you've provided, we know that gangs aren't having such an easy time recruiting new members right now. That's all us. Besides, you've been cheated and overlooked throughout your career. You've been passed over for promotions and treated like an outsider right from the start. If the cops played it straight and rewarded the people who deserved it, you'd be a commander by now. The police department is corrupt, and as far as I'm concerned, they're fair game. They're not my target, but I'm not going to let them stand in my way. If they did their jobs, I wouldn't have to do what I'm doing. Why don't you get that?"

"I get it, but I don't agree with it. As cops, we're limited by law in what we can do. A lot of the time, we know who the perpetrators are, but we can only do what the law allows. That's not the fault of cops. It's the law. It's really hard to gather the proof necessary to win convictions. If a gang member is brought to trial with inadequate proof in a murder case and he is not convicted, he can't be tried again for the same murder. We're better off not bringing that thug to trial unless we have a great case. At least we still leave the possibility of nailing him at a later date."

"That's where I come in," said the killer. "I don't have to wait to get lucky. The people I'm taking out have earned their fate. They don't get a chance to kill some more or to destroy another family. You know that what we're doing is right."

"You've become a hypocrite. You talk about destroying families after you destroyed DuKane's and are threatening to destroy Jefferson's. You've become just as evil as the men you so despise. Don't you see that?"

"Bullshit! The gangs are killing for personal gain. I'm risking my life with what I'm doing, and none of it makes my life any better or makes me richer. I sacrifice for the good of society. Gang members are selfish. They're only in it for themselves."

"You're doing what you're doing to avenge the deaths of your brothers. You may not be doing it for riches, but you are doing it to make yourself feel better. Your motive is selfish too."

"I started out doing it for revenge, but that's changed. Now I'm working to eliminate the dregs of our society. I'm receiving no gain and no pleasure. I'm doing what has to be done."

The companion realized that he was getting nowhere. The men sat in silence. The waiter brought their food. The killer began to eat. The companion sat motionless, deep in thought. The killer said, "Why aren't you eating?"

"I think I'm going to get them to wrap up my dinner. I'm not really ready to eat right now."

"Relax, things will be okay. I commit to you that for now, I'll back off from Jefferson. I'll start being even more careful. I'll change my routines so there is no way they'll know where or when I might strike again. I'll start targeting some lower tier gangs with equally bad members. I'll make sure that I don't get caught. Jefferson or anybody else won't have a clue, and therefore won't pose a threat to us. It'll all work out."

"I guess that's okay, but know this: I meant what I said earlier. If you go after another cop or the family of one, I will turn myself in. Being a cop means protecting good people, and that still hasn't changed with me. I won't stand for another incident like the one earlier today. Do I make myself clear?"

"I get it." With that, the killer returned to eating his dinner. The companion reflected for a while and then started eating too. He felt like he finally broke through. He was tired of feeling bad and carrying guilt. He couldn't bring DuKane back, but he wasn't going to sit idly by while some other innocent found himself in harm's way. The men finished their dinner, settled up with the waiter, and went in opposite directions.

179

CHAPTER 41

Jefferson and Hector both arrived at the station earlier than usual the next morning. They had a lot on their minds. Before jumping into work, they talked for a little while. Hector asked Jefferson about his wife's reaction to the shooting the day before. Jefferson said, "I didn't tell her about it. I need to be calm when I tell her so that I don't panic her too much. I wasn't calm last night. I was upset, and I remain upset. I've never had a sniper shoot at me before. It's unnerving."

"I'm trying to understand this marriage thing. Shouldn't you tell your wife everything?"

Jefferson's response was, "That's easy for you to say because you don't have a wife. I do think Aubrey has a right to know the truth, but the timing is important. When I tell her about the shooting, I need to appear confident and under control. If I seem scared or panicky, she doesn't stand a chance of being supportive of my doing what I have to do. I hope to get a lot accomplished today and feel good about the day. If that happens, I'll be more relaxed this evening, and I'll share everything with Aubrey then."

Hector nodded, then quickly moved on. "I'm ready to work. I was able to find a phone number for Alphonso Burton's friend, Benton Wever. I plan to call him now. What are you going to do?"

"I'm going to research the backgrounds of the people who are of interest as possible co-conspirators. I'm pretty sure that will take up my whole day, even with your help after you're finished with Wever."

Hector got lucky. He got through to the man on his first attempt. The voice on the other end said, "Hello?" in a questioning tone.

"This is Detective Jerome Hector with the Chicago Police Department. Is this Benton Wever?" Hector asked.

"Yes, that's me. What can I do for you?" Wever couldn't understand why a detective would be calling him.

"I'm guessing that you're aware that Alphonso Burton was found dead?"

"Yes, I heard about it on the news. I was very sorry to hear that. But I haven't been in touch with Alphonso for a number of years."

"When a situation like this occurs, we always research the person's background to try to understand if there's a reason to be suspicious of the cause of death. I'm calling today to get some background on Mr. Burton. Somebody told me that you and he were best friends. Is that true?"

"We were really good friends at one time. But as I said, I haven't been in touch with him. Our friendship kind of fell apart."

"Why?"

"It's a long story. The quick version is that I grew up and realized that I didn't like him all that much."

"I'd like the longer version, if you wouldn't mind. It might be helpful to us in understanding him."

Wever thought about it for a few seconds and said, "I guess it'll be okay. We met in speech class our freshman year in high school. He was into fishing and hunting. He made a speech on hunting. My family was dirt-poor. The idea of fishing and hunting to be able to eat better, made sense to me. After class, I told him I enjoyed his speech. I expressed an interest in learning to fish and hunt. He seemed to like the idea of mentoring me. He offered to teach me, but I told him that I couldn't afford equipment. He said that it wouldn't be a problem. He had extra equipment to lend me. It sounded too good to be true.

"Alphonso had everything when we were teenagers. His folks were wealthy. I had the clothes on my back, and they were hand-me-downs from my older brothers. Alphonso not only taught me to hunt and fish, but he was also generous in other ways. He was actually generous to a fault, and as a kid, that was seductive. I couldn't resist."

"What went wrong for you?" Hector asked.

"There were a few things that seemed wrong right from the start, but I looked right past them. Alphonso acted as if he was entitled. He was a spoiled only child, and he thought he could and should have everything he wanted, including people."

"Give me an example of how that played out."

"We were at a McDonald's when a popular girl from our school came in with a few of her friends. He was excited because he had been eyeing her for a while. After she sat down with her friends, he went over and started talking to her, almost like he was doing her a favor. He tried to get her phone number, but she told him that she had a boyfriend and wasn't interested. He got indignant with her. I don't remember what he said, but it was loud and abrasive. The manager came over and asked him to leave. He shouted some vulgarities as he walked out the door. Frankly, it was embarrassing for me to be with him. He continued to stalk the girl until her boyfriend threatened to kick his ass. The boyfriend was not necessarily all that big, but he wasn't a guy you wanted to mess with."

"Were there a lot of incidents like that one?"

"I wouldn't say there were a lot, but there were a few. As I got older, I realized that he wasn't that great of a friend. He did a lot for me, but I think he was buying my friendship and at the time, I guess it was for sale. I do have to say, in my defense, when he wanted to be, Alphonso could be charismatic. He could be really charming. If he showed that side to girls instead of being a pompous ass, I think he would have done well. He wasn't a bad-looking guy, and he wasn't stupid. I blame his parents for making him into what he was."

"You told me that Burton did a few things that bothered you. What else did he do?"

"It always had to be his way," Wever said. "In my case, he probably thought I owed it to him because of all he did for me. I came to realize that relationships don't work that way. In true friendship, it should be a partnership, not a dictatorship."

"Was there a turning point for you?" Hector asked.

"He was the best man at my wedding. I had other friends, and actually, he was no longer my best friend. I asked him to be the best man to honor him because he had done so much for me. I thought it would be okay because he had grown. He had learned that charm was a much better way

182

to get what he wanted. However, right before our wedding rehearsal took place, he told my fiancée and me that he wanted to march down the aisle with someone other than the maid of honor. One of the other bridesmaids was single, and she was a looker. My wife wouldn't agree to make that change. It was our wedding and our decision to make. It was out of place for him to even ask. He didn't give my wife a hard time, but he berated me privately and questioned what kind of friend I was. I knew then that in some ways, Alphonso would never change. My wife already had a bad feeling about him. Maybe that was my fault for the things I told her about him. I'm not sure. I just knew that my marriage and my life would be better off without him."

"How did you get him out of your life?"

"I tried to do the right thing. A few weeks after we got home from our honeymoon, I met him for a beer. I thanked him for the things he did for me, but told him that our friendship had to end. I explained why. He got very angry with me. It was a lot like the scene that I described at the McDonald's several years earlier. A bouncer asked us to either put a lid on it or to leave. Alphonso shoved me hard, and I fell over. He went walking out the door. For the next few weeks, he called my cell phone a bunch of times, but I never picked up. He left messages on my phone, but I deleted them without listening. I guess it was my way of establishing that he was no longer in control. He sent me nasty e-mails. I never answered them. A few weeks later, I changed my phone number and e-mail address. I never saw him or talked to him after that, but I'm still sorry to hear that he's dead."

Hector said, "I have one last question for you, at least for now. Do you think Burton was capable of abducting a woman if she was rejecting his advances?"

"That's a hard one to answer, Detective. I told you that he shoved me. That was the most physical aggression that I'd ever seen from him. I didn't think it was a big deal at that time, just a dose of testosterone. He was driven to get what he wanted, and he certainly wasn't laid-back about it. Yet, I don't think he was capable of abduction back in the day. But if I'm being perfectly honest, it wouldn't shock me. He loved his women, and as I said before, he thought he was entitled."

Hector thought about what Wever had said for a second and then thanked the man for his time and hung up.

CHAPTER 42

When Hector finished his call with Benton Wever, he looked over at Jefferson. Jefferson was typing away at his keyboard. Hector said, "That was Burton's friend Wever that I was just talking with. It was an interesting call."

"I heard the tail end," said Jefferson. "What did you learn?"

"He didn't paint a very rosy picture of Burton. In fact, he went so far as to unfriend Burton. My take is that Burton could've been capable of abducting a woman. Bertha Brown doesn't seem like an innocent victim to me, but based on what Wever had to say, it's possible." Hector recapped his conversation with Wever for Jefferson.

When Hector finished, Jefferson said, "Why aren't these cases ever easy? What do you think our next step should be?"

"Wever hasn't been in touch with Burton for a number of years. I think we have to try to find more current friends to try to understand if Burton's antisocial tendencies became more pronounced. We have to know everything we can about Burton before Bertha goes on trial, if she does."

"I agree with all that you're saying, but I'm not clear on where you stand in this case now. Do you believe that Burton abducted Bertha when she tried to end their affair, or do you believe that she voluntarily ran off with him?"

Hector's brow creased as he said, "My gut tells me that Bertha is not a victim. But even if she voluntarily moved in with him, it's possible that she decided to move back in with her family and he then kept her captive. Personally, I'd like to be able to prove that her story is a fabrication, but I'm stuck on trying to figure out how to do that."

Jefferson gave it thought. Then he said, "We need to look a little deeper into Bertha's background. We know about her family life somewhat, from the time she moved to Chicago until she disappeared. We haven't talked to friends. We haven't explored her life prior to the move, in depth. It's going to be a ton of work. Also, I think we also have to talk to Burton's more recent acquaintances as you indicated. Does that make sense?"

"It does. How about if I dig in, while you continue to do your research in trying to find the Vigilante Killer's conspirator?"

"That works for me," Jefferson said. "Before we get back to it, I do have a little to share with you." In a hushed voice, Jefferson said, "Let's take a walk so that I can talk to you in private." Hector nodded, and the men headed for the exit to take a walk around the block.

Once they were away from the station, Jefferson said, "I had a brief conversation with the man Trout reported to when he was a detective. The guy is still a sergeant. His name is Gillis. He didn't have time to go into detail. He said that he'd call me back when he had more time to talk. He told me about a case that Trout was assigned involving a gang member. The gang member's pregnant girlfriend disappeared. From all appearances, the boyfriend killed the girl and got rid of the body. This was at a time when Trout and his wife were expecting. It's hard to picture this today, but this case really hit home with Trout. He was determined to nail the guy. But he mishandled the case and got accused of being a racist. It almost killed his career. Trout had been up for promotion. But the internal investigation went on for months. The whole time, Trout was assigned to desk duty, and his opportunity for promotion dissipated. Trout was a basket case through the whole ordeal. Eventually, he was cleared, but his career took a major hit. That's why he was only promoted to sergeant within the last few years. I asked Gillis, before he hung up, if he thought Trout really was a racist. He told me that he defended Trout at the time, but he was torn."

Hector said, "That's interesting. It certainly could be an explanation for Trout not being invested in the Vigilante Killer case, and maybe even motive for aiding and abetting."

"Let's not jump to conclusions," Jefferson advised. "I've never investigated a boss before, and I don't like it. I feel like I'm working for internal affairs, not a good place to be. In any case, Trout's innocent until proven guilty, and we have a long way to go to prove anything."

"How will you follow up?" Hector asked.

"I'll continue to dig into Trout's background. It's going to be tricky to do it without him finding out, though."

● ● ● ●

After spending most of the day on their phones, the detectives were both worn out. They agreed to discuss their findings for the day the next morning. Jefferson was anxious to get home. He knew he had to tell Aubrey about the shooting. When he pulled into his driveway, he saw Aubrey sitting on their front porch with Bossy lying by her side. Instead of pulling into the garage, he left the car in the driveway and got out. When he opened the door, Aubrey stood up, and Bossy came charging. He made it to the front of the car before Bossy got close. He braced himself for the obvious onslaught. Aubrey called out, "Don't get any ideas. I won't let you arrest Bossy for assault and battery."

Jefferson called back, "You need to learn to control your beast, Lady. You're responsible for the damages." Once Jefferson pulled Bossy's paws from his shoulders and put them on the ground, Bossy stuck her nose where it didn't belong, and Jefferson let out a groan. Aubrey laughed so hard she almost fell down. Jefferson said, "You sure have a sick sense of humor. I can't believe how much joy my pain brings you. We may never be able to have kids again."

Aubrey replied, "Thank goodness."

Jefferson just smiled.

Aubrey said, "You're home early. Why didn't you call me and tell me you were coming home?"

"I probably should have, but I was hoping to catch you doing the bad things you do when I'm not around."

"Like what?"

"I don't know. That's why I sneaked home early, to find out."

Aubrey asked, "What did you discover?"

"I discovered that I got home too late and missed the bad stuff. I'll catch you eventually."

Aubrey gave him an I-don't-think-so look. Jefferson turned serious and told Aubrey that the real reason he was home early was because he needed to share something with her. He proceeded to fill her in on the shooting incident. She didn't take the news well.

There was a long silence. Aubrey was mad, something Jefferson rarely saw. She was an upbeat person who saw the good in people and the humor in most situations. The two of them just stared into each other's eyes. Jefferson waited for Aubrey to say something. Finally, she did. "I want you off the case. I've been supportive of your career right from the start. I never tell you what to do. Being the wife of a cop is a scary position to be in, but no wife should have to live with having a cold-blooded killer pursuing her husband specifically. Marcus, I can't live with this."

Jefferson couldn't let Aubrey know how scared he was. He said, "If the killer wanted me dead, he would've killed me. He knows that if he kills me, another detective will take my place. He's just frustrated, and we have to believe this was his last-ditch effort in trying to intimidate us."

"Tell that to Mrs. DuKane."

"We're pretty sure that DuKane's death was an accident. We don't believe that he meant to kill him."

"Why should I believe that the idiot won't have another accident? Marcus, I can't take this."

Jefferson tried to take Aubrey's hand, but she pulled it away. That had never happened before. Jefferson adored his wife. It was killing him to see her this way. It was so unlike her. He realized that she was even more upset than he had expected. He said, "Listen, I'm really torn. I hate seeing you this upset, but it makes me sick when I think about letting the bad guys intimidate us into quitting. Let me just sleep on this and figure it out tomorrow with a clearer mind."

Without a word, Aubrey got up and walked into the house. Jefferson was left sitting alone, teary-eyed.

CHAPTER 43

For the rest of the evening, Aubrey went mute. She didn't even talk during dinner. Her kids sensed that something wasn't right. Most dinners in their house were lighthearted affairs. Aubrey was typically an active participant. This dinner was different. The only conversation that took place was because Jefferson asked a few questions about the things going on in his kids' lives. It was apparent his heart wasn't in it. After dinner, the kitchen was cleaned up quickly, and the kids headed to their rooms. Aubrey went to the family room, but when Jefferson walked in, she got up and left. She glared at him as she walked by.

Jefferson had never seen Aubrey like this. He could just feel the hate emanating from her. He was crushed. He had to deal with his own fears; a killer had him in his sights. A situation that had seemed like it couldn't get worse was suddenly much worse. It was devastating for him to see Aubrey so pained. He heard Aubrey in the kitchen. It sounded like she might be doing some baking. He wanted to talk to her, but he realized that he had nothing to say that was going to make things better. He wasn't ready to give up. A man can't kill a good human being like DuKane, a good cop, and get away with it. Jefferson turned on the television. He sat in front of it for close to three hours, but he couldn't tell you what was happening in the programs he was watching. He kept thinking about the case and about Aubrey, wrestling with all of his options. He didn't come to any conclusion. He decided to try to get some sleep.

Aubrey was already in bed when Jefferson entered the bedroom. In all the years they had been married, he had never gone to bed without kissing his wife. He didn't know if she was sleeping or not, but he walked over to her and put a kiss on her cheek. She rolled away without a word being said. He tossed and turned all night, dozing off for shorts spurts. He was up early, before the alarm went off, and was out of the house within twenty minutes. He stopped and picked up a large cup of coffee and headed to work.

He had been hoping that a good night's sleep would help him put things in perspective. But without a good rest, he was no further ahead than he had been the day before. He felt more conflicted than ever. It was too early to start making calls. He sat silently by himself and started hashing things over and over again in his head. He'd love to be off of the case. It would be good for his sanity, and it would help bring back the Aubrey he so loved. But how does a real man do that? A man needs to stand up for what's right. He was raising kids, good kids. He needed to continue to be a role model. He would rather go down doing the right thing than survive as a coward. Why the hell didn't Aubrey get that about him? Then he realized that he was painting Aubrey as being the bad guy in fighting him, but he knew that she was fighting him out of love. He was back to square one.

Jefferson had a headache. He popped some aspirins. He crossed his arms on top of his desk and laid his head down on them. He must have dozed off because, suddenly, he felt someone tap on one of his arms. He flinched, looked up, and saw Hector standing over him.

Hector said, "Rough night?"

"You might say that, but I don't want to talk about it right now," Jefferson replied. "Why don't we recap our phone conversations from yesterday for each other?"

"That's good by me. I couldn't track down any of Alphonso Burton's more recent friends. I talked to two of his neighbors and the trainer from his gym. None of them were aware of Burton's friends, other than Bella. He has no living relatives. I can't think of another way to uncover possible friends. I wonder if the guy had any. He wouldn't want to entertain people with Bella around. A friend might ask Bella questions about herself that could lead to some very uncomfortable moments. My guess is that Burton avoided being with other people. As one neighbor said, Burton was friendly but not sociable. Contact with Burton seemed to be minimal for most people."

Jefferson said, "Did you have any luck finding out more about Bertha?"

"I was able to find her father, and I contacted him," said Hector. "When I introduced myself, he asked me if Bertha was okay. I assured him that she was. He told me that he worried about the guy who abducted her coming after her again. I told him not to worry because we got the guy and that I was calling just to complete our case file. He thanked me for capturing the guy and was very cooperative. I wanted to ask him if his daughter was always a liar, but it didn't seem to be the best way to go."

"My, how you've grown," Jefferson said and gave Hector a smile. Jefferson realized that he was feeling more relaxed. Work was good therapy, he concluded.

Hector smiled back and continued his story. "Bertha's father was interviewed when she went missing. He told me many of the same things I saw in the case file. He believes Bertha and her husband, Charles, are doing better now than before the abduction. He said Bertha was headstrong and had a dominant personality. The father worried about her marriage because she was not that nice to Charles. She always seemed to resent Charles, but her father never could understand what she had to be bitter about. He believes that Charles is a good person and, evidently, a good provider. He is a loving father, and his daughters are close to him. Since the abduction, Bertha treats Charles more like an equal, although she still has her moments."

"Did the father say anything that would make you more suspicious of Bertha?"

"Not really. The short version is that Bertha has always had a strong personality. He admitted that she fought a lot with her mother before the woman passed away when Bertha was fifteen. He said the women in his family all had strong personalities, but they all meant well. It was almost like he was apologizing. He described Bertha's childhood as normal. They didn't have much, but they never missed a meal, and they had a roof over their heads. I asked a lot of questions but never got any new information that I thought could help us."

Jefferson said, "The man said something about the women in his life. Was he just referring to Bertha and her mother?"

"Not just them, but a sister too. The father gave me the number for her. I talked to her too. This conversation was much more interesting. The sister and Bertha quit talking to each other a few years before Bertha disappeared. They resumed their relationship when Bertha returned home. The sister was relieved and seemed genuinely pleased that her sister was still alive. But within a few months, they quit talking again. The sister said that she was through with Bertha."

"Why did they quit talking the first time, and then again more recently?"

"To net it out, her sister said that Bertha is a scheming liar. Bertha thinks a lot of herself. She thinks that she's smarter than everyone else and can get away with whatever she chooses to do, right or wrong. The sister had hoped the horrible experience would humble Bertha and help her to be a better person, but if anything, she's worse. When her sister confronted her, Bertha hung up the phone and hasn't accepted any of her calls since. She quit trying to contact Bertha after months of being ignored."

"There's nothing like sisterly love. Although the sister's description of Bertha sounds damning, we have to ask if it's Bertha who's wrong or the sister who's warped, or a combination of both."

"I've talked to both Bertha and her sister. Bertha seemed arrogant to me, a little too sure of herself for someone who went through what she supposedly experienced. Her sister seemed like she was down-to-earth. She was sincere and genuine. She apologized because she thought she sounded vindictive. She expressed love for her sister. She really wants Bertha in her life but realizes that it doesn't seem possible."

Jefferson responded, "Bertha's sister learned what Burton learned. Don't piss Bertha off. Did the sister talk about Bertha's marriage?"

"Yes. She had positive things to say about Charles, but also said that he let Bertha walk all over him. I asked her why she thought Bertha treated him that way. She told me that Bertha was boy-crazy when they were growing up. Her sister said that she was a world-class flirt. She had plenty of suitors. The sister thought it was strange that Bertha chose to marry Charles. Bertha liked excitement and adventure. She said Charles is anything but excitement and adventure. She thinks Bertha resents Charles for taking her away from the things she loved, although it was her choice to marry the guy. I think she called it a conundrum." Both men laughed, and Hector continued his recap of the conversation with the sister. "I asked her why she thought Bertha married Charles if he didn't appear to be her ideal match. She didn't hesitate in answering my question. She always suspected that it was the money. Charles came from a wealthy family, and he was making a really good income and had a promising career. Bertha was always attracted to money. When they were growing up, they didn't have much. Bertha always wanted more. The sister told me something else that was curious. She said that Bertha needed to support her pen collection."

His interest piqued, Jefferson asked, "What kind of a pen collection?"

"Bertha started collecting Parker Pens when she was only six or seven years old. According to the sister, Parker comes out with new pens relatively frequently. Bertha started purchasing them with allowance money. She started babysitting at twelve, and then as she got older, she worked as a waitress while attending high school and college. Almost every cent she made went into pen purchases. I guess Bertha has one of the largest known collections. Some of the pens are relatively inexpensive. Others are ridiculously priced. Here's the crazy part." Hector stopped talking and looked at his notes. Then he said, "As a wedding gift, Charles gave Bertha something called the Parker Duofold Limited Addition Fountain Pen. It cost him $35,000."

Jefferson visibly flinched. "You can't be serious?"

"That's what her sister told me. She said that Bertha really wanted that pen but couldn't swing it. She thinks Charles promised her the pen if she agreed to marry him."

"If Bertha did run off, I think I'm beginning to see why. Hers was not a marriage built on a great foundation of love," Jefferson said. "Apparently, pen collections must be a good investment, worth a lot of money. Maybe I'll start collecting Bic Pens." Hector smiled. Jefferson wondered out loud, "Why would she run off and not take her collection of pens with her? I can't believe she would just turn her back on them."

Hector said, "If she ran off, she turned her back on her daughters. I'd like to think she valued them more than the pens."

"Another thought crossed my mind. Maybe she ran off knowing that eventually she would return home. She hooked up with Burton to experience the things that Charles wasn't giving her with the idea that it wasn't permanent." Hector nodded, indicating he agreed. Jefferson said, "Just for the heck of it, why don't you check and see if the pen Bertha left behind with the journal was a Parker Pen. Who knows, it could be worth a fortune."

Hector made a quick call and confirmed that the pen was indeed a Parker.

Jefferson asked, "Did the tech find any other prints on the pen other than Bertha's?"

"No. The journal and the pen only had Bertha's prints on them."

"I can't tell you why because I don't know myself, but I think we should retrieve the pen and take another look at it."

"Why, what could a pen possibly tell us?" Hector asked.

"I have no idea, but I want to look at it. One day, I can say I held a pen from the valuable collection of Bertha Brown."

"It doesn't sound that impressive to me."

"That's because you're just a peasant, unlike me." Both men laughed. Jefferson asked, "Did the sister give you anything else?"

"She gave me the names of two women who were close friends with Bertha. I talked to one of them. She said that she and Bertha had fallen out of touch years ago. There was no reason for it, but neither of them put the effort into maintaining the relationship. I asked her why. She said they just grew apart. She talked about how some women seem to prefer men friends over girlfriends and Bertha was that kind of woman. I asked her about Bertha's character. She said it was questionable and laughed. She saw some of the same things that Bertha's sister described."

Just then, Jefferson's phone rang. He looked at the caller ID and said, "I think this is Trout's old sergeant. Let me take the call."

CHAPTER 44

Sergeant Gillis was at the other end of Jefferson's phone. The two men made some small talk and then got down to business.

Gillis said, "I'm getting back to you about Dirk Trout. I didn't have time to ask you why you wanted information on him yesterday. How about filling me in?"

Jefferson needed to be careful. He didn't know Gillis. To be on the safe side, he had to assume that Gillis couldn't be trusted. He said to Gillis, "As you may know, I'm heading up the task force responsible for the capture of the Vigilante Killer. The mayor, my commander, and everyone else seems gung ho on getting the job done. Trout is being less enthusiastic. I'm trying to figure out if it's because he's got it out for gangs or if he's burnt out. If he's burnt out, I feel that it's up to me to try to raise his level of enthusiasm. If he has an aversion to gangs, I want to work around him as much as I can." Jefferson realized that what he was saying sounded a little fishy, but he really couldn't think of anything else to say without giving up too much information. It could be a costly mistake.

Gillis let out a non-committal grunt and said, "Getting back to the story I told you yesterday, that case changed Trout. After Trout got accused of being a racist, a powerful minister in the community started speaking out against him. He went to the press and made a big deal about Trout's arrest record. If I remember it correctly, he spouted off something like ninety-six percent of Trout's busts were black men. The minister never mentioned that Trout's district was predominantly black. He painted an inaccurate picture from what I could see. But we were working alongside racist cops and Trout didn't seem to mind them. After a long and thorough investigation, the conclusion was that there were no grounds for the charges. Unfortunately, the damage was already done. Of course, when he was cleared, it barely got any mention by the press."

"How did the case change Trout?"

"He seemed to lose confidence and enthusiasm. He carried several partners before the incident. It seemed to me that his partner was carrying him afterward. He went from being a very good detective to being a careful one. As you know, in our line of work, you sometimes have to take chances. He went from arguing for what he believed in to going with the flow. The only reason he made sergeant is because he endured and had a good record in spite of the incident. If you could get him to regain his enthusiasm, that would be terrific. I think you would be real pleased."

Jefferson asked if Trout had experienced any other incidents or problems with gangs. Gillis told him not that he could remember. They ended their call with Gillis wishing Jefferson luck with the case. He knew the kind of scrutiny and pressure that came with a high-profile case like the one Jefferson was working on.

Once he was off the phone, Jefferson shared the new information with Hector. Hector asked Jefferson what he was thinking. Jefferson said, "It sure gives us insight into who Trout is today. But I'm still not convinced that Trout is the guy. He got into a jam because of one gang member. He didn't have problems with gangs in general from what Gillis had to say. I can see how the incident scarred him, but I can't believe that it would be enough for him to want to get involved in killing gang members. I thought of asking Gillis the name of the minister who spoke out against Trout. Perhaps he could fill us in on other things that Trout might have done or said. But I realized that if we talked to the minister, he might make noise to the press about Trout. I would like to talk to the guy, but I don't think we can risk it."

Hector agreed. Then he asked, "Did you come up with anything on Trout's son?"

"I talked to a few people about him. Everything was very positive. It seems that Trout and his wife raised a good kid. He's doing a bang-up job as a cop. He's going to law school at night. I won't hold that against him. He's expressed interest in getting involved in politics down the road. Apparently, he is careful to lead an exemplary life so that he won't have any baggage if he does get into politics."

"A lawyer, politics, what could he be thinking?"

Jefferson replied, "Don't worry; there's still time for him to come to his senses."

"Were you able to check on anybody else?"

"No," Jefferson replied. "I did talk to a few other people who knew Trout Senior back in the day. I didn't come up with anything else. Today, I'll start working on the backgrounds of other task force members."

Jefferson's phone rang again. This time, it was the commander. When he answered, the commander told him that he needed to see him. Jefferson said he was on his way. He got up and said to Hector, "The commander requests my company. He must have heard that my life hasn't been that great lately and just wanted to cheer me up." Both men laughed.

The commander couldn't make Jefferson any more uptight. He had a sniper taking a shot at him and a wife who was hating him. The commander was small potatoes compared to those things. He knew he wasn't going to take any crap. Subconsciously, he was hoping that the commander would give him a reason to quit the case.

When he arrived at the office, the door was open, and the commander was pacing. Jefferson walked in. The commander motioned for him to sit, and he did. The commander stopped walking and turned toward Jefferson, seeming to stare right through him. He said, "How are you doing in your investigation into Trout's background?" The commander didn't sound very friendly, but at least he wasn't screaming or glaring.

Jefferson detailed what he had discovered about Trout and his son. The commander wanted to know what Jefferson was thinking. He got the same explanation that Jefferson had given Hector minutes earlier. The commander nodded his head in agreement.

"Have you checked into the backgrounds of the other people on the task force?" he asked next.

"No, Commander. I plan to do that today."

"What the hell is Hector doing?" the commander asked.

"He's working on our other case."

Jefferson knew what was coming. The commander was suddenly glaring at him, his nostrils flaring like a bull ready to charge. "What the hell are you thinking?"

Jefferson thought, *The man has transformed himself from a bulldog into a full-blown bull.* Calmly, he said aloud, "Even if we land on someone whose background leads to suspicion, we can't really make a move until the killer strikes again. The FBI is still monitoring Waul. He's overdue to make a move. Once we grab him, we can get to the bottom of things quickly."

"Let me be blunt. As far as I can tell, your MO is to do next to nothing until the killer strikes again. And you call that detective work. The guy shot at you. I would think you would be in overdrive in trying to find the guy. And what am I going to tell the press? Our investigation has come to a halt while we wait for the killer to off somebody else." The commander raised his voice and said, "Are you serious?"

Jefferson sat expressionless. He didn't reply right away. He knew what he was going to say, but he wanted to irritate the commander. It was working because the glaring became more intense. Jefferson said, "I told you when I agreed to head the investigation, I didn't want your shit unless you had a useful suggestion. You're giving me shit, so I'm guessing you have a useful suggestion. What is it?"

The commander's expression changed for a second. He had a half-smile on his face, but then he was right back to the charging bull. "I do have a suggestion. I suggest you get your ass back to your desk and put together a much more aggressive plan. I've been patient, but that isn't getting us anywhere. I'm really disappointed in you. Now get the hell out of here, and let me know what you come up with."

Jefferson was surprised. Nothing that the commander said really bothered him until the man told him that he was disappointed in him. That seemed so personal. Nobody on the job had ever said anything like that to him before. He realized that he couldn't walk off of the case. His reputation and his legacy meant a lot to him. He wasn't going to let the killer or the commander take that away from him. The commander was right. He needed to step it up.

CHAPTER 45

Jefferson filled Hector in on what transpired in his meeting with the commander. Hector could see that Jefferson was in a somber mood, but he also seemed like a man possessed. He delivered his information quickly and said, "Let's get to work. The commander was correct when he told me that I needed to get you focused in on the Vigilante Killer case. We have plenty of time before Bertha Brown actually goes to trial, if she does. How about helping me to check out the backgrounds of the people who could be aiding the killer?"

Hector agreed. They divided up their list of people they thought might be of interest. They dug in, checking records and making phone calls. Another detective took sandwich orders from the people in the department just before noon. He came back with the sandwiches a little after twelve, and Jefferson and Hector ate at their desks while they continued to work. At two forty-five p.m. Jefferson said, "I need to take off early today, but I'll make up for it tomorrow."

Hector looked up from his desk. "What's up? Is everything okay?"

"I need to talk to Aubrey," Jefferson said. "As you can imagine, she wants me off of the case. We had a bad night last night, and I want to make it up to her."

Hector didn't tell his partner that Aubrey had called him earlier that morning. He had agreed with her to keep their conversation between the two of them. She told Hector about the argument that she had with her husband. She felt bad about it, although her heart had been in the right place, worrying about the man she loved. She had told him that as she had lain in bed, awake, trying to fall asleep, she couldn't help but rehash their disagreement over and over. Initially, she got angrier. But as the hours passed by, she was able to let go of the anger, and she realized that Jefferson couldn't be expected to drop the case. He wasn't built that way.

It was unlike Aubrey to pour out her heart, especially to someone she didn't have a real close relationship. She and Hector were friendly enough, but they didn't really know each other well. Most of what they knew was what Jefferson had told them about each other. She had a purpose in making the call to Hector. She asked him to try to keep Jefferson out of harm's way. He said, "I promise you that I'll do the best that I can. I'll talk to the commander and ask him to assign a few patrol cars to make regular checks on your neighborhood." Hector realized that there was no way to guarantee Jefferson's safety when they were outside or driving in their car. He didn't tell Aubrey that, but he didn't have to. She had been married to a police officer for years and was well aware of that. That's what really bothered her.

Jefferson stopped at a flower shop and picked up a dozen red roses. He drove to Aubrey's school. He knew that she would still be there. He hoped that by coming to the school, it would make more of a statement than if he met up with her at home. Students were just leaving when he walked up to an entrance. Jefferson knew the teacher who was monitoring the entrance. The man let Jefferson go in, and he headed toward the library. There were a few students in the library when he walked in. He spotted Aubrey at the counter, apparently typing on a keyboard. He walked up to her. She looked up and saw Jefferson with the flowers in his hands. A tear rolled down her cheek as she half-smiled at him. She looked around at the students and said to Jefferson, "Why don't you come back to my office with me?" The students were all staring at them. It's not often they saw a man carrying flowers in school.

When they got to the office, she closed the door. Jefferson asked, "Don't you have to keep an eye on the students?"

"No, I have two student assistants who will keep tabs for me. What are you doing here?"

"I'm really sorry about last night," he said. He handed Aubrey the flowers. She smelled them and put them down on her desk. Jefferson continued, "I should be flattered that you care as much as you do. I'm a lucky man. I never want to feel like I felt last night. You are the most important thing in the world to me."

Aubrey wanted to ask Jefferson if that meant that he begged off of the case, but she knew better, and she didn't want a repeat of the previous evening any more than he did. "You've got that right. You are lucky. I'm an idiot for loving you as much as I do." The two of them just smiled at each other.

"Please don't hate me, but I just can't quit on this case. If I were the one who had been killed, I know DuKane would do everything he could to solve the murder. Besides, once we let the bad guys intimidate us, we might as well give up."

Jefferson had more to say, but Aubrey put up a hand, indicating that she either didn't want to hear it or that she wanted a chance to speak. Jefferson studied her, trying to determine which it was. Then Aubrey said, "I get it. I don't like it, and no matter what you say, I still won't like it. But I get it. I'll stand behind you, but you better nail this guy quickly because living this way is much too hard. The kids wonder why I'm crabby, and I don't dare tell them." Aubrey's eyes welled up with tears as she spoke.

Jefferson leaned in, and he and Aubrey shared a long kiss and a hug. As they hugged, the tears rolled down Aubrey's cheeks. Jefferson whispered, "Hector and I are putting everything into this case now. If we don't come up with something in the next day or two, I have a plan to fully utilize the task force. We will make something happen very soon. I'm sure of it."

"I'm counting on it," she said.

Forcing a change of subject, Jefferson said, "I'm going to make you dinner. Tonight will be about us. What do you want to eat?" "How sweet of you, a romantic dinner for just the four of us." She gave him an impish look. "I took pork chops out of the freezer this morning. Why don't you see what you can do with those?" He gave her another kiss and a hug and headed for home.

Bossy must have been asleep in another part of the house because she didn't hear him walk in. He called out. "Bossy, I'm home." She immediately got up and started bounding toward the sound of his voice. She had her paws up on his shoulders in no time. He thought to himself, *Bossy is the only one who shows me as much love as Aubrey.* He took Bossy out to the backyard and sat on a lawn chair while she did her business and went around the yard sniffing at the ground in various places. It didn't take much to make Bossy happy. He gave her ten minutes of bliss and then got to work on creating his soon-to-be-famous pork chops.

CHAPTER 46

It was Friday morning, and the Vigilante Killer remained absent from the scene. Tuesday through Thursday evenings had been uneventful. Normally, that would be a good thing. But it wasn't good because the FBI had been conducting surveillance on the suspected killer. Jefferson had been anticipating an opportunity to catch the perp in action, and he wasn't happy. He knew that the commander could go bonkers at any moment. The lack of progress was sure to set the man off.

Jefferson and Hector spent Friday going through the backgrounds of all of the people they believed could possibly be working with the killer. The work was tedious. It took a lot of effort to check files, records, and make calls. To complicate things, they couldn't tell people why they were calling to get feedback on their possible suspects. It meant deceiving people and making up stories. It was one thing to lie to possible felons. It was quite another thing to lie to fellow police department personnel. It was uncomfortable, but it had to be done.

Just as he was getting ready to wrap up the day, Jefferson thought he might be onto something. He needed more time to dig in, but he didn't have it. He was still involved in repairing his relationship with Aubrey. She had warmed up after he appeared at her school, but he still sensed a certain distance in their relationship that he had never noticed before. He decided to try to make her feel special. He had asked her to go out for a nice dinner and to see a movie of her choosing. He needed to get home in time for their dinner reservation. He justified leaving the station by reminding himself that the killer seemed to be idle. Another day or two shouldn't matter. Besides, he could come down to the station the following morning and finish his work. He told Hector that he planned to come to work on Saturday morning and why he thought that it was necessary. Hector agreed to come in the next morning as well.

The movie let out around ten p.m. The evening turned out to be a good thing. Aubrey appreciated the effort. They had a good conversation during dinner. She seemed to be the most comfortable she had been since the shooting incident. Jefferson was hoping that the worst was over. He told her that he might be getting close to a breakthrough in the case. They agreed not to talk about it. Jefferson needed to clear his mind as best he could. Although Aubrey was optimistic, she didn't want to get her hopes too high. She agreed that it was important that he go to work on Saturday morning and follow up on whatever it was he thought he'd found.

They were both tired. It had been a tough week, and sleep hadn't come easy for either of them all week. But they both seemed to be in a better place now. They were in bed by eleven, and they were finally able to sleep soundly.

At just after one thirty a.m., Jefferson's cell phone began ringing. It woke Aubrey. She had to wake Jefferson. He was in a fog but picked up the phone. It was a patrolman. The Vigilante Killer had struck again. Two gang members had been shot. The police had received several calls about gunshots. One lady said that she could see two bodies lying on a sidewalk, but she was too afraid to go outside and check to see if they were alive. Several patrol cars were sent to the scene. The officer told Jefferson where the shootings had taken place. Jefferson said that he was on his way.

Aubrey could tell from what she could hear of the conversation that there had been a killing. She said, "It sounded like someone was shot."

Jefferson was still for a few seconds, then said, "This doesn't make sense. Two people were shot. The officer said that one man was shot in the middle of his forehead, and the other took at least two bullets to his torso. I guess it could be the Vigilante Killer, but this doesn't fit the pattern. It's Friday night. The killer has always struck on a Tuesday, Wednesday, or Thursday. Also, the killer has never killed more than one person at a time. I need to get going."

He called Hector, who was on his way home from a night out with friends. They both headed to the crime scene.

By the time Jefferson arrived, Hector was already there. There were eight squad cars, a fire truck, and two ambulances at the scene. Hector was already talking to the officer who was in charge. Jefferson joined in the conversation. The officer told them all that he knew. He had already assigned other officers to conduct a thorough search of the neighborhood. They were able to pinpoint where they believed the shots came from—an empty building across the street and down the block a little. They came up with nothing else. The detectives walked up to the bodies, and without touching anything, got as close as they could. From the positioning of the bodies, it appeared as though, after the first man was shot, the second had been trying to run away. He didn't make it far.

They walked toward the building where the shots were most likely from. Jefferson said, "It's a Friday night, and we have two victims. I hope this isn't some kind of copycat killer."

"There's more conflicting information. Both victims had identification on them. We ran their names. They're known gang members, but they don't belong to any of the five gangs that have been targeted to this point."

"Like I said, I wonder if we have a copycat killer," Jefferson said. "I haven't heard from the FBI. I'm assuming that they still have eyes on Waul. I think they would have called me if they lost him. And if he did the shooting, they would be here. I better make a call and see what they can tell me."

After talking to his FBI counterpart, Pete Berz, Jefferson told Hector what he learned. "Waul was last seen going into a nightclub around eleven. He didn't have a bag with him. As far as Berz knows, he's still inside. They're sending in one of their guys to be sure that he didn't somehow leave and get past them."

The detectives were looking through holes in a boarded-up window. It was the window that the killer most likely used to fire his shots. Jefferson said, "Not only might we have a copycat, but the copycat might have a partner. Even a trained sniper would be challenged to take out two guys at once with no time for set up between shots, particularly at this distance."

Jefferson's phone rang. It was a call from the Agent Berz. Somehow, Waul had gotten past them. He wasn't in the club. They found a back door that led to a fenced-in area behind the club, but it had a gate leading to an alley. Waul could easily have left through the back. Jefferson asked if Waul's car was still there. The agent told him that it was. The agent apologized for the slip-up. Jefferson accepted the apology, although he was frustrated.

After Jefferson shared the information, he said to Hector, "We can't wait any longer. We have to pull Waul in. I'll call the commander around six and get his blessings."

"Shouldn't you call Trout?"

"Normally, that would be the way to go, but if Trout is the partner, that could be disastrous. We need it to be the commander."

Hector nodded. He understood.

•   •   •   •

The detectives were at their desks by six thirty a.m. At six, Jefferson had called the commander. The commander was already awake and grumpy, as usual. Jefferson figured it must be horrible starting each day grumpy and then having it go downhill from there. The commander issued the order to have Waul picked up and brought in for questioning. He said that he wanted to be there for the interview and asked Jefferson to call him once Waul was apprehended.

Shortly after the order was given, Waul was picked up at his home. He acted shocked when he found six police officers at his door. He probably was. They wouldn't tell him what it was about, only that he had to come with them. They couldn't tell him because they didn't know. They only knew that they were warned that he could be armed and dangerous. Waul was cooperative. He knew that he had an exemplary record as a cop, and there was no reason to believe that this was something serious, even with the overkill of having six cops come to his door. He rode to the station in the back of the squad car without a word being spoken.

Upon his arrival, Waul was placed in an interview room. Jefferson and Hector waited in the observation room for the commander to appear. As the detectives studied Waul, Jefferson said, "In spite of the beard, Waul has an innocent appearance, almost sweet-looking. It's hard to believe he was a sniper, let alone a serial killer." Waul fit the description of the killer.

He was of average size in both height and weight. He was black and had a beard. Those things proved very little because there were thousands of men in Chicago who fit that description.

When the commander arrived, he chatted with Jefferson and Hector, warning them to get this right. He took a seat in the observation booth as the detectives entered the interview room. They had decided to treat Waul with respect. They had no real evidence that he was the killer, and there was a chance that he wasn't. He had been a good cop, and he deserved to be treated as one until there was a solid reason not to do so. They entered the room and introduced themselves. Waul said, "I'm kind of in shock. Why am I here?" He wasn't hostile and didn't even seem angry. He was sure that it was a mistake.

Jefferson said, "We will get to that, but we have some questions for you." Waul looked at him and then at Hector and back again at Jefferson. He nodded. Jefferson said, "Let's start with last night. Why don't you tell us what you did after you left work last night?"

Waul smiled and said, "Do you mean before or after I robbed the bank?" He smiled, and the detectives returned it. Waul continued, "Apparently, something happened last night. I'm not sure why you're talking to me about it, but I'll tell you what you want to know. After I got home, I had dinner. I took a nap. I showered and went to a club, where I met a few friends."

Hector said, "What about after you left the club?"

"If you must know, I walked over to a friend's house. She lives a few blocks from the club. We went to that club near her home so none of us would have to drive afterward. We were celebrating my friend's birthday, and we knew there was a chance we might have a little too much to drink."

"What time did you leave the club?" Hector asked.

"I'm not exactly sure. I'm guessing around midnight."

"Was it just you and this woman who went back to her place?"

"No. There were two other guys with us."

Hector asked, "What time did you leave this woman's home?"

"I know the answer to that. When I woke up, it was just before five. I got up and went home."

"Will this woman and the other two friends verify your story?"

"Yes. The reason we went back to the apartment so early last night was because my woman friend had a babysitter who couldn't stay late. After we got there, we stayed up talking until maybe two. Then we all ended up sleeping there because we did have a little too much to drink."

Hector asked, "Is this woman your girlfriend?"

"No, we're all just good friends."

Jefferson spoke up this time. "How do you know these friends?"

"They're high school friends. They've always been there for me."

"Were any of them in the service?" Hector asked next.

"No, after high school, they all went directly to college and then started their careers."

Jefferson said, "Write down your friends' names and give us their contact information. We're going to keep you here until we have a chance to verify what you've told us. I'm assuming we will. If your friends corroborate your account of last night, we'll tell you what this is all about and let you go. We apologize for any inconvenience, but as you can appreciate, we're just doing our jobs." Waul looked frustrated. He nodded. The detectives walked out of the room and joined the commander.

The commander said, "Do you believe the guy?"

"Unfortunately, I do," Jefferson answered. "In talking to him, my sense is that he is what he seems to be, a good person. I was hoping he was our guy so we could get this thing wrapped up, but now I'm glad that he probably isn't."

"Do you think his friends are in on it and that they're also his alibi?" the commander asked.

"I don't think so, but we'll try to figure all of that out when we talk to them. We better get going. We have a long day ahead of us."

As they walked away, Hector made a good point. "Earlier, you talked about a copycat killer. Even if Waul's friends back his story, he could still be the Vigilante Killer."

"I know, but I didn't want the commander to get that into his head. I don't want him trampling all over Waul's career if he's not our guy."

CHAPTER 47

The detectives were able to reach Ernie Waul's lady friend, Samantha Polse, by phone. They told her that they needed to verify some information that Waul had given them. She thought it was odd, but she seemed relaxed about meeting them and helping. They met at a coffee shop. Jefferson felt uneasy, remembering the last time he sat in a coffee shop. When the woman entered the shop, Hector asked her if she was Ms. Polse. "Yes, but please, call me Samantha." She was friendly and had a very upbeat way about her. She had a great smile, and although she wasn't a classical beauty, there was something about her that made her very attractive. Hector was immediately drawn to her. He thought it might be best if he let Jefferson conduct most of the interview.

Jefferson started by saying, "We can't get into the specifics of why we need information from you, but we do have some questions."

"I'd sure like to know what this is all about," she said, her smile fading somewhat. "Ernie is all right, isn't he?" Jefferson assured her that he was fine. Samantha said, "If I can answer your questions, I will." She looked at Jefferson as she talked, but her eyes flashed over to Hector when she finished. He felt like he was blushing. He had to look away.

Jefferson asked Samantha to tell them what she had done the night before. She went through the activities of the previous evening. It lined up with what Waul had told them. Jefferson asked, "When you got back home, did the three guys you were with all stay over?"

"Yes."

"What time did each of them leave?"

"I heard someone stirring around five, I believe. I know the sun was just coming up. Later, when I got up at about eight, there were two guys still sleeping on the living room floor. Ernie was the only one who wasn't there, so he must have been the one who left around five. The other two guys had breakfast with me and my son, and then they both left together, maybe around nine or so."

"Is it possible someone left after you were asleep and returned later?"

"No, that isn't possible. I have a big German Shepherd. He barks loudly whenever someone enters my house, including me. If someone left and came back, my dog would have awakened all of us."

Samantha looked over at Hector. He was ready this time. He stared back at her. His heart was melting. She must have sensed something because she gave him a half-smile, and his pulse raced. He couldn't remember ever reacting this way to a woman before.

Jefferson said, "That helps clear up some things for us. We appreciate that. We have a few other questions, specifically about Officer Waul."

"That's fine, but to be honest, I'm somewhat uncomfortable. Why would detectives be asking questions about Ernie? He couldn't have possibly done anything wrong."

Jefferson replied, "He fits the description of someone we're looking for. We're trying to eliminate any suspicions. I'm afraid that's as far as I can go at this time. Officer Waul has a child. Do you know if he has joint custody?"

"His son is really cute. Ernie was granted joint custody. Maybe about a year ago, his ex-wife was offered a job at North Carolina University. She's a college professor. The school is doing some cutting-edge research in her field. The job offer was a once-in-a-lifetime opportunity. It broke his heart, but he conceded to let her take the boy. He never stopped caring about his ex, and he's too good of a person to hold her back. His son spent a month with him this past summer, and he has a generous visitation schedule. Ernie sees him a lot."

"How did Waul manage to have his son for a month while working every day?" Jefferson asked.

"His sister works nights, and she was with the boy during the day. He babysits for her routinely too."

"Have you ever met Daniel Trout?" was Jefferson's next question.

"Sure. Ernie went through training with him. They became good friends. He hangs out with us from time to time."

"Do you know Daniel's father, Dirk?" Jefferson asked.

"No. I've heard about him, but I've never met him. Daniel is close with his father from what I hear. It's apparent that he wants to make his father proud. Daniel is a good guy."

Hector spoke up for the first time. "Have you ever dated any of these male friends of yours?"

Jefferson was trying to figure out what Hector's angle was for asking that question, and then it hit him, and he had to bite back a chuckle. He saw the way Hector was looking at Samantha.

Samantha looked slightly confused at the turn in topic, but she still answered readily enough. "No. I got married while in college. My husband was a pharmacist. On his way home from work, he got caught in the crossfire of two opposing gang members and was killed. It was about a year and a half ago, and I haven't been ready to start dating." Samantha got teary-eyed as she told the story.

His expression sympathetic, but his mind racing, Jefferson said, "We're truly sorry. Was Officer Waul close to your husband?"

"They became friends because of me. My husband liked Ernie. Most people do, I suspect. Ernie seemed to enjoy spending time with my husband as well."

"Do you know if Ernie is close to Dirk Trout?" Jefferson asked.

"Last year, I know Ernie accompanied Daniel and Daniel's girlfriend to the Trouts' home for Thanksgiving. Ernie sees Daniel's father from time to time. The relationship is solid."

Jefferson asked Hector if he had any other questions. Hector didn't. They thanked Samantha for her time and for sharing information with them. She shook hands with Jefferson and then with Hector as she stared into his eyes. He was just happy that he couldn't be arrested for his thoughts.

As they walked back to the car, Jefferson began talking. "We know for sure that the sergeant knows Waul. Hell, he had him over for Thanksgiving dinner. Why wouldn't Trout reveal that to us? It's almost like he couldn't care less that we're investigating his son's friend. You know that he has to care. It makes it look real bad for Trout."

After a period of silence, Jefferson said, "Based on what Samantha had to say, Waul couldn't have been the shooter last night. But she helped to establish a possible motive for Waul to go after gang members. It would seem that Waul could be the killer, and Trout or his son could be working with him. Either one of them could've been the shooter last night." Jefferson waited for Hector to speak, but he didn't. Jefferson's head was spinning, but it seemed to him that Hector was disengaged. "Samantha really got to you, didn't she?"

Hector looked slightly guilty as he answered, "There's something about her. She's attractive and all, but it goes beyond that. She's amazing."

"Before I react to that, did you hear anything that I had to say?"

"I heard it all," Hector said. "I don't know what to think."

"I can see this isn't going anywhere with you right now. You have Samantha on the brain. It seems that you're forgetting about your girlfriend again."

"I don't have a girlfriend anymore."

"Since when?" Jefferson asked.

"I ended up going out with my high school crush, and my girlfriend found out. She dumped me."

Jefferson looked surprised. "I thought you told me that your mother convinced you not to go out with the other girl. You told me something about love being more important than lust."

"That's what my mother said. My mother's a wise lady. Unfortunately, I'm not bright enough to always listen to her. To make matters worse, I didn't enjoy the evening with my old high school crush at all. I never realized it before, probably because I didn't really know her, but the girl has a nervous laugh. If it was occasional, I could live with it, but it's constant. After a couple of hours with her, I just wanted to get away. I tried to make it up to my ex-girlfriend, but she wouldn't give me the time of day. A friend of hers told me that she's crushed. I feel bad, but if the relationship was the real thing, I don't think I would have done what I did in the first place. I'm looking at it as being all for the best."

Jefferson chuckled. "I wondered why you were swooning over Samantha. You're horny."

211

"That might be true, but that girl really got to me. I'm really hoping Waul is innocent. I doubt that Samantha would go out with the guy who threw her friend in prison."

"Wow, you already have plans to date the woman. You're something else."

"Thank you for noticing," Hector said.

The two men laughed.

CHAPTER 48

Before walking to the conference room to talk with Ernie Waul, the detectives sat down at their desks. Jefferson said, "I got quite a bit of work done yesterday. I was just checking into Bill Small's background when I ran out of day. I have more work to do, but one of the things I discovered was that Small has a son, Wallace, who was a sniper in the Marines."

Hector was caught off-guard with that news. He said, "Why didn't you say something sooner?"

"For now, I don't want Trout or the commander to know. I don't want to raise any suspicion. Small lost his partner. I'm going to give him the benefit of doubt for now. I was going to tell you on the way to our meeting with Samantha Polse but thought it might throw you off your game."

Hector's face darkened. "I had my game face on all the way. I'm a big boy. I can handle new developments."

Jefferson said, "I have bad news for you. You lost that game face the moment you saw Samantha."

"Guilty as charged."

"I kind of messed up. I should have asked Samantha if she knows Bill's son, Wallace."

Hector said, "Why would she know Wallace Small?"

"He and Ernie Waul were both snipers. It's possible that they know each other, and may even be friends."

"That may be a stretch, but I'll gladly contact Samantha and ask her," Hector volunteered a bit too eagerly. "I'll give her a call and see what she can tell us." Jefferson smiled. He said, "I was thinking that you might say that. Go ahead and call."

Hector dialed the number, and when Polse answered the phone, he identified himself. As she responded, her voice registered a certain inquisitiveness. "Detective Hector, I wasn't expecting a call this soon. Did you have another question for me?"

Hector's interpretation was that she expected a more personal call from him some time in the future, but not so soon. He didn't know if he was reading it right and didn't want to embarrass himself. He had a strong urge to flirt with her but thought better of it. He played it straight. He said, "I do have another question for you. Have you ever met a man by the name of Wallace Small?"

Without hesitation, Samantha responded, "No. That name's not familiar."

"Do you usually have a good memory for names?"

"I'm not bad. I have an uncle named Wallace. He's the only Wallace I know. If I met another one, I'm pretty sure that I would remember the name because of the connection with my uncle. Why are you asking?"

"I have to apologize, but I can't get into that at this time."

"I'll let you off the hook this time, but the next time I see you, I expect an explanation."

Hector was dumbfounded. He wondered if this was her way of telling him that she wanted to see him again. He wanted to suggest meeting up with her later that night, but he hesitated. He realized that he was intimidated by this woman. He just froze and then clumsily got off the phone. He was deep in thought when Jefferson was returning to his desk from using the restroom. Hector didn't acknowledge his return. He stared into space until Jefferson poked him on the way past and asked, "What did Samantha have to say?"

"I think she wants to go out with me."

"That's what she had to say?" Jefferson asked.

"No. But I think she hinted at it."

"I'd love to hear the misadventures of your love life at some other time, but for now, I'm kind of anxious to hear if she knows Wallace Small."

Hector muttered, "She doesn't know him."

"If you can come out of your trance, I'd like to go talk to Waul. How soon can you be ready, Romeo?"

Hector scowled. "You're a riot. I'm ready. Let's go."

The detectives walked over to the conference room. Waul was still there. Someone had brought him a sandwich and a bottle of water.

As they entered the room, Jefferson said, "I'm glad to see that we're being good hosts." Waul didn't respond. He looked at Jefferson and then Hector. He wasn't happy to be spending a nice day in this dark and drab room with no windows and nothing to do.

There was tension in the room. Jefferson told Waul that, so far, his story was holding up. Waul showed no expression. Jefferson asked Waul if he knew detective Bill Small. Waul said, "No, should I?" He wasn't being unfriendly, but it was apparent that he wasn't happy.

Jefferson answered, "Not necessarily. His son, Wallace, was a sniper in the Marines about the same time you were serving. Did you ever meet him or hear about him?"

Waul thought about it for a while. He said, "I don't remember that name, but for what it's worth, I was in the Army, not the Marines."

"I'm sorry for the mistake," Jefferson said. "Why did you enlist in the Army specifically, as opposed to the other branches of the service?"

"I had an older cousin who was an Army recruiter. I always looked up to him. It just seemed like the thing to do."

"How close were you with Samantha Polse's husband?"

Waul looked puzzled by the question, but he answered readily. "I've been friends with Samantha since grammar school. She's one of my best friends. I met her husband when they were dating. I liked him from the start. He became a good friend. He was a little nerdy but a real nice guy. He was good to Samantha."

Jefferson looked over at Hector and said, "Do you want to ask Officer Waul anything before we let him go?"

Waul interrupted. He asked, "Are you going to tell me why I'm here?"

Jefferson just stared at Waul as if he were measuring him. After several seconds, he said, "I can't today, but soon, we'll tell you everything." Waul just shook his head in frustration.

Hector said, "We met with Samantha Polse to try to verify your story. She was able to do that. I'm wondering if we can trust her. Tell us about her character."

Waul glanced at Hector with a cockeyed look. He said, "I'm guessing I'm a suspect for some crime or irregularity. I can't imagine why else I'm sitting here with you. Is it normal for you to ask a potential suspect about the character of the person supplying his alibi?"

Hector could feel himself turning red. He was sure that Waul was on to him. Jefferson couldn't stop the grin that took over his face. Hector said, "I'm just trying to determine the relationship that you have with her."

"Detective, I'm not dating her, if that's what you're asking. We're just good friends." Hector realized that Jefferson was right. He had lost his game face the moment he met Samantha, and he still didn't have it back. It was time to shut up and not embarrass himself any more.

"Officer Waul, you're free to go," Jefferson informed him. "I had a lot of time to sit and think while the two of you were gone." Waul said. "At first, I couldn't figure out why you brought me in. I'm pretty careful in how I conduct myself, and I know that I haven't been involved in any suspicious activities. As I thought about it, I remembered hearing on the radio, on the way home, that some other gang members were gunned down by the Vigilante Killer. You asked me about another ex-sniper. The Vigilante Killer appears to be an ex-sniper. Do you suspect me of being the killer?"

Jefferson was caught off guard. He considered how he wanted to answer the question. He decided since Waul was onto them, it might make sense to put him on the spot and see where he went with it. He said, "Apparently, you're a good cop. You've got that one right. What do you want to say for yourself?"

Waul got a disgusted look on his face. He stared at Jefferson for the longest time. Finally, he spoke. His voice was calm, but his eyes were staring bullets. He said, "Let me say, even though it occurred to me that I might be a suspect, it's shocking. Other than the fact that I was a sniper, what else led you to me?"

Jefferson sighed. "Don't take it personally. Frankly, we're hoping it's not you. But we suspect someone with the department has some involvement.

You match the description that we have for the killer, and there's that sniper piece."

Waul asked, "Is that it?" After Jefferson told him that it was, he asked what they thought his motive could possibly be.

Jefferson replied, "From what we hear, Samantha Polse's husband was killed by gang members. You told us that you're good friends."

"I don't like it, but I see where you're coming from. I guarantee you that I don't operate that way. I can prove that I'm not your guy. I remember being in a hotel room in North Carolina listening to the morning news. It was reported that the Vigilante Killer struck again in Chicago the night before. My son and I were getting ready to go to breakfast. I had arrived in North Carolina the Friday before and didn't come home until three days after the incident. My credit card receipts will prove that I was gone then. My flights, hotel, meals, and gifts for my kid were all charged to my credit card."

Jefferson said, "That's good news. Are you willing to give us a copy of your credit card statement?"

"Of course," Waul said. "I'll scan the one in question and e-mail it to you today."

Jefferson thanked Waul and walked him out the lobby. He said, "Thanks for your cooperation. I'm sorry for the confusion, but we have a dangerous killer on the loose, and we need to look under every rock. Wait here, and I'll have an officer drive you home."

Jefferson walked back to his desk. Hector had already returned to his. Hector asked, "What do you think?"

"Do you mean about you embarrassing yourself, or about Waul?" Jefferson chuckled. Hector bit his tongue. He knew what he wanted to say but held it back. Jefferson said, "Assuming that his credit card charges clear him of one murder, then we know if he's doing some of the killings, he's not doing all of them. He seems like a good enough person. My gut says that he's not our guy."

CHAPTER 49

The rest of the day was spent investigating the backgrounds of each of the possible suspects. The detectives worked hard and fast. Hector seemed to know every computer shortcut and was able to uncover information quickly. Jefferson, not so much, but he plodded along and came up with the biggest piece. It came during a conversation with a retired commander Bill Small had worked under. Small had worked for the man just prior to transferring to their current station and partnering with Fred DuKane. When the conversation ended, Jefferson sat staring into space. Hector saw the dazed look on his face and asked, "What's up?"

Jefferson blinked and brought his eyes down to meet Hector's. He said, "You're not going to believe this. Bill Small had three sons. One was a gang member and was killed in a gang war. A second son was a good student and a basketball player who was going to attend college on a basketball scholarship. He was killed by a gang member too. Small's third son, his oldest, was the Marine sniper. I never would have suspected Small, but it seems obvious now that he's our mole, and his son is the Vigilante Killer."

Hector blanched. "I don't think we can jump to that conclusion so readily."

Jefferson was upset. He didn't know if it pained him more that Small had to suffer through the death of two children or the thought of Small being involved in this whole mess. He wasn't in the mood to be challenged by Hector. He said, "Why is it that you always contradict everything that I have to say?"

"Whoa, Marcus, that's not true. I usually agree with you," Hector responded. "Don't take it out on me that a colleague has apparently gone rogue."

Jefferson sat quietly trying to come to terms with what Hector said and with how he was feeling about Bill Small. Hector was waiting for some response, but it wasn't coming. Hector felt in his heart of hearts, that they had their answer. He let it go and got back to work.

As he worked, Jefferson's mind began to drift. He was growing more and more upset. He came to realize that it wasn't Hector's fault, but it sure would help if Hector was more supportive at times. It occurred to him that he and Hector mostly got along, but they were always going to have their moments. He just wished those moments didn't seem to come when he felt he needed some support the most.

Hector finished his work. He looked over at Jefferson. Jefferson was staring into space again. He looked tired and down. Hector felt bad for him. He'd had a tough week. He decided to break the ice. "Marcus, where are you at right now with this?"

"In spite of your doubts, I think Small and his son are our best suspects," Jefferson said.

"I don't have doubts. But I think there are other possibilities. The Smalls could be innocent. One or both of the Trouts and Waul could still be a possibility. It's not impossible that Small and Sergeant Trout have teamed up with Small's son and Waul. That would explain how Waul could be out of town when one killing took place but still be a killer."

"Christ, you think the whole department is teaming up on this. I can't think that way."

There was anger in Jefferson's voice. Hector decided not to pursue it. If he had to guess, Jefferson was correct in suspecting the Smalls, but he learned early on to challenge every theory. Jefferson had taught him that good police work demanded it. He wanted to remind Jefferson of that, but he knew it wasn't the right time. Instead he asked, "What do you want to do next?"

Jefferson replied with a question. "Did you come up with anything else?"

"No. There was nothing in anyone else's background to suggest a vendetta against gangs."

"I think we let this go for the rest of the weekend. It will give me a chance to clear my mind and to sleep on this whole situation. Be ready to meet with the commander first thing Monday morning." From Jefferson's tone of voice, he wasn't suggesting a course of action. He sounded like he was giving a command. Hector didn't like it. He had the urge to go off on him. He didn't enjoy being treated like a junior partner, but he stayed under control and just nodded his head in agreement. The detectives headed for the exit without another word being spoken, even as they headed in opposite directions to their cars.

When Jefferson walked into his house a short time later, he was prepared to defend himself from the siege he expected from Bossy, but there was no Bossy. He called out for Aubrey. There was no answer. Her car was in the garage, so he assumed that she was home. He called a little louder and got a response from his daughter: "Mom's on a walk with Bossy." Jefferson went to his daughter's room. The door was open. He walked in and gave her a kiss on the cheek. He said, "I'm going to change clothes, and then I'm going to hunt down your mother." His daughter nodded at him.

Jefferson was about halfway down the block when Aubrey and Bossy came around the corner. He was about fifty yards away from them when Bossy spotted him. She tore away from Aubrey, her leash dangling behind her. She charged Jefferson. He was actually scared because she had a head of steam. Although he braced himself for the onslaught, he went tumbling backwards as Bossy leaped up on him. Aubrey couldn't help herself. She laughed so hard that she cried. As she approached the two of them with a wide grin, Jefferson was still flat on his back with Bossy hunched over him, licking his face. Aubrey said, "Are you okay?" She was trying to hold her laughter back as she spoke.

"Do I look okay? And don't think I didn't see you laughing. Too bad you didn't get it on video. Then you could laugh over and over again." With that, Aubrey broke out into a full-blown belly laugh. She laughed so hard, Jefferson couldn't help but laugh too. She helped him up. They shared a kiss and headed toward home.

Jefferson started telling her about his day. As they approached the house, she said, "Let's go around the block so you can finish filling me in." As they continued to walk, he told her about their interviews with Waul and Samantha Polse. He told her about Hector's attraction to Polse. She, of course, brought up Hector's girlfriend, and he filled her in on that situation. He went on to tell her about the situation with Bill Small, and finally, his little tiff with Hector.

"You had quite the day," was all she said. She didn't want to, but she couldn't help herself. She started laughing again.

Jefferson peered at her and asked, "What are you laughing about now? Did you see somebody else get driven into the ground?"

"No. It just occurred to me that you had a really challenging day, and then you get assailed by Bossy as soon as you get home. I can't tell you why, but it made me laugh." She broke out laughing again. So did Jefferson. Once they were back under control, Aubrey asked, "Which do you want me to help you with, your most recent issue with Hector or solving the case?"

Jefferson realized that he had his Aubrey back. She no longer seemed distant. He had Bossy to thank for that. Her Lambeau Leap had saved the day. Aubrey knew how to relax him, and he appreciated her sense of humor, even in his most trying times. He said, "Hector and I will be fine. He's going to dream of Samantha Polse for the rest of the weekend and will forget all about everything else." "Do you think he'll pursue her when the dust settles?"

"Unless her friend Waul is arrested, I'm sure he will. Even then, I wouldn't put it past him. He's like a dog with a bone in his mouth. There's no getting it away from him."

"I honestly feel bad for you because either option in solving this case involves arresting a cop. That's got to be tough. It's hard for me to believe that Small would take part in the shooting of his partner."

Still troubled about it himself, Jefferson said, "That part doesn't make sense. I believe the shot wasn't intended to kill Fred and was fired as a warning, but still. Who has his partner shot as a warning? Small seems so laid-back. But one thing does make sense. If Small's involved, it explains why he never seemed to be engaged in solving the case."

Aubrey said, "I'm so happy that this whole thing is coming to an end. What's the game plan?"

"I have to give it some thought, but Hector and I will meet with the commander Monday morning, and I'll be ready to make my recommendations. I think for now, I want to leave it at that. I need to put some distance between myself and the case so I can come back later with a fresh perspective."

CHAPTER 50

Jefferson was already at his desk when he saw the commander walking toward the break room. He walked over and told the commander that he expected Hector any minute and that when he arrived, they needed a few minutes with him. The commander agreed. Ten minutes later, the detectives went to his office.

They caught the commander in a rare moment. He actually seemed mellow, almost decent. He said, "Fill me in on what happened after your interview with Officer Waul." Jefferson told him the story. He then filled him in on what he had discovered about Bill Small and his son Wallace. It caught the commander by surprise. He thought about the conflicting theories. It could be Trout was involved with Waul or that the Smalls could be behind the killings. Either theory was a possibility. He said, "Let's start with Trout. I'll get him in here, but let me do the talking. You two just observe. At least to start out, I don't want him to know that he's a person of interest."

A few minutes later, Trout came to the commander's doorway and walked into the office. He was surprised to see the two detectives. The commander told Trout to take a seat. He asked Trout, "Do you have any theories as to who the Vigilante Killer could be and who his inside contact is?"

"I know just what Jefferson has told us to date. I believe Officer Waul is the only suspect."

The commander asked, "From what you know, how do you feel about Waul being a suspect?"

"We don't have anything concrete. He's a cop. My natural inclination is to give him the benefit of the doubt."

"What if he is the shooter? Who do you think could be his inside contact?"

"Honestly, I have no idea," Trout responded.

"Okay, we'll get back to that later," the commander said. "Not to change the subject, but how is your son doing these days?"

Trout sat silent for a few seconds. His face turned red. When he finally spoke, anger rang in his voice. "I'm not stupid. I know where you're going with this. Neither my son nor I are working with the Vigilante Killer, even if it's Waul, and I'd bet my life it's not him. I can't believe you even went there. This is insulting. It's even low for you."

Jefferson was amazed. It was the first time he had ever seen Trout actually come back at the commander. He felt the need to jump into the conversation. He said, "I'm the one you should be upset with. But really, you need to look at yourself. I know about your connection with Waul. Hell, you even had him to your house for Thanksgiving last year. You're well aware that he is a prime suspect, yet you never mentioned your relationship with him. I find that very suspicious."

"My relationship with him has no bearing on the situation. I didn't say anything because I didn't want to prejudice the investigation. If I told you that I knew him, you would've asked me about his character. I would have nothing but good things to say. I didn't want you backing off. Unfortunately, he is our only suspect."

Not quite buying it, Jefferson said, "You know me better than that. I'm not going to back off because you know a suspect. I have to be suspicious of your motives, and that makes me suspicious of you."

Hector was thinking to himself that if Trout wasn't involved, his relationship with Jefferson just went to hell. He had been silent till now, but it was time to back his partner. "Look, Sergeant, Jefferson and I have been sitting on this for a while now. We don't want to believe that you're involved. But we can't wait another minute. It's time to let you clear your name before this goes any higher than the commander. It may sound like we're out to get you, but it's just the opposite. We want to prove you're not involved. How can you help us?"

Jefferson was impressed. Hector had handled a precarious situation with tact and something close to warmth. Trout was giving the situation thought. The room fell silent. After a while, he said, "I get it. There's only one way that I can prove my son and I are not involved. It's to prove that Waul's innocent. I'm confident that if you check into Waul's whereabouts when the killings took place, you'll find that he had alibis for some of the killings. I actually have wondered why you hadn't done that research."

Jefferson thought about what Trout had said. They should have had Waul account for his time during the other murders. Nonetheless, Jefferson was bothered that Trout seemed so confident that Waul would have alibis for some of the killings. Perhaps the two men worked together to help establish alibis for some of the other murders. Jefferson remained suspicious.

The commander's shouting caught Jefferson by surprise. "That's the best that you can do, Sergeant? The killer knew our every move. He either has a copy of our Gang Audit, or someone is feeding him information directly from it. You have nothing to say to vindicate yourself. Why don't you take the rest of the day off and figure out how you're going to clear your name. I want to help you, but you need to be part of the solution." Jefferson realized that it was the first time he had seen Trout staring at the commander instead of his hands when sitting in this office.

Trout got up. "Why don't you call me when you're ready to apologize. I really can't believe this is happening," he said, then stalked off.

The commander watched him walk away. Jefferson said, "At this point, Trout is right. We need to investigate possible alibis for Waul."

"I'm going to call Small and tell him to come down here," the commander said. "Let's figure out where we are in terms of his situation before we do anything else." The detectives agreed.

It was a good ten minutes before Small showed. The time spent waiting was used to discuss whether Trout was guilty or not. The commander seemed to be more suspicious of Trout than prior to the meeting with him. Jefferson wondered if it was because Trout had no real defense or because he just didn't like the man.

The commander said to Small, "Take a seat." The big man plopped himself down. He had never been summoned by the commander before. He was concerned. When he saw Jefferson and Hector, his anxiety let up a little bit. He was thinking that maybe this was some kind of group meeting. But then he realized that his worst fears were being realized when the commander said, "Tell me about your son."

Small didn't answer. He sat quietly, staring down at the table. He was trying to figure out a way for things to come out right for his son. He came up with nothing. The four men continued to sit in silence. Small wished that he knew why the commander was asking the question about his son. He wondered if it was possible that they had hard evidence or if it was just a hunch. "Why do you ask?" he finally asked.

The commander bluffed. "We know all about what he's done. With your cooperation, we have a better chance of taking him alive."

Small felt like he had just been hit by a train. His chest felt heavy. He thought that the commander might be bluffing, but he couldn't be sure. He came to the realization that even if were a bluff, they were onto his son. He knew that Jefferson and Hector would be able to put a case together rather easily at this point. Small felt like there was no way out. He didn't want his son jailed, but he couldn't allow him to be killed. Tears started streaming down his cheeks. None of the other men moved. They didn't try to comfort him. When he was able to stop crying, he said, "Please don't kill him. Take him alive."

Jefferson was teeming with emotion. There was a certain joy of victory and agony of defeat all at once. The case was solved. His family was safe, and he was still alive. The pressure of the case was dissipating quickly. But there was Bill Small, this decent man, who had lost two children and was now facing his worst nightmare.

Gently, Hector said, "Why don't you tell us about it?"

Small seemed relieved to get the monkey off of his back. He said, "I'm sure you figured it out. While Wallace was at war, his two younger brothers were killed by gangs. We all knew who committed the murders, yet we couldn't come up with proof. Shortly after he returned to the States, his mother committed suicide. In his mind, gang members killed her too. He was bitter. I think he initially just wanted retribution for his brothers' deaths. He began to realize that plenty of other innocent people were being injured and killed by these thugs. To him, going after the worst of the gangs was his civic duty. There was no stopping him."

The commander asked, "Why didn't you turn him in or warn us before he started down this path?"

"Believe me, I thought about it. I wrestled with it, and I argued with him. In the end, there was no stopping him. There was no way I was going to turn on him. From your vantage point, he's an evil killer, but he's my son, and in spite of what anybody thinks, he's a good person who tried to do what was right, something few people could do. He did it with no thought for his own safety or quality of life. It's been a horrible life for him. Even as a sniper in the service, he never derived any pleasure from killing. It was his job. When he got home, he still saw it as his job, only with a different enemy. Please don't hurt him. He's all that I have."

The commander said, "It would be a lot easier to have mercy if not for DuKane. There's no forgiving that."

Looking crestfallen, Small said, "It was a mistake."

"Knowing that will bring DuKane's family great comfort," the commander said sarcastically. "Why did you help him?"

Small looked like he was on the verge of crying again. "I wasn't going to at first, but when I realized that he was going to kill gang members, I wanted to be sure that only the most deserving would be his victims. There are enough young kids who still have a chance to straighten out their lives. I was hopeful that when they saw the most rotten members being killed, it might get them to re-think things."

"Does Wallace live with you?" Jefferson asked.

"No," Small replied.

"I'll give you one more chance to do the right thing. I want you to set up a meeting with him. Your home might be perfect. I don't want it to be in a public place in case it turns bad. This will give us the best chance of taking him in alive," Jefferson said.

Small thought it over. It made sense to him. The only thing that he cared about now was his son's safety. "Okay," he agreed.

"Let's do it now," the commander said. "But first, give me your gun."

Small slowly pulled his gun out of his holster, leaned forward, and put it on the desk. He sat back in his chair and pulled out his phone. He looked at it for a long time. Nobody said anything. He brought up his son's contact information and placed the call.

"Hey, Wallace, how's it going today?" he said, once the connection had been made. Small's voice seemed a little flat, but it didn't seem that he was trying to convey a message. Small, responding to his son, said, "I'm okay.

When can you get over to the house?" After a pause, he said, "Nothing's wrong, I just wanted to fill you in on the latest developments." Again, there was silence on Small's end of the line. "I'm not home right now, but I'm going to take the rest of the day off." Small nodded at the other three and said, "Okay, I'll see you then." He hung up the phone and said, "Wallace will arrive around three thirty this afternoon. I'd like to come with you to my house."

The commander said, "That's not going to happen. If he cooperates, everything should work out for him."

Tears started rolling down Small's face again.

• • • •

The commander looked at Jefferson and said, "Get him out of here." He made no effort to hide his disdain. "I'll arrange for a welcoming party for Wallace," he said.

The detectives didn't cuff Small. They got up from their chairs, as did Small. The big man followed Jefferson out of the office, with Hector close behind. They walked to an interrogation room. The three of them sat down. Small looked around the room like he had never been there before. At first, Jefferson thought that was strange, but then he realized that Small had never sat on that side of the table before. It had to feel weird.

Jefferson read Small his rights. He said, "We want to ask you some questions." Small nodded in agreement. Jefferson said, "Do you admit aiding your son, Wallace, in the killing of gang members?"

Small sat silent for what seemed a long time. The detectives did the same. Small swallowed hard and said, "Yes. The only reason I'm cooperating is because I don't want any harm to come to my son. I expect you guys to honor that request in exchange for my confession."

"We have no interest in hurting anybody," Jefferson said. "Tell us how you participated."

"I provided my son with the gang audit. He used it to target his victims. I also kept him informed of police activity in the investigation."

"Did you participate in any of the shootings?" Hector asked.

"No."

"Were you ever with your son when he actually shot anybody?" Hector asked.

"No."

"Why did Wallace pick victims in alphabetical order?" Jefferson asked.

Small hesitated, then said, "If you want the truth, it was to make the police look stupid. He assumed that it would be figured out eventually. He thought that once it was, the press would have a field day with the information, making the police look inept for not noticing sooner."

Jefferson asked, "Why was he so intent on making us look bad, especially with you being a cop?"

"There were two reasons. He was very upset that we never came up with the evidence needed to convict his brothers' killers. And he was bitter that my career never took off. It took me much longer than it should've to become a detective. During my first few years as a detective, I had a high conviction rate. I never got real consideration to continue to advance my career. That upset my whole family when it was intact. Frankly, they were right. Look what we have at this station. First there's Trout, who was burned out years ago and has no leadership qualities. Then we have the commander. That selfish son of a bitch only cares about himself. It's embarrassing that these men are considered to demonstrate better leadership qualities. It's a farce."

The detectives could've easily agreed with Small, but they were taping the interview. They knew the video would be seen by several different people, including Trout and the commander.

Instead, Hector asked, "Why did your son shoot DuKane, and why did he shoot at us?"

"He shot at DuKane as a warning because DuKane was beginning to make some serious progress. He knew that if DuKane was left alone, he would soon put the whole thing together. He shot at you to deter you from gaining any traction. Think what you want about me, but know that I didn't agree with Wallace shooting at DuKane or shooting at you. If there's a second reason I'm cooperating, it's because I feel so bad for DuKane's family. I know what it's like to lose someone through violence and not get closure. They at least deserve that."

Hector glared. "You know, that sounds great now that it's over for you. Why the hell didn't you end this right after DuKane was killed if you're carrying so much guilt and concern for his family?"

Small said, "That's fair." Tears rolled down his cheeks. "I put my son before them, and I don't feel bad about that. Somebody had to put my son first. He served his country. He didn't go into the service to be a sniper. That's where he was assigned. He never shot at anybody prior to serving. He was a good boy growing up. He took care of his younger brothers. He never got into any trouble. Then he was trained to be a killer. He came home with serious issues. He got his discharge, and it was like he never existed. The experience of being a sniper screwed Wallace up. The government's response was 'Thanks for everything. Now go back to civilian life and be normal.' Wallace still has nightmares. He believes his brothers and his mother would still be alive if he hadn't been sent to fight in a foreign land. He came home and did what he was trained to do, kill. Who's to blame? The government, that's who." Small wiped tears away from his eyes as he began to sob.

Jefferson said, "We'll give you a break so you can relax for a few minutes. I'll bring you a bottle of water when we come back." He motioned for Hector to get up. The two of them walked out and moved to the observation room.

Hector asked Jefferson, "Why are we taking a break?"

"I'm not worrying about him clamming up. He wants to talk. It's therapy for him. I just wanted to give him the chance to regain his composure. It's impossible to agree with what Small did for his son, but it's not impossible to feel bad for the guy. None of us can say what we would've done if life had beaten us up like it did the Smalls."

"If DuKane hadn't been killed, I could be more sympathetic," Hector said. "But one thing that Small said did resonate with me. The government obviously isn't doing what it should to help our soldiers try to move productively back into society. Between this case and the one involving the ex-military guy who committed suicide in the hotel room, I really get it. These guys are risking their lives, and we aren't coming close to paying them back for what they risked and continue to risk."

Jefferson was feeling the same thing. He didn't say so, but part of the reason he wanted to give Small a break was because he needed one himself. He was stuck on exactly what Hector put into words. It was very disturbing. He felt just slightly better that Hector felt it too.

CHAPTER 51

Jefferson walked over to the commander's office. The door was open. The commander was on the phone. He saw Jefferson standing in the doorway and motioned for him to come in and take a seat. The commander said, "Okay, I'll see you a little later," and hung up the phone. "How did it go with Small?" he asked Jefferson.

"It went okay. He confessed to assisting his son, and we got it on video."

"Great," the commander said. "It's guys like him who give us all a bad name."

Jefferson replied, "It doesn't feel all that great. I feel some relief, but there is no joy here. Small started his career with such high aspirations, and then his life came crashing down on him. I can't imagine living through what he has."

The commander contemplated what Jefferson said for a few seconds and then said, "Why don't you take me through the whole interview." Jefferson gave him a recap. The commander had a stoic look on his face as Jefferson told the story. When Jefferson finished, the commander said, "Let me tell you where things are at on my end." Jefferson was surprised that the commander would actually share with him. He seldom confided or even really communicated with his team, unless it was to scream at them.

"When you walked in, I was just finishing a conversation with Trout. He's relieved to be off the hook but still pissed that we were even looking at him. He's on his way back in. He'll direct a team of people in the apprehension of Wallace Small. I've arranged for manpower, including members of the SWAT Team. Starting around one o'clock, we will position an unmarked van near to the house. I want you and Hector to arrive at Small's house around one thirty. When you get there, we'll already have four other men inside the house. I want you and Hector to make the collar. There can't be any mistakes. We can't lose this case on a technicality."

The commander was emphatic. He purposely quit talking so that he could scowl at Jefferson. Jefferson thought, *That's more like it.* For a moment, he had been thinking the commander had been replaced by an alien. Jefferson found his own thoughts amusing. He had to do everything he could not to break out in a grin.

The commander picked up where he left off. "We've already scouted the house. There are only two entrances, a front and a back. You'll cover one door from inside, with two other guys. Hector will take the other door, also from the inside, with the other two guys. I'm concerned that if we have too many people, you'll end up shooting each other. Meanwhile, we'll have men outside of the house, sharpshooters watching each of the doors, in case Small makes a run for it. We can't give him a chance of escaping."

"It all sounds good, except you're talking about shooting the guy. From the way you've laid things out, we shouldn't have to shoot him."

"His dad may see Wallace as a victim, but I see him as a killer first. I'm not going to allow him to take any more of our men. If you can capture him alive, that's fine, but I just want him off of the streets, whatever it takes. Are we on the same page?"

"As long as you understand that we're going to try to get him without any violence and you're okay with that."

The commander said, "Of course I'm okay with that."

"How will Trout participate?"

"He'll be in the van, and he'll be communicating with the rest of the team. You'll each have earbuds. All communication will go through him."

"Does he know that we want to take Small alive?"

"He knows that we want to take Small off of the street. I'm sure he knows that we don't kill suspects if we don't have to."

Jefferson was a little frustrated. It sure sounded like the commander didn't care if Small was killed or not. Jefferson felt obligated to do his best to protect Small from harm. He had assured Detective Small that he would do all that he could to protect the man's son. He decided not to get into it any deeper with the commander. He would communicate directly with Trout. Jefferson said, "Unless there's anything else, I'm going to talk to Small one more time. There are a few things to clear up." The commander nodded as if to say okay. Jefferson collected Hector, and they returned to the interview room.

They hadn't cuffed Small to the table, and he was pacing when they returned. He knew the routine. He went back to his chair and sat down. Jefferson said, "We have a few more questions for you. Did your son ever work with a partner, someone who spotted for him or someone who actually did some of the shooting?"

"No. I'm the only one he worked with, and I never physically participated in any of the shootings."

"Does your son carry a gun or other weapons on him?"

"He has a small handgun that he carries everywhere he goes. He carries it in a holster that is usually hidden under a jacket or vest. He doesn't carry any other weapons."

Jefferson asked, "Is your son usually punctual, or does he tend to be early or late?"

Small responded, "He's usually on time, but he might be a tad early."

"Tell me about Wallace's routine when he comes to visit."

"Is all of this necessary?" Small said.

"If we're going to protect Wallace, we need as much information as we can get."

Small thought about it and said, "First, there is no routine. Wallace and I usually meet at restaurants, not at my home. When he does visit, he comes right on time usually. He rings the front doorbell and then walks in. I don't lock the door when I know he's coming."

Hector asked, "How do you think Wallace will react when he opens the front door and sees us standing there with guns drawn?"

"I honestly don't know. My hope is that he'll cooperate, but he no longer values his own life. That's what scares me. You have to jump on him before he has time to react." Jefferson nodded his understanding. "We'll do our best. Does Wallace have advanced training in hand-to-hand combat skills?"

"He's a tough kid, and he can handle himself, but his experience with martial arts is very limited. I don't see him trying to get into a physical altercation with you. He'll give up, go for his gun, or try to run. Wallace has his mother's genes. He's average size. I'm sure it won't just be the two of you trying to arrest him. You should be able to handle him without too much trouble."

The detectives felt like they knew all that they needed to know. By the time they finished with Small, Trout had arrived at the station. The detectives went to his office so they could talk to him. Trout's door was closed. Jefferson knocked. From the other side of the door, they heard, "Come in." He gave them a disgusted look when they entered. Without waiting for an invitation, they sat down. Jefferson filled Trout in on all that they uncovered during their two interviews with Small. Surprisingly, Trout listened attentively, like he actually cared. When Jefferson was done relaying the information, he said, "Small was totally cooperative. He only asked for one thing in exchange. He doesn't want Wallace killed, or even harmed, if possible. We need to do everything we can to honor that request."

"You don't have to tell me that. It could have been my son. These kids come back, and their lives can go in any direction. I'm one of the lucky ones. We have a close family friend who is a psychologist, and he helped Daniel work through some heavy-duty issues. Who knows what might have happened if it weren't for the counseling? We're going to take this kid in without incident, if he'll let us."

Jefferson felt some relief hearing that. "Look, we're sorry about what occurred first thing this morning. I know it was hurtful for you and upsetting. It wasn't so good for us either. Hopefully you can see that it was actually good police work that led us to you and your son. We had to do what we did. It wasn't personal."

Trout was silent for several seconds. Then he said, "This isn't the time for it, but we'll have that conversation after we nab Small. You can be assured that I'll do my best not to harm Wallace Small, but at the same time, your safety will be my priority."

The detectives thanked Trout and went to prepare for their encounter with Wallace.

CHAPTER 52

By one thirty, when Jefferson and Hector arrived at Small's house, the other four men were already there. Trout was sitting in the control van with another man. He spotted the detectives walking up the street and instructed the officers in the house to let them in. The detectives walked up the four stairs leading to the front door. The house was a well-maintained bungalow. It had a front porch. There were two wooden chairs to the left of the front door. Hector knocked, and the door immediately swung open.

An officer greeted the detectives. He escorted them to the living room, where the other three men were waiting. The man in charge told the detectives that his name was Bill Malley. He said, "Before introductions, please put on a Kevlar vest." He handed a vest to each detective. The detectives were happy to cooperate. Malley then gave each of the detectives a two-way radio. Attached to each radio was a headset, so they could put their radios in their pockets. He instructed them on the usage. "This button on the headset has to be pressed when you want to speak," he said as he pointed to it. "The six of us will each have a radio, as will the two sharpshooters and the two men in the van. We'll all be operating on the same radio frequency, and we'll be the only ones using it. Any questions?" There weren't any.

After Jefferson and Hector put on their vests, Malley introduced them to his team. Jefferson had never met any of them before. After introductions, Malley went through instructions with his three men, as well as the detectives. The instructions were simple, and everybody knew exactly what was expected of them. Malley wrapped it up by saying, "Trout will warn us when Small arrives. His communication with us will be constant as of that moment. Until he arrives, we always want to have someone on guard at each door, just in case Small slips by without being seen. The rest of us are free to move around."

Malley pressed the button on his headset and said, "Sergeant Trout, we are up to speed and ready to go. Are you ready?"

Trout responded, "Yes, we're ready. We have cameras facing the front door and back door, as well as the walkways leading up to the doors. The cameras are placed far enough away to give us a full view surrounding the house. There's no way for Small to get into the house without us seeing him." Trout went on to say, "To be sure there are no misunderstandings, let's clear up one other thing. Bill Malley is in charge of this operation up until the time the arrest is being made. The detectives are responsible for making the arrest." Malley and his team already knew this, but Trout wanted to be sure the detectives did too.

After Trout finished, Jefferson began walking around. When he and Hector had first arrived, they entered into a small foyer. The living room was adjacent to the foyer. The room was small. It had a sofa, a coffee table, one end table, and two chairs. The furniture wasn't big, but it filled up the whole room. On the largest wall, over the sofa, there was one large painting and two smaller ones. They were all summer scenes. The paintings depicted scenes that appeared to be from the vantage point of a boat. The scenes went from water to land. They were colorful and made the room feel comfortable and tranquil. On a smaller wall, facing the sofa, was a big-screen television.

The detectives walked through the house to get a feel for it. As they passed through the foyer, they entered the dining room. Hector was surprised at how small that room was too. He couldn't imagine someone as large as Bill Small living comfortably in this house. The dining room had a table and four chairs. There was a small cabinet with a hutch taking up the remaining space in the room, leaving just enough room to navigate around the furniture. On the wall dividing the dining room from the foyer, there were family photographs hanging. Both detectives studied the pictures. It appeared that Small's wife had been a tiny woman. One picture showed the family on the front porch, the boys standing behind Mom and Dad, who were sitting in the same chairs that the detectives had seen when they arrived. The boys were teenagers. The youngest son couldn't have been much more than thirteen, but he was a head taller than the other two boys. Hector studied the oldest boy. That was Wallace. Nothing in the picture indicated that he would someday become a killer.

As with the other rooms, the kitchen was small, but it was also serviceable. It had an eating area with a table and chairs. The appliances were stainless steel, and the countertops were granite. The room was bright and up-to-date.

Behind the kitchen was a door leading to a laundry room. There was just enough room for a washer, dryer, and sink. The back door to the home was in the laundry area. There were two other rooms on the first floor. One was a bedroom, presumably the master. The room contained a queen-sized bed and one dresser. The other room was a bathroom containing a sink, a toilet, and a shower.

The detectives checked out the cellar. It looked like it was used mostly for storage, but like the rest of the house, it was neat and well-organized. Jefferson noticed that there were a few windows, but they would be too small for Wallace to enter if he suspected something and wanted to sneak up on them.

The detectives walked up to the staircase. There were two bedrooms and a full bath on the second floor. The bedrooms were furnished but had the bare minimum, a bed and dresser in each.

The detectives returned to the living room. The two men who weren't on guard duty were sitting and talking. The detectives joined them. They discussed their expectations once Small arrived. They all felt like things should go smoothly. Considering they were going to be confronting a dangerous killer, they were calm and under control.

At two thirty, the detectives took their turn for guard duty. Hector got the bad end of the deal. He was positioned in the tiny laundry room. Jefferson got the front door. Although Jefferson couldn't actively participate in the discussion in the living room, he could hear it, and time passed relatively quickly for him.

Hector had a small window next to the back door to look out. There was a curtain covering the window. When it got closer to the moment, the curtain would be closed, but for now, Hector kept it open so he could at least see out. He watched squirrels chasing each other up and down a big oak tree. His mind started wandering. He started thinking about Bertha Brown. As bad as Wallace Small was, he disliked Brown much more. Wallace was a killer. There was no doubt about it. But as strange as it sounded, there was something pure and real in what he was doing. He was eliminating bad people. On the other hand, to him, Brown had killed a man just because she got tired of him. He agonized over that case. She was an admitted killer. She was a liar and a cheater. Yet, there was a good chance she would get away with it because of her journal. He wished there was some way he could invalidate the journal. Unless a witness came forward, the case against the woman was all circumstantial. The journal could be viewed as evidence that she acted in self-defense. Once Wallace Small was captured, Hector was going to put every working hour into proving her guilt.

Thirty minutes before Small was scheduled to arrive, the men took their places at their stations. Jefferson was at the front door with Malley and one other man. Hector was at the back door with the other two men. As three thirty approached, there was no word from Trout. Malley spoke. "Sergeant Trout, are you still there?" There was no response. Malley tried again, and there still was no answer. Jefferson walked over to the front window. He pulled back the drape enough to look down the street. He spotted the van Trout was using. The doors were all shut, and there was no activity around the van. He reported what he was seeing to the other two men. He walked to the back door. The men had their headsets on and were aware that there was no answer from Trout. Jefferson told the three men that as far as he could see, the van was clear, at least on the outside. He walked back to the front of the house.

Malley said, "The only reason Trout isn't answering us is because he can't. I think we have to assume that Small got to Trout and the other man in the van with him."

"How could Small get past the sharpshooters in the street?" Jefferson shot back, irritated.

Malley responded, "We only have two sharpshooters in the street, as per your commander's instructions. He believed that fewer men made the most sense in dealing with Small's highly trained observational skills. One shooter was to focus on the back door of the house and the other took the front door. Nobody was keeping an eye on the van."

With that, a new voice could be heard on the headsets. "This is Wallace Small. I appreciate having this welcoming committee here to greet me. I have Trout, one of your sharpshooters, and another guy here with me. By the way, my dad was right. Trout isn't sergeant material. I'm not impressed. I want to know what happened to my dad. Tell me now, or Trout will lose a knee."

There was a silence. Then Jefferson said, "This is Marcus Jefferson. Your dad has been placed under arrest."

"Why? What are the charges?"

Jefferson responded. "Do you really have to ask? You've killed a bunch of people, and your dad admitted to his part in all of this."

"Who arrested him?"

"I did," Jefferson said.

"Listen carefully, Jefferson. I need you to disarm yourself and come out of my dad's house. Walk slowly to the van with your hands clasped behind your head. Do it now."

Jefferson responded, "I'm not doing anything until I hear Trout's voice. I need to know that he's okay." There was an eerie silence for a few seconds, and then Trout could be heard to say that he was okay. Jefferson said, "I need a few minutes to think things through."

"I'm timing you," Small responded. "If I don't see you in five minutes, I start taking Trout and his partner apart, piece by piece."

"Why do you want to see me?"

"I want to be eyeball to eyeball with you," Small said.

"Let's just talk through this," Jefferson said. "What do you want to accomplish?"

"I want to look you in the eye. That's what I want."

"It won't do you or your dad any good if you kill another cop or do harm to the men you have taken as hostages. I'm sure that your dad will serve his time protected from the other inmates. I'm also sure that if you harm or kill anybody else, that will change. Instead, your dad will be thrown in with the general population at one of our worst prisons. Even as big as your dad is, he doesn't stand a chance."

"I didn't say anything about killing someone. Quit talking, and get your ass over here. You're on the clock."

• • • •

Jefferson and Hector conferred with Malley. Malley told them that he had already called for backup, and several cars had already arrived. Within the five-minute window, they could have the van completely surrounded with men. Jefferson said, "That doesn't do us any good. Small isn't worried about being killed. He expects to be killed. If we do anything but abide by his demand, he will start shooting the men in the van."

"Why don't we get a hostage negotiator involved?" Malley suggested.

Jefferson said, "There's not enough time. I don't see any alternative other than for me to do what he wants."

Hector shook his head adamantly. "That's crazy. If you go, he'll kill you, and we still have no guarantee that he won't kill the other guys he has captive. There's got to be another way."

Jefferson knew that Hector was probably right. He pressed the button on his headset and said, "Wallace, if you give us more time, perhaps we could work out a deal to cut some of your dad's prison time." Jefferson didn't expect a positive response, but he had to give it a try.

Small shot right back, "No deals. You're down to two and a half minutes."

Jefferson tried to think of another way, but he couldn't. He attempted to hide it, but the other men could see that he was shaking. Jefferson was scared. He was real scared. He remembered what he told Vicky Soderheim when she admitted to him that she wasn't brave; that she was scared as she pursued the Vigilante Killer after he shot DuKane. He had told her, "Brave doesn't mean not being scared. The definition of brave is doing what needs to be done, in spite of being deathly afraid to do it." He was going to have his opportunity to walk the walk. He thought about his family, and despite Hector's vigorous protest, started walking toward the front door, dropping his gun along the way.

CHAPTER 53

Jefferson stepped out of the front doorway. He folded his hands on top of his head. He looked around as if he was trying to find a solution. There had to be a dozen police cars on the street. They were keeping their distance from the van. They didn't want to panic Small and have him do something rash. Meanwhile, Jefferson didn't see a solution. Nothing was coming to him. He walked slowly toward the van. As he walked, he thought about Aubrey and how much he loved her. It pained him to think that she was going to hate him for eternity for not giving up this case when she asked him to. He thought to himself, *I love you so much, Aubrey. I pray that you realize how much you mean to me.* He thought about his son and daughter. He was so proud of them. He hoped this didn't screw up their lives. In his mind, sadly, he said goodbye to all three of them. Then he thought of Bossy. Even in his time of duress, the thought of Bossy eased some of his anxiety.

There was a curtain that separated the front cabin of the van from the back of it. Small pulled the curtain partially open. He watched Jefferson walk up to the van. The van didn't have a side door, so Jefferson walked around to the back. Small maneuvered to the back of the van and opened the door. He said to Jefferson, "Listen very closely. Keep your hands on top of your head. Sit down on the floor of the van." This was the opportunity for a shooter to try to take Small out, but there were three men sitting directly behind him. Too many things could go wrong, injuring, or even possibly killing, one of the innocent men.

For some reason, Jefferson felt less scared now. He realized that being in the moment as opposed to worrying about the future made things more manageable. He sat as he was told to do. He had his back to Small. Small said, "You can take your hands down now. I want you to remove the vest. You won't need it." Jefferson didn't know how to take that comment. Did Small mean that he wouldn't be shooting Jefferson or did he mean that he was going to shoot him in the head? Jefferson decided to take the glass half-full attitude. He took the vest off and laid it on the van floor.

Small instructed Jefferson to fold his hands and put them back on his head. He strapped Jefferson's hands together with a plastic cable tie. He grabbed the top of Jefferson's jacket and pulled him completely into the van and closed the door. He said, "Since you won't need the vest, I think I'll wear it." He put it on.

Jefferson looked around. He saw Trout and the other two men in a sitting position on the floor near the front compartment. Their hands and feet were tied together with the same ties used on Jefferson. He nodded at the men, and they nodded back. Nobody said a thing. Trout didn't look good. His face was red, and his ears were an even brighter red. He looked helpless and hopeless. It made Jefferson feel more anxious. He said to Small, "How did you know we were here waiting for you?"

"My father never meets me during the day. If you check his personnel file, you'll see that he doesn't take time off of work other than when he grieved for my mother and brothers. That was my first clue. He also never wants to meet me at his house. Now that my mother is gone, he has nobody to go out to dinner with. If he wants to meet, it's over dinner. I came over here right after he called. I was watching as you set up to meet and greet me. There were no surprises for me. I appreciate that you made it easy."

To Jefferson, that wasn't a good thing. If Small saw that they were setting a trap for him, he could've vanished. He didn't. Instead, he created the opportunity to make Jefferson his captive. Jefferson's stomach knotted up. He said, "I guess I didn't do my homework. I have one other question for you: Why have you done most of your work on Monday, Tuesday, Wednesday, or Thursday nights?" Jefferson was interested in hearing Small's answer, but he was mostly trying to create dialogue to help Small see that he was dealing with another real person and not just a target.

"I'm a waiter. I work three shifts, each for twelve hours. I have Monday through Thursday off."

"That never occurred to me. I thought it was possible that you might have joint custody of kids and had them on weekends." Jefferson tried to maintain eye contact with Small. He was trying to demonstrate that he was very human, capable of screwing up like everyone else. Jefferson was feeling good about the conversation. The tone was not unfriendly, and Small seemed calm and poised. It could mean that he was confident, or it could mean that he didn't plan to harm anybody.

Small said, "I don't have kids. Unfortunately, neither of my brothers had the chance to have kids and now, I won't either." Small seemed at peace that things were not going to have a happy ending for him. That bothered Jefferson. Small seemed to realize that he had nothing to gain from cooperating. The man was prepared for the worst, and he seemed to be okay with it. Jefferson repeated to himself: *glass half-full, glass half-full*.

Jefferson had one real question on his mind. He finally built up the courage to ask it. "Why did you want to talk to me?"

A crooked smile spread across his face. "I'm not interested in chatting with you. I wanted to make you my prisoner. You made my dad a prisoner. I thought it might be good if you saw how that feels, having no control and probably no future."

The glass suddenly looked half-empty for Jefferson. This couldn't be good. He wanted to blame Small for getting his father in trouble. After all, Small was the one who convinced his father to assist him. He thought better of challenging him. He realized that if he had any chance at all, it didn't make sense to piss Small off.

Jefferson said, "If I'm the guy you want, you've got me. Why not let these other men go?"

"I don't think so. When you and I are done with our business, I plan to have one of these guys drive us out of here. These other men are my insurance policy."

Jefferson knew what he wanted to ask, but he had trouble getting it out. He remembered something his father often reminded him of when he was growing up in a tough neighborhood. "A coward dies a thousand times. A hero dies but once." Jefferson took a deep breath and asked, "What is our business?"

"I'm going to use you," Small said. There was a long silence before Jefferson asked how. Small said, "I'm going to give one final message to the world about the Chicago Police."

"What's that message going to be?"

"Look how incompetent the Chicago Police Department is. In spite of having the upper hand, they got one of their best killed."

Jefferson sat, stunned. He had to remind himself to breathe. He had known when he agreed to give himself up that this was a possibility. But ever the optimist, he never completely came to terms with this truly being his end.

Small said, "I think it's time we get this over with." He moved closer to Jefferson, the gun pointed at his head.

All through the conversation, Trout had sat motionless and quiet. Now he spoke. He said, "Wallace, you don't have to do this. If your goal is to make us look incompetent, you've been doing that for months. And now that you captured four of us, you've put an exclamation mark on it. The brass won't be able to let this one slide. The press will have a field day. What's to gain from killing an innocent man?"

"Shut up. Maybe I'll take you out too." Trout looked at Small defiantly. Jefferson realized that if he wasn't so sick to his stomach, he would be impressed with Trout. He really was a man after all. As Small threatened Trout, he brought the gun around and pointed it at Trout. Trout didn't flinch. Small peered at Trout for several seconds and turned the gun back on Jefferson. He said, "Any last thoughts, Detective?" Jefferson's heart was pounding. He realized that he had nothing. On a vacation to the Grand Canyon with his family, he had taken a picture of Aubrey and the kids with a side of the canyon in the background. He ended up enlarging the picture and had hung it in a frame in their living room. It was his favorite photograph of his family. He pictured the photo in his mind and braced himself.

Suddenly, the back door to the van was yanked open. Small turned and fired. Hector went flying backwards. He had managed to get off a shot at the same time Small did. It hit Small, and he went flying backwards too. The gun was knocked out of Small's hand. Jefferson's feet weren't tied together. He moved quicker than he had in years. His hands were bound in front of him, and that made it possible for him to grab the gun. Almost instantly, there were at least a dozen cops surrounding the back door of the van. Jefferson couldn't see Hector. The cops could see that Jefferson was trying to get out of the van and made a path for him. He hopped out, and one of the officers cut the restraint from his wrists. Meanwhile, a paramedic was already heading toward Hector, who was still lying on the ground.

Jefferson and Hector made eye contact. Hector was gasping for air. He had a panicky look on his face. Jefferson felt his own heart beating in his chest. He knelt next to Hector. "The paramedic is here. You'll be okay." Jefferson was praying that he was right. Hector caught a deep breath and let out a moan.

When Hector was able to speak, he said, "The vest saved my life. The bullet just knocked the wind out of me. Breathing is a little hard, so I wouldn't be surprised to find that I have a few broken ribs. But I'm okay, and glad that you're alive." The paramedic started working on Hector. Jefferson turned his head and saw that the officers had already pulled Small up into a sitting position and cuffed him. Jefferson's vest had saved Small's life. The other three captives were all standing, and they were no longer bound. Trout started moving toward Hector.

"Thank you, Sergeant, for standing up for me," Jefferson said. "I know that you've been upset with me. You showed me a lot by what you did." Trout just nodded. Jefferson turned his eyes back to Hector. He said, "What you did was incredibly brave. You risked your life for mine, and I'm sure that Small would have killed me if you hadn't come when you did. There are no words to express how grateful I am."

"Look, man, that's what partners do. I know you'd do the same for me. Hell, you did it for Trout. You risked your life to try to keep him alive." Hector looked over at Trout and said, "If Jefferson stays my partner, I want to start receiving hazardous duty pay." Jefferson chuckled, and even Trout smiled.

Trout said, "I owe my knees, and maybe my life, to both of you. All is forgiven. You represented yourselves and the department in the most positive way. I can guarantee both of you that I will strongly recommend you for Carter Harrison Awards." Jefferson reflected on what Trout said. The award was the highest one a police officer in Chicago could receive for bravery. Jefferson thought he would be satisfied if his heart would slow down for now. The adrenaline seemed to still be pumping wildly through his body.

"I guess I'm really lucky you acted when you did," he told Hector.

"It wasn't luck. We were able to hear the conversation on the two-way radio. Someone in the van must have been pushing the talk button on their radio the whole time you were in there. We knew it was time to act." They looked at Trout, and he nodded his head, indicating that it had been him.

Jefferson asked, "How did you know the back door to the van was unlocked?"

"We didn't know. As quietly as I could, I pushed on the button, and it went in. I set myself and pulled on the door as quickly as I could without losing balance, and it opened."

"Small could have shot you in the head. I guess we're all lucky today. I can't believe that Small didn't lock the back door. He's a marksman to be sure, but he isn't a mastermind criminal, apparently." He smiled at Hector and said, "I guess this means that I'm buying lunch tomorrow."

"You don't get off of the hook that easily. You're responsible for coffee and doughnuts until further notice," Hector said in response. Jefferson nodded in agreement. By now, Hector was standing. Jefferson gave him a long hug. Hector said, "Ow, are you trying to hurt me because I said you were in charge of doughnuts?"

"Oops, I forgot about the ribs. I'm sorry." Jefferson let go of Hector and said, "I have one other thing to take care of, then we can get to the hospital and have them check out your ribs." Small was standing next to the rear bumper of the van with his hands cuffed behind his back. He had three officers surrounding him. Jefferson walked up to him and started reading him his rights. Small tried to interrupt him to tell him that he had already heard them. Jefferson didn't stop talking. He wanted to be sure that Small didn't get off on a technicality. Jefferson then said to the three officers, "Please take him to the station. I don't want anybody talking to him, and whatever you do, don't lay a hand on him." Jefferson was taking no chances of something going wrong with this case.

He walked back to Hector and Trout, who had been watching him. Trout put an arm around each of the detectives' shoulders, and the three men walked away.

CHAPTER 54

Jefferson took Hector to the hospital. Hector had two broken ribs and some serious bruising. The doctor wrapped his chest, prescribed some pain pills, and sent him on his way. By the time the detectives left the hospital, it was after six. It would have been later, but the emergency room personnel had put him at the top of the list. While Hector was being treated, Jefferson called Aubrey to let her know that he would be late and not to wait up for him. He told her that he didn't have time to get into it, but she could rest comfortably. The Vigilante Killer was behind bars. She wanted more information, but he told her that he would share everything with her when he saw her. He wanted to be able to tell her the whole story, but he wanted to deliver it in person. He wasn't sure how she would take it.

The detectives returned to the station. Jefferson found a note from the commander, telling him to report to his office as soon as he returned to the station. He and Hector walked down to the commander's office together. Trout and the commander were talking when the detectives walked up. The commander told them to come in. He said, "I already got an account of the events today from Sergeant Trout. I want to hear your version to be sure I have everything. I know that for the next couple of days, I'll need to repeat the story for different people within the department, and possibly with the press. But before either of you speak, I have something to say. I couldn't be prouder. You both went above and beyond in my book. I always knew that you could do it. On behalf of the department and the community, thank you." The commander maintained a serious look, but he wasn't scowling. That in itself was some reward for the detectives. They knew it was only temporary, but at least they now knew the man was capable of looking like a normal human being.

Jefferson said, "You should know, Commander, Sergeant Trout risked his own safety in trying to convince Small not to shoot me. He didn't have to say anything, but he spoke up when Small implied he was going to kill me. I would've been impressed if I hadn't been shaking so hard." Trout and the detectives smiled. The commander came close to smiling but controlled himself.

"It wasn't that big of a deal," Trout said. "When it became apparent that Small was ready to take action, I just wanted to create extra time, hoping that someone would initiate a move. We got lucky. It turned out to be just enough time."

The commander looked at Trout and nodded his head. "That's good information. Thanks goes to you too, Sergeant. You did real good. This was a horrible case, but some good came out of it. I think we're growing as a unit. Very nice."

Jefferson reviewed the situation from his perspective for the commander. When he finished, Hector said, "My version matches perfectly with Marcus's."

The commander asked Hector, "Why were you the one chosen to try the back door?"

"It was simple," Hector said. "I insisted on being the one. I had the most to lose, my partner, so I had the highest motivation to be sure that the bad guy was the only one to get shot. We heard that Small had put on the vest. We became less concerned that a bullet might ricochet or pass through Small and hit someone else. We believed that the bullet would get lodged in the vest. The only question was whether the back door was unlocked. Obviously, it was. That was a huge break."

The four men talked for a while longer and then concluded their meeting. Jefferson and Hector had Bill Small brought to an interview room. Small had been a decent man until family tragedy hit. He had done a lot of good things as a cop. They felt that they owed it to him to let him know how things turned out. When they walked into the room, Small looked concerned. Hector said, "Wallace is in custody. He's probably a little sore, but otherwise, physically, he's okay." He proceeded to tell Small the story.

When he was finished, Small thanked the detectives for not killing his son and asked to see him. Jefferson said, "I don't think that's a good idea."

"Listen, Marcus, I might never see my son again. I know you don't owe me anything, but put yourself in my shoes. Just give me ten minutes with him. You've got me cuffed to the table. It's not like I can do anything."

Jefferson pondered it. He wasn't concerned with what either Small could do. He just didn't want to give them a chance to concoct a plan for rewriting history. Then he realized that there was nothing the Smalls could do now. They were going down. He said, "Okay, but we'll be listening in on your conversation from the observation room and taping it."

Small agreed to being taped and thanked Jefferson.

Twenty minutes later, Wallace Small was accompanied to the conference room. His face held nothing but apology when faced with the sight of his father in cuffs. Bill just looked sad. Wallace was cuffed to the table across from his father. "I'm sorry, Dad. You don't deserve to be sitting here," he said. "But I wouldn't take back what I did. I know that I killed some people, but I also know that I avenged the deaths in our family and saved a lot of innocent lives along the way."

"It's okay, Son. It's partially my fault. I raised you to stick up for your younger brothers. You gave up your own life in the names of your brothers. I forgive you." Wallace cast his eyes down at the table. He had nothing else to say. His father said, "One thing really bothers me. You were going to kill Detective Jefferson. There's no rationale for that. What were you thinking?"

"I wasn't really going to kill him. I wanted him to suffer through the experience of facing his own demise. After all, he's the one who put you behind bars. I also wanted the department to know that I could've put Jefferson down if I really wanted to."

The father looked at his son, trying to decide what to think. He said, "I believe you. Once you went into the van, how did you think this was going to end?"

"When they started setting up a trap for me, I knew that they had figured everything out. I was positive that they had you in custody. I thought about running, but I couldn't do that. After all, the reason you're here is because of me. I couldn't start a new life somewhere else knowing that I put you behind bars. I decided to take the opportunity to show the world how incompetent the department is. If they killed me or captured me, it didn't matter. I have nothing to look forward to. Eventually, I would've given myself up. Is there anything that I can do or say at this time that could benefit you?"

Bill Small contemplated what to say next. As he was thinking, Jefferson entered the room. "I'm sorry, Gentlemen, but this conversation is over." Right behind Jefferson were two officers. They disengaged Bill's cuff from the table and cuffed his wrists behind his back. They escorted him out of the room.

As he was led away, Small called out, "I love you, Son, and I always will."

Wallace shouted back, "Me too, Dad, me too."

Hector joined Jefferson in the conference room. He read Small his rights again. He wanted to get it on tape. Hector asked Small if he wanted a lawyer. Small said that he didn't. Hector said, "Do you want to tell us your side of the story?"

Small thought about it for a while. The room fell silent. Then he said, "Sure." For the next fifty-five minutes, Small walked the detectives through everything from motive, weapon, and the names of people he killed. He also told the detectives why each victim had been selected. His confession was thorough and honest. It was all on video. The detectives were feeling good about things. Hector said, "Thank you. There's just one other piece where we need your input. Please tell us about your father's involvement."

"That's not going to happen, Detective. My father wasn't involved. If he said he was, he just did it to take the heat off of me. Leave him out of this."

Hector was going to challenge Small on that point, but thought better of it. They already had Bill Small's confession. He had given them enough information to document that what he told them had to be true. Hector was satisfied with what they had and was ready to call it a day. He wanted to get home and start taking some heavy-duty pain pills. He ended the interview. He said, "We may want to talk to you again tomorrow."

With that, the detectives got off their chairs and left the room. Once outside the room, they shook hands. They'd had a very nerve-racking day, but a successful one. They still had work to do. They needed to talk to some people and to file the appropriate reports. They were both tired and anxious to get home, but they coordinated their efforts and got finished as quickly as they could.

As they headed for the exit, Jefferson said, "I have one more job to do tonight. I called Fred DuKane's widow. She's waiting up for my visit. She deserves to get all of the details firsthand and not from the press."

"I never thought of that," Hector said. "Thank you. I'll follow you there."

"You don't have to come. I can take care of it."

"I do have to be there," Hector insisted.

Jefferson understood.

The detectives met with Mrs. DuKane and her children. There was lots of crying and hugs as the details were discussed. Mrs. DuKane was shocked that Bill Small was involved. In the end, although she felt good with the case being solved, she said, "None of this will bring Fred back. There will be no celebrating here tonight." There was no real way to relieve the grief that the DuKanes were feeling and would continue to feel. The detectives left with very mixed emotions, relief in solving the case, but with heavy hearts.

To change the mood, as they walked to their cars, Hector said, "Now we have to go after a scarier monster, Bertha Brown."

"You've got that right," Jefferson agreed with a light chuckle.

CHAPTER 55

All of the local news stations carried the story of the capture of the Vigilante Killer on the five o'clock news. It was the lead story, and at least half of the telecasts were devoted to it. The details were still sketchy, pieces coming in bit by bit. Because there were more than a dozen police cars, a fire truck, and several ambulances at the scene, it attracted a crowd. People alerted the media. Onlookers in the crowd were taking pictures and videos. Several of the videos made it to the viewing audiences. Bystanders were interviewed. Neighbors identified Wallace Small as the person who was led away in handcuffs. Reporters tried hard to get someone from the police department to give them details, but they weren't successful.

By the time the ten o'clock news came on, still no information had come from the Chicago Police Department. The mayor's office gave a written statement, confirming that the police had arrested a suspect in the Vigilante Killer case. The stations devoted nearly a full half-hour to reporting the story. Even with limited information from the authorities, the entire story had been pieced together. Details of the backgrounds of Wallace and Bill Small were delivered. It had become known that the father and son had worked together and that Bill was also in custody. The stations had been able to gather the names of the hostages and discussed each briefly. The heroism shown by Detectives Jefferson and Hector received major attention.

Jefferson arrived home just after eleven thirty. Bossy had been sleeping in the kitchen. She usually followed Aubrey or Marcus around when they were home. Her customary position was sleeping at the foot of their bed. But when Marcus wasn't home, she tended to wait for him in the kitchen. She was startled when he came in. She had been in a deep sleep and didn't hear him until the door opened. It took her about three seconds to put it all together, but then her tail started swinging wildly as she got up and leaped at him. He was able to catch her before she got her paws on his shoulders. He made a fuss over her. He loved Bossy, and it didn't take a genius to figure out that she loved him.

Aubrey had stayed up waiting for Marcus. She flew into the kitchen once she realized he was home. Jefferson saw her come through the doorway. He straightened up and headed to her. They hugged and kissed and hugged some more. Aubrey cried. Jefferson pulled her in tighter. By this time, the kids had come in too. They joined their mother and father and had a family hug. Bossy did her best to push between everybody.

Jefferson's son said, "Dad, we saw the news. Weren't you scared?"

"The truth is that I was very scared."

The four people uncoupled and stood facing each other. Aubrey had regained her composure. She offered to serve some leftover pie to everybody, and they were all quick to say yes. She dished it out, and the Jeffersons sat down at the kitchen table. As they ate, his family asked Marcus a lot of questions. He answered them and shared the story with them. He was worried Aubrey might be upset with him, but she was so elated that he was home safe, it trumped whatever other feelings she had.

Aubrey had recorded the news so that Jefferson could see it. After Jefferson finished giving his family a recap, the kids went to their rooms, supposedly to go to bed. Jefferson watched the recording with Aubrey sitting by his side, squeezing his hand. He didn't show any emotion. It almost felt unreal to him, watching the story unfold on television. When the story turned to him and Hector, it felt weird. Aubrey was all smiles.

"I need to get to bed," he finally said. "I have to be downtown at seven tomorrow morning to prepare for the ten o'clock news conference."

"What preparation do you have to do?" Aubrey asked, still beaming with pride.

"The brass want to be sure that Hector and I say the right things. They are going to let us know what we can say, what not to say, and when to reply with no comment."

"You're definitely going to be speaking during the news conference?" Aubrey asked.

"That's what we were told."

"Are you nervous?"

"I'm too tired to be nervous right now, but I can assure you I will be tomorrow. Public speaking is not my strong suit."

Aubrey said, "Oh, go on." They both laughed. She asked, "Who else is going to speak?"

"I believe the commissioner is going to represent the department. I can guarantee you that my commander will be in view of the camera too. He can never get too much publicity. Hector and I will be asked to answer questions."

"Let's make sure that I pick your clothes for tomorrow. If Hollywood's going to discover you, this is your chance. We can't have Hector outshining you."

"Any guy who saves my life can outshine me all that he wants."

Her look quickly sobering, Aubrey nodded in agreement.

Jefferson was up and about early the next morning. He went for a run, shaved, showered, and had a bowl of cereal. Aubrey made sure he looked perfect before sending him on his way. He made it downtown at ten minutes to seven. He and Hector were given their instructions. They rehearsed answering the expected questions. They did well. They were comfortable because they had each other to lean on, and all they needed to do was tell the truth.

The news conference went well. There were questions about how the detectives came to view Wallace Small as a suspect. The press wanted to know more about Bill Small. The detectives answered what they could, and for some of the questions, they either side-stepped them or said, "We can't comment on that at this time." They came across as professional and friendly. They were a hit.

Near the end of the session, the questions started getting personal. Neither detective wanted to get too deep into their personal lives. When a female reporter asked Hector if he was seeing anyone, he turned red. He said, "No, but I'm available if you're asking me out." It evoked laughter.

Jefferson leaned over and whispered to Hector, "I hope this doesn't mean that you're falling in love again." Hector just grimaced. With that, the commissioner took back the podium and ended the conference, thanking everybody for their attendance.

After the news conference, there was a debriefing. Then the detectives were told to take the rest of the day off. They were both very willing to do that. They needed to regroup. They still had one more mountain to climb.

CHAPTER 56

The rest of the week was spent in activities related to the cases against Bill and Wallace Small. The detectives met with the people who would be involved in the prosecution of both the father and the son. Search warrants were issued for Bill Small's home, Wallace Small's apartment, and Wallace's car. The detectives found the rifle that would later be identified as the murder weapon for all of the victims, in a carrying case in the trunk of Wallace's car. They found other evidence, including a printed copy of the Gang Audit, in Wallace's apartment. Between the confessions and the evidence collected, both cases would be airtight. They had their men and were anxious to devote their time to the other case that had been haunting them. That would be their mission during the following week.

Jefferson spent the entire weekend with his family. They did something they hadn't done as a family for at least a few years. They went to a movie. Jefferson didn't particularly like going to the movies if for no other reason than it was expensive. But he wanted to have family time, and he knew that his kids would enjoy it.

Bossy was included in the family weekend as much as possible. The kids joined their parents in taking her for a long walk. Bossy got lots of attention during the walk. There seemed to be an extra bounce in her step.

Jefferson felt lucky to be alive. Although he and his family didn't do anything all that exciting, it was one of the best weekends for him in a long time. He had always appreciated his family, but the recent events made that sentiment even stronger. Also, not having the Vigilante Killer case hanging over his head, and all of the ramifications that came with it, made it much easier for him to just relax and enjoy.

Hector had his own style for unwinding. He hit the clubs on Friday and Saturday nights with friends. He partied hard. On Sunday, he slept until two in the afternoon after getting home at close to three in the morning. He hadn't slept that late in years, but he was spent. Sunday was all about chilling, at least what was left of it after sleeping so long. He had taped the Bears, and after brunch, he lay on the sofa watching the game until he dozed off. He slept for another hour. He had laundry to do and some other chores, but he let them go and just relaxed.

• • • •

Monday morning, the detectives were both refreshed and ready to work. Together, they outlined a plan to continue their investigation into the death of Alphonso Burton. They were going to prove it was murder and bring Bertha Brown to trial, one way or another. Their first move was to visit Burton's neighborhood one more time and see if anybody, besides the next-door neighbors could provide additional information. On the ride there, Hector said, "You'll never guess who called me yesterday."

"If I'm never going to guess, why don't you just tell me? I don't know if I can handle the suspense."

"Drum roll please," Hector said. After a short silence, he said, "Samantha Polse."

Hector could see that Jefferson was trying to remember who that was, and then it apparently dawned on him. Jefferson said, "That's Ernie Waul's friend, the one you went nuts over. Well played. What did she have to say?"

"She said that she called to thank me for solving the case and clearing Waul. She also wanted to say how impressed she was with, as she called it, my act of heroism."

Jefferson responded, "I'm sure your modesty shone through."

"Listen, Marcus, I feel a sense of accomplishment, but it wasn't as big a deal as people seem to think it was. I just did what I had to do. I'm ready to move on. But I have to admit, it was cool for Samantha to comment on it."

Jefferson queried, "Did she ask you out?"

"No, she didn't."

"Did you ask her out?"

"That's another no."

"Why not? Aren't you still hot on her?"

"More than ever. She was so easy to talk to. She has a sexy giggle. She's warm and just such a decent person."

Jefferson shot back, "You know what they say? Opposites attract."

Hector winced and said, "You really know how to blow a guy's self-confidence."

"So what's the answer? Why didn't you ask her out?"

"I plan to very soon, but I want this relationship to be perfect right from the start. I want to call her specifically to ask her out. I don't want her to think that it was just a spur of the moment reaction to her call. I want her to feel special."

"Wow, it sounds like you're ready to pick out the ring."

Hector didn't respond. They had arrived in front of Burton's home. They canvassed the neighborhood. Nobody answered the door at several of the neighboring homes. But they did get to talk to six different people. Unfortunately, the detectives didn't learn anything new. A few of the people reaffirmed what they already knew, and a few didn't have anything at all to offer.

They returned to the station. Their next step was to interview Bertha's husband, Charles, again, as well as their daughters. They hoped that if they upped the intensity of the interviews, they might be able to extract something that could help them. Charles and the twins declined to meet with them. Jefferson said, "I'm just shocked that Bertha's family is standing behind her. She not only cheated on her husband, but she cheated the girls too. From what we've been told, she never was a loving wife—in fact, just the opposite. Their loyalty doesn't make sense."

Hector said, "We need to figure out another angle. I'm sure that we're missing something."

Jefferson agreed. "I know this doesn't seem like much, but something about the pen Bertha used to write in her journal bothers me. She has a big collection of Parker Pens, maybe the biggest other than the Parker Pen Company. She values the pens. Here's where I'm stuck. The pen she left at the crime scene is a really nice pen. It wasn't a Bic or some other inexpensive pen. I don't know pens, but it appears to me that this pen is not an ordinary Parker Pen. It seems like a very expensive model. For someone who has spent most of her life collecting these things, I'd think she would've taken the pen with her instead of leaving it behind."

"I think you make a good point. But she had just killed a man," Hector pointed out, "and she may have been in a hurry to get out of there. She probably wasn't thinking straight."

"That doesn't work. After she killed Burton, she took the time to write a final chapter. She didn't just rush out of there. She was under control. This is my theory: I believe that she wrote the journal after killing Burton, to give credence to her assertion that what she did was in self-defense. By leaving an expensive pen, I think she is trying to show that the journal was written in real time. She's guessing that we would believe that if she wrote the journal after the fact, she would have left a cheap pen behind, not a collector's item. Does that make any sense?"

"Wow, that's deep, Brother. Do you really think that she analyzed the situation to that degree?"

"Absolutely," Jefferson answered. "I think we should make an appointment with someone who is somewhat of a historian on Parker Pen and see what they can tell us about the pen that she used. I know it sounds strange, but I think it might offer up a clue. Parker Pens is based in Wisconsin. It will be a nice day trip for us."

"I'm in," Hector agreed readily.

CHAPTER 57

Hector did some research on the Parker Pen Company. He discovered that the company was owned by Newell Rubbermaid. They had purchased it from Gillette. Although the company had its start over one hundred years ago in Janesville, Wisconsin, the headquarters was now based in England. The company still had a presence in Janesville with somewhere around one hundred fifty employees, though. Hector called the Janesville facility. He was passed on to three different people before he was connected with someone who thought he could help and was willing to meet with representatives of the Chicago Police Department. Hector made an appointment with the man, Grady Bingham, for ten thirty the next morning. Bingham didn't want to meet at the Parker facility. Instead, he gave Hector the name and address of a coffee shop a few blocks away from his office.

Packed with the pen Bertha Brown used to write in her journal, the detectives headed up to Janesville the next morning. The drive wasn't especially scenic. It was expressway all the way, with very little to see. The terrain was flat. It would have been a boring ride if they didn't have each other for company. They arrived in Janesville a little before ten and headed to the coffee shop.

The detectives were drinking coffee and discussing the case when a man who appeared to be in his sixties walked into the shop. He looked directly at the detectives and walked over to them. He said, "One of

261

you must be Detective Hector, I presume?" The detectives stood and introduced themselves to Bingham. He was a distinguished-looking man. He was clean-shaven, with a full head of white hair. He was wearing a gray pair of dress pants and a long-sleeved shirt with a button-down collar. He carried a leather briefcase with him that looked like it had a lot of miles on it. Jefferson's first impression was positive. Bingham seemed like a decent man with a friendly demeanor. Hector offered to get Bingham a cup of coffee. Bingham said, "Thank you, I'd appreciate that." He told Hector what he wanted, and Hector went to get it.

Jefferson and Bingham talked about Janesville. Jefferson had been through Janesville before on the way to Madison, but he never stopped other than to fill his tank with gas. Bingham was born and raised in Janesville. He was a third generation Parker Pen employee. Jefferson mentioned that to Hector when he returned to their table.

The three men made small talk for several minutes. Hector asked Bingham why he wanted to meet them at the coffee shop rather than at the office. Bingham told them, "I just thought it might be more relaxing. We have coffee at the office, but it's not that good. Why don't you let me see that pen that you had mentioned to me on the phone?"

Hector had it in his jacket pocket in a clear plastic bag. He handed it to Bingham. Bingham immediately said, "This is a nice pen. It's a pen that a collector would want to have, but it's not one of our real expensive ones. It probably goes for somewhere around $300.00. What do you want to know about it?"

"As I believe Detective Hector mentioned to you on the phone, the woman who owns this pen is a collector of Parker Pens. When I first heard that, I was a little surprised. It never occurred to me that people collect pens. Is that common?"

"It's probably more common than you would think. It's really a smart investment. We sell what I would call everyday pens to a wide variety of retailers. Parkers are readily available. But at the same time, we manufacture very high-end, limited edition pens for collectors and as mementos for special occasions. Those pens are very pricy, going for upwards of ten thousand dollars."

Hector, looking taken aback, asked, "Do those pens come with power steering and brakes? We're talking pens, right?"

All three men laughed. Bingham said, "People, more than ever, understand that collection quality pens will go up in value. Writing instruments are becoming less necessary now that we're in the age of computers. In fact, some schools anticipate a time when they'll no longer be teaching cursive. At some point in the not too distant future, we'll be doing everything by computer. Pens will become like the horse and buggy. They're still around, but they don't serve a purpose for most of us."

Hector said, "If somebody is a big-time collector and they have to give up one of their pens, is this one that they would be willing to part with?"

"Yes. There are enough of these around that it wouldn't be hard to replace it at a fair price. Collector pens don't come a lot cheaper than this one."

Jefferson asked, "Is there anything else you can tell us about this pen?"

Bingham reached into his briefcase and pulled out a catalog. He flipped through the pages. When he found the right one, he stopped and scanned the page. He said, "This pen is a Jotter Jubilee Premier Edition Ball Point Pen. This particular pen is Saffron Yellow, and it's also available in Licorice Black. The design is based on the original Jotter Filigree, a pen that was sold almost exclusively at the 1959 New York World's Fair. This pen was introduced in 2004. You won't find a lot of people using it as their everyday pen. It's definitely a collector's item. What more can I tell you?"

Hector started asking if there was a way to know where the pen was purchased. Before he finished the question, Jefferson grabbed his forearm. Hector looked over at Jefferson, who had a wry smile on his face. Jefferson said, "We got her."

Hector asked, "How do you figure?"

Jefferson looked at Bingham and said, "Are you positive that the pen didn't become available until 2004? It's not like cars, where a 2004 model can actually become available in 2003?"

Bingham responded, "I'm positive. A pen that's introduced in 2004 is not available to the public, including collectors, until 2004." Hector got it. He broke out in a wide grin. Bingham asked, "Why does that help you?"

Jefferson gave Bingham a brief explanation. "The woman we're investigating claimed to have been held captive, starting in 2003. She kept a journal documenting her captivity. She claimed that she started writing in her journal almost immediately upon being captured. She also stated that the pen found at the crime scene was the only pen she used. If the pen in question was not introduced until 2004, she has to be lying. We have a relatively strong case against her. The only hang up was the journal. If it was to be believed, it could create some doubt for a jury. With this information, we can prove that the journal was not written in real time, but after the fact. We can document that she's a liar. When this is added to the mix, we have a stronger case against her. Can you send us some sort of documentation proving the exact date this pen became available?"

"Sure. I can scan a document and e-mail it to you. It will be waiting for you when you return to Chicago. I'll mail a hard copy to you too."

Hector gave Bingham his card. It had all of his contact information. The detectives thanked him and walked out to their car.

Jefferson smiled. "This has become a rather successful week for us, Partner. We need to enjoy it. They don't come that often."

CHAPTER 58

Bertha Brown started becoming nervous as her trial approached. Her husband was indignant. Her attorney, Anthony Cavitello, assured them that they had nothing to worry about. As he started to understand the case that was going to be presented by the prosecutor, he became less confident. He recommended to her and her husband that they hire additional attorneys to work with him. They agreed.

Cavitello asked for continuance after continuance. It was good for Bertha. She was out on bail and was trying to go about her life as if nothing had happened. But all good things must end, and the trial eventually began.

Bertha's legal team was a strong one. During the trial, the attorneys fought every piece of evidence and every point made by the prosecution. They were good, very good. But the case against Brown was strong. Midway through the trial, it appeared as though the jury was teetering back and forth.

Initially, the defense hadn't planned to call Bertha to the stand. But something happened deeper into the trial that had the attorneys rethinking their strategy. Bertha's husband, Charles, of course, was present for each day of the trial. The couple had assured their twins, who were away at college, that the trial was just a formality and to stay at school. Initially, Charles appeared to be calm and one hundred percent behind his wife. He began to waver as the trial moved forward. The prosecutor asserted that

Bertha had voluntarily left her family to be with Alphonso Burton. It was no secret that the prosecution would be trying to show that to be true. What Charles didn't expect was the evidence that demonstrated the truth of what they were claiming.

As the evidence mounted, Charles started realizing that he had been in denial. It hit him that he had been a fool to buy into Bertha's story. Things went downhill for him. When evidence was presented that Bertha had ample opportunities to escape, such as at the gym or the airport, Charles really started doubting his wife.

Jefferson was called to the stand to document that the detectives had caught Bertha in a variety of lies. The defense tried to neutralize his testimony, but the prosecution had already introduced into evidence videos that demonstrated she had been lying. Their only option was to try to minimize the damage. The jury seemed to understand what was happening. It was a score for the prosecution team.

Charles went from being calm to becoming twitchy. It was apparent to everybody that his demeanor changed. Cavitello found himself in a difficult position. The jury certainly was aware that Charles was Bertha's husband. His newfound demeanor might have an influence on them. Cavitello could ask Charles not to attend court, but that might look to the jury as though he had given up on his wife. Cavitello talked to Charles, sharing his concern. He asked Charles to act confident and to make it clear to the jury through his actions and posture that he was behind Bertha all the way, that he truly believed in her.

Charles committed to trying, but he told Cavitello that he couldn't help being upset.

Charles tried, but it didn't last for long. As the trial moved forward, when he and his wife exchanged glances, his face no longer expressed love and concern; his expression bordered on disdain. Initially, after the first two days of the trial, Bertha and Charles could be seen leaving the courtroom holding hands. After the third day, they didn't even walk out together. The other two attorneys who were working along with Cavitello were concerned that the changing relationship could affect the outcome of the trial. They recommended that Bertha be put on the stand in an effort to improve her image. They realized that it was a very risky move, but they were beginning to feel that the case was getting away from them.

The evidence proved that Bertha was a liar and strongly suggested that she fabricated the story of being held hostage. Charles had become a liability.

Hector was called to the stand to document that the pen Bertha used to write her journal was not available until the year after Bertha claimed to have been abducted. The court already had in evidence the document that Grady Bingham of Parker Pens had sent to Hector. The defense asked Hector if it was possible that Bertha ran out of ink and needed to get a new pen. Hector conceded that possibility, but Bertha had told them that the pen was the only one she had used. Cavitello said, "When Mrs. Brown talked to you, she had gone through a very traumatic experience. Isn't it possible she got a little confused with some of the details?" Again, Hector conceded that possibility. The prosecutors weren't worried. From the jury's faces, it was apparent that they weren't buying in.

Bertha took the stand. She came across as a sweet person. Cavitello led her through a rather lengthy testimony. She told the story of the abduction and her life as a prisoner. If you believed her, it was clear why she thought that she had to kill Burton. Cavitello had her read passages from her journal so the jury could feel the emotion that Bertha had experienced. She sobbed as she read, having to stop to regain her composure several times. The attorney wanted to play on the jury's sympathy, and it seemed to be working. One of the jury members visibly flinched when one passage was read. The journal was the effective tool it was meant to be.

Cavitello had Bertha explain why she had lied. Her explanation was that the ordeal left her confused and disoriented. She had tried to give the police answers when, in reality, her memories were blurred. Cavitello suggested that she had suffered from post-traumatic stress disorder after her escape. He claimed that the condition explained the inconsistencies in her stories. Bertha did a credible job. She seemed to evoke sympathy from the jury. Her attorneys began to feel optimistic again. Bertha performed well.

In the cross examination, the prosecutor asked Bertha how she came to use a pen that wasn't available until 2004 while writing in 2003. She said that she had been confused. She said that she started writing with one pen, but it was replaced the following year. She couldn't remember why. He said, "So, Mrs. Brown, you want the jury to believe that you started writing your journal with one pen and that it was replaced the next year?" She indicated that he was correct.

He said, "I'll get back to that, but I want to clear something else up first. I read your journal from cover to cover. It paints a picture of Burton being an ogre. You claim that he used and abused you. You indicated that you were scared for your life and the life of your family the whole time. Do I have that right?"

"Yes." He asked her if Burton ever did anything nice for her or treated her nicely. She replied, "Only when we were in front of other people."

"Did he ever buy you gifts?"

"No, he had no reason to. He didn't need to charm me. He was an animal. He took what he wanted."

The prosecutor said, "Let's get back to the pen. How did you get the second pen, the one that was manufactured in 2004?"

"Burton bought it for me."

"Didn't you just tell us that he didn't buy you gifts?"

She replied, "My gosh. It was just a pen."

"Why would he buy you a pen? You said in your journal that he wasn't aware that you had a pen. You hid it beneath his workbench. What did he think you were going to do with the pen?"

"I really can't remember."

"A few seconds ago, you said it was just a pen. What you didn't mention was that it's worth $300.00." Bertha recoiled slightly. It hadn't occurred to her that the price of the pen would come up. It hadn't been mentioned during Hector's testimony. The prosecutor said, "Wouldn't it seem to you that a $300.00 pen would be considered a gift and an awful nice thing for this ogre to do for you?"

She responded, "I have no idea what he was thinking. I certainly didn't question it."

The prosecutor went on to challenge different pieces of Bertha's story. On some of them, she came out okay, but others were backbreakers for her. Her attorneys tried to protect her as much as they could, but things went downhill fast. By the time Bertha left the stand, she had gone from appearing sweet to conniving and dishonest.

Cavitello needed a last-ditch effort to pull this one out of the fire. He tried to prove that Burton was an antisocial monster. He had several people testify. The picture painted for the jury would suggest that Burton was a bottom feeder. The takeaway for the jury was that he could be a creep.

But there was doubt that he would abduct a woman and treat her in a way Bertha's journal stated. It wasn't so much a reflection of how they felt about Burton. It was more that they had come to believe Bertha manufactured the entire story.

During his closing argument, the prosecutor reviewed the facts that had been presented. He felt confident that they would be more than enough for a conviction. "There is no question that Mrs. Brown killed Burton. She admitted it. The real question is motive. Did she murder him out of fear or for some other reason? Ladies and Gentlemen of the jury, I feel confident, with all of the evidence presented, you see that the journal was a piece of fiction. Fear was not the motive. We will never know for sure, but here is what I believe it was. Bertha Brown left her family, leaving them to mourn her loss. Meanwhile, she was off enjoying the good life with her new found lover. When the relationship grew stale, she wanted to go back to her family. She couldn't admit to them what she'd been up to. She concocted her abduction story. She had one problem. Mr. Burton could contradict her story. She wasn't willing to chance it. Apparently, she believed that the deception of her family was worth more than another person's life. Hers was an act of total selfishness.

The jury deliberated for less than three hours before they came back with a guilty verdict. She was convicted of first-degree murder. When sentencing took place, she begged for the court's mercy, but none was given. She was sentenced to life in prison with no chance of parole. Bertha looked over to her husband as she was led away in handcuffs. She was crying. Cavitello said, "We'll fight this. Just hang in there." Her husband just looked right through her. He knew that the jury had got it right. He was a broken man. What was he going to tell Caron and Carla? He bit his lips to try not to cry out loud as tears streamed down his face.

CHAPTER 59

As Jefferson drove home at the conclusion of the Bertha Brown trial, he found himself reflecting on life, both during the time he and Hector had been building this case and now. Simultaneously, they had investigated the Vigilante case. They had also looked into the death of a man in a hotel room.

Jefferson thought about how war damages people. Both the suicide victim and the Vigilante Killer came back from overseas as changed men. The changes weren't good for either of them, or for society. He was aware of the negative effect war had on both men, but he realized that it was much worse than he had ever imagined. Millions of people, most of them innocent, had their lives changed, and in many cases destroyed, by war.

His mood improved as he realized some good came out of the Vigilante Killer case. Word got around the station that Sergeant Trout spoke up in Jefferson's behalf when it appeared the killer was about to end his life. It was a gutsy thing to do. Although Trout didn't get the publicity that the detectives received, his bravery was recognized by those who worked with him. The incident and the recognition within the department seemed to raise his confidence. He became much more engaged. There was a difference in how he went about working with and protecting his men. Even Hector had said, "Trout has gone from being irrelevant to being a good boss."

Jefferson and Hector had worked a myriad of cases since Bertha was first arrested. This gave the commander the opportunity to berate them on a regular basis. They never seemed to solve their cases in a timely enough fashion for him. There were cases they hadn't solved at all, and The Bulldog had a field day with those. It was almost like he preferred they didn't solve their cases so that he had a reason to beat them down. Oh yeah, he had been almost human when they brought down the Vigilante Killer and Bertha Brown in the same week. But that didn't last.

Something did change. Trout no longer sat silently, with his eyes staring at his folded hands in the presence of the commander. When appropriate, he took exception to the commander's comments. He actually challenged the commander on certain points. He also agreed with the commander at times. When that occurred, he came at the detectives just as hard as the commander did, although he was more civil in the way that he handled it. He wasn't intimidated by anybody. When the commander screamed at Trout, he gave it right back. He stood for what he believed. The transformation was dramatic and amazing at the same time.

Jefferson thought about Vicky Soderheim, the detective who had been with Fred DuKane when he was shot by the Vigilante Killer. The event had a profound effect on her. She returned to work but had become depressed and seemed to keep her distance from people, including her regular partner. She had been assigned to work with a police psychologist. He recommended to Sergeant Trout that she be given a leave of absence to devote the time needed to get intensive therapy. Trout agreed, and she realized it was for the best. After thirteen weeks away, she came back. She had come to terms with things. She still found herself thinking about DuKane and the incident, but she was functional and continued to make progress.

Jefferson's mind continued to drift. He thought of the family and friends those three cases had impacted. The ex-soldier who committed suicide came to mind first. He left behind family, friends, and other soldiers whose lives he had touched. Sad, he thought.

The Smalls came to mind as well. Wallace had killed a lot of men. Other than DuKane, they weren't good men, but many of their families were composed of some very good people. And then Jefferson thought about Bertha Brown. What she had done to her family was a crime in itself, and she did it twice, by disappearing and then coming back to them as a liar and a killer.

Slowly, a smile came to Jefferson's face. He was thinking about Hector. He realized that Hector had become the best partner that he ever had. He had grown by leaps and bounds as a detective and as a man. There weren't many laughs their first few months together. They seemed always to be stoic and proper with each other. But that had changed. They found plenty of things to laugh about now, even while investigating some very serious crimes. They laughed with each other and at each other. Jefferson was really enjoying the relationship.

It had taken Hector a few months to actually ask Samantha Polse out. He had her on a pedestal, and he had to convince himself that he was worthy. Jefferson found this amusing because Hector never seemed to lack for confidence.

Samantha accepted his offer. Hector admitted to Jefferson that he knew he loved her from the day he met her. Things were going well until she realized that they were getting serious. She told him, "I like you, and I enjoy being with you, but I think we need to back off." He told her that he had strong feelings for her. He wanted to tell her that he loved her, but he wasn't quite ready to put it out there yet. He asked her why she wanted to back off. She said, "That's the problem, Jerome. I'm developing feelings for you too. I went out with you because I could tell that you were someone whose company I could enjoy. I didn't expect to develop deep feelings. I lost my husband to a violent crime. I don't think that I can commit to a cop, especially one like you, who is maybe too brave. I don't believe I could handle losing someone else while still in the prime of life."

Hector didn't know where to go with that. He couldn't promise her that he'd be safe. His wasn't that kind of a career. He couldn't tell her that he'd be more careful. Too often, you just have to react. In the moment of truth, there's not enough time to analyze all of the options. He had never lied to her, and he wasn't about to start. After several discussions, she agreed to continue to spend some time with Hector, purely as a friend. He was disheartened, but he thought, with time, he could get the relationship back on track.

Through his relationship with Samantha, he got to know Ernie Waul. He and Ernie actually developed a friendship, in spite of the fact that

Hector had looked at Waul as a suspect in the Vigilante case. Hector being Hector, he coaxed Waul into supporting his relationship with Samantha. Waul began to work on her. Jefferson wasn't sure how this one was going to end, but he knew to never count Hector out.

Jefferson turned onto his street. He began to think of his own family. The Vigilante Killer case could have made him appreciate his family even more, but it hadn't because he had always treasured them. It reminded him that he needed to make sure they knew it every day. Whatever Samantha was to Hector, Aubrey was always more to him. He was so lucky to have found her and to have won her over. He realized that the case had caused him to invest more of himself into the lives of his family. That turned out to be good for everybody but Bossy. She wanted him all to herself.

Printed in the United States
By Bookmasters